DEADLY REVENGE

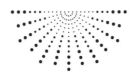

D. S. BUTLER

✸ Created with Vellum

DEADLY REVENGE IS THE third book in the DS Jack Mackinnon Crime Series.

One by one, they will pay for the past...

DS Jack Mackinnon's career is in serious trouble. Still in the Detective Chief Inspector's bad books and excluded from the Major Investigation team, Mackinnon is assigned a case nobody wants.

As Jack Mackinnon investigates, he discovers a horrifying link to a crime committed a decade ago.

Not forgotten. And never forgiven...

DEADLY REVENGE is a British police procedural, perfect for fans of Peter James and his Roy Grace series.

CHAPTER ONE

2001

TEN YEARS AGO...

Grace stepped inside the lift, lowered her heavy shopping bags to the ground and pressed the button for the third floor. The smell of pine cleaning fluid was so strong, it made her nose twitch.

Mrs. Anderson, who lived on the floor above Grace and her father, must have been cleaning again. She had a thing about germs. Grace was always catching her polishing the handrails on the stairs, and the smell of bleach often wafted down to their floor when Mrs. Anderson was scrubbing her landing, which she did practically every day.

When Grace once commented on how the whole block of flats smelled of cleaning products, Mrs. Anderson took it as a compliment, and folded her arms underneath her matronly bosom and beamed. "Thank you, Grace. You can never be too careful with germs. As you know, after all the time you have had to spend in hospital with your troubles."

Grace never mentioned the cleaning again. She didn't like to be reminded of "her troubles," as Mrs. Anderson called them.

When the lift reached the third floor, Grace bent down to lift up the plastic carrier bags. Just as she was about to step out of the lift, she felt one of the handles give way, and the bag fell to the floor with a thud, followed by an ominous shattering sound.

Damn.

She quickly inspected the damage. A glass jar of pasta sauce had smashed open and the red sauce had leaked over the rest of the shopping. Grace held the bag out in front of her, so the sauce wouldn't drip onto her clothes.

The little yappy dog next door was barking like mad. Mrs. Rainer, who owned the dog, was stone deaf and never seemed to notice the barking. Grace wondered what set it off this time? Something on the TV? Or a car alarm?

Swearing under her breath, Grace lifted her key to the lock.

She froze.

The door was open.

That was strange. Her father wasn't due home from work until after eight. Maybe he had come home early, and hadn't closed the door properly.

Grace pushed open the door and stepped into the flat. She was about to call out when she heard voices.

It wasn't her dad.

Had she left the television on? She entered the hallway and set down the bags, the leaking pasta sauce forgotten. She walked on, towards the voices. Maybe it was the radio?

There was a crash, followed by a laugh. Too late, she realised these were real voices, they weren't on the television or radio.

For a second, she hesitated, something she would later regret bitterly, then adrenaline kicked in. She needed to get out of here; she needed to call for help.

She turned to run, but tripped over the shopping bags and fell against the hall table, sending the vase on top clattering to the floor.

"Who's that?" A male voice shouted out from inside the flat.

Grace scrambled to her feet, her heart thumping, and clambered over the shopping. She made it into the hallway, but before she could get away, she felt hands grab her, pulling her back inside the flat.

"Let me go!" Grace struggled, turning to face the intruder. She kicked out at him. "Let me go."

The man's cheeks were covered in old acne scars. His eyes didn't focus properly as he stared at her. "You're not going anywhere." He grasped a handful of her hair and yanked it hard.

Grace pushed against him, but he pulled her closer. She could smell his stale sweat and rancid breath.

"Please just let me go."

The intruder smiled, pulling out a knife.

If he hadn't been holding her up by her hair, Grace would have sunk to her knees.

He ran the knife along the hollow of her exposed throat. "I've got plans for you."

He nudged Grace forward with his body. "Get inside. Here, Gordon, look what I found."

In Grace's front room, another man stood in the corner, unplugging the television set.

He turned to face them, and his eyes widened when he saw Grace. "What are you doing? Don't let her see our faces." He pulled up his sweatshirt so it covered the lower half of his face.

"Thought she could tell us where she keeps the cash," the first intruder said, grinning.

"You're an idiot." Gordon staggered over, clutching the DVD player. "She's seen us. Now she can identify us. And if that's not bad enough, you just said my name!"

They argued back and forth, getting more and more agitated, and Grace waited for her chance. When the first intruder released her arms so he could wave his arms about to emphasise a point, she took off.

She spun around and made for the door.

One of the men yelled in anger, and she could hear things being knocked over as they chased her.

She almost made it. She was almost at the door when she felt a heavy blow to the back of her head.

Grace slumped to the floor.

CHAPTER TWO

2011

PRESENT DAY...

RONNIE sat in the squat, leaning back against the wall. He loosened the tourniquet on his arm and stretched out his legs in front of him. He looked over at Scott and grinned at him.

"It's good stuff..." Scott said as his eyelids fluttered.

Ronnie agreed. This was good stuff. He settled back to enjoy the high, oblivious to the squalor of the room.

None of that mattered now. He didn't care about the food wrappers and drink cans scattered on the floor, or about the toothache that had been gnawing at him all day. All that stuff just slipped away. He felt good. Really good.

Even the sound of Letitia in the bedroom down the hall, servicing one of her clients, faded into the background.

He floated into his little bit of paradise. He felt warm and safe and knew everything was going to work out just fine. Soon, his life would turn around, and he would get himself a job and a nice place to live, and when his ex saw just how well he had sorted his life out, she would be impressed. She would want him back, she would let him see his little girl, and they would be a family again.

Some minutes later, Ronnie heard the sound of retching. He tried to block it out, to get back to his high. He didn't want to come down yet. Reality sucked.

But the sound got worse.

"Here, Ron. I don't feel so good," Scott said.

Ronnie opened his eyes, blinked and tried to focus on Scott, who was swaying from side to side. At least he thought Scott was swaying, maybe he was the one swaying?

Suddenly Scott groaned and doubled over, clutching his stomach. He cried out in pain. "It hurts!"

Ronnie rubbed a hand over his face, willing himself to snap out of it. He shuffled over on his knees to Scott who was crouched on the floor.

"What's wrong?" Ronnie asked, trying to get Scott to face him. "Come on, mate. What's the matter?"

But Scott stayed clenched in a tight ball, trembling and muttering, "It hurts," over and over.

It was probably a bad trip, Ronnie thought. He put a hand on Scott's shoulder. "It's all right, Scotty. Just try and relax."

Scott stayed like that for a little while, and Ronnie felt himself drifting again, so nice and so peaceful. He kept his hand on Scott's shoulder.

Just when Ronnie thought Scott was over the worst of it. He felt Scott's entire body shudder violently.

He was having a fit.

Ronnie tried to pull Scott onto his side. He thought that was right. He had heard about the recovery position, but wasn't there something about making sure the person having the fit didn't bite through their tongue? Or maybe that was just an old wives' tale?

Scott relaxed and his body flopped back against the floor.

"Scott?" Ronnie shook Scott's arm. "You all right?"

Scott rolled over onto his back and stared up at the ceiling with blank, un-seeing eyes.

Ronnie looked down at him, and saw a miracle.

From the corner of Scott's eyes, two red teardrops appeared. Ronnie reverently made the sign of the cross. It was just like that statue of the saint Ronnie had read about. Scott was crying tears of blood.

Ronnie stood, transfixed, stunned into silence.

Then the silence was broken by a roar from Scott.

The veins in Scott's temples bulged and the tendons in his neck strained under the skin. He vomited blood. It splattered everywhere.

It was like a horror film. Ronnie had never seen so much blood. It was on his clothes, even under his shoes. The floor was slick with it.

Ronnie staggered out of the room, trying to control his rapid breathing. This isn't real. This is just a bad trip. It can't be real.

He went into the filthy bathroom, ignoring the dirt-encrusted floor and stained sink. He turned the taps on full, then splashed water on his face.

Come on, Ronnie, think!

He looked down at his shirt. It was covered in blood. Oh God, it was real. This was really happening. What the hell was he supposed to do?

Ronnie hammered on Letitia's door.

"Go away." Letitia's shrill voice carried through the thick door.

Ronnie tried the handle, but they'd locked it. "It's an emergency. I need a phone." He kicked the door. "Open up. Now."

The door was wrenched open, leaving Ronnie off balance. He staggered, then steadied himself against the door frame.

In front of him stood an obese man, wearing only a pair of white, grubby boxer shorts. "What the hell do you think you're doing?" he snarled at Ronnie, getting in his face, before suddenly taking a step back. "Is that blood?" he asked, pointing at Ronnie's shirt.

Ronnie nodded. "I need to use your phone... to call an ambulance. My friend..." Ronnie's voice trailed off as he looked back along the corridor.

"You're not using mine. No way." The fat man yanked on a pair of black trousers. "I'm not getting involved. I'm out of here." He picked up his shirt and pushed past Letitia, heading out of the room.

Letitia handed Ronnie her mobile phone. "You can use mine."

Ronnie took the phone and called for an ambulance. The operator asked him to stay on the line, but Ronnie hung up. Letitia had disappeared.

"Letitia?"

"In here."

Ronnie found Letitia kneeling over Scott. As Ronnie entered the room, she turned. "He's still alive. I think I can see him breathing."

Ronnie leaned over, and sure enough, he could see the faint rise and fall of Scott's chest, along with bubbles of blood foaming at the corners of his mouth.

CHAPTER THREE

DOCTOR ANNA SORENSEN WAS sleeping in the on-call room when her pager went off. For a moment, she looked around the poky little cubicle, no bigger than a cupboard, and wondered where on earth she was.

She had been dreaming about suturing a wound, which kept getting bigger and bigger, no matter how long she worked on it. She groaned into the pillow. She would give almost anything right now to be in her own bed, with nothing to do for the rest of the night, but sleep.

She sat up, and slipped on her shoes. Rubbing sleep from her eyes, she looked at her pager. It was Accident and Emergency.

She left the on-call room and walked along the corridor to Accident and Emergency. The junior sister on duty greeted her and told her they were expecting an emergency admission, ETA five minutes.

Anna thanked her and headed to the ambulance bay.

Claire, an experienced nurse, was already out there, waiting. She rubbed the goosebumps on her arms.

"What are we expecting?" Anna asked.

"Drug overdose. Breathing problems and vomiting blood."

Anna sighed. "Sounds like a GI bleed. Looks like it's going to be a long night."

Sirens sounded in the distance, and both Anna and Claire turned as the ambulance pulled into the bay.

The first paramedic clambered out of the back and secured the doors open. "It's a bad one." He adjusted the pulleys on the trolley.

They got the patient out of the ambulance and started to wheel him inside while the paramedic reeled off information. They'd already started a drip to maintain the patient's blood pressure.

"There was so much blood," the paramedic said, shaking his head. "I can't believe the poor bloke has any left."

They entered the double doors to the department.

"First name's Scott. Got that from his friend here." The paramedic nodded behind him, indicating a short, black man with an afro.

It looked like Scott's friend had taken something, too. His eyes were glassy, and his pupils were like pinpoints. He followed them in a daze.

"Last name?" Anna asked.

The paramedic shook his head. "Don't know."

Anna turned to Scott's friend. "What's your name?"

The man blinked. "Uh, Ronnie."

"Okay, Ronnie, can you tell me what your friend has taken?"

Ronnie opened and closed his mouth a couple of times.

"It's important, Ronnie. I can't treat him properly if I don't know what he has taken."

Ronnie looked down at his shoes and scratched his arms. "I think he took heroin." He rocked slightly, his eyes closing as he spoke.

And so have you, by the looks of it, Anna thought.

After the paramedic left to fill out his paperwork, Anna asked Ronnie to wait outside. Inside the trauma room, Anna checked Scott's vital signs, which were better than she expected from the look of him.

She took four blood samples. The first had a light pink lid. She would send that to haematology, to find out how much blood Scott had lost. The second vial had a red lid, and this sample would be used for cross-matching donor blood, as Scott would need a few units soon if he was going to make it through the night. A third tube, with a yellow lid, would go to biochemistry for standard analysis, and the final tube, with a purple lid, was the sample for the coagulation tests, which would hopefully tell her why Scott was bleeding.

Anna labelled each tube of blood with a bright yellow "danger of infection" sticker. Claire took the samples and a request form and packed them inside a plastic capsule. She inserted the plastic capsule into the pneumatic tube, which was directly linked to the laboratory downstairs.

Once they had managed to stabilise Scott and get the O-negative blood hooked up, Claire took some damp cotton wool and tried to clean away some of the blood from his face. "Poor kid," she said. "He looks so young. Not much older than my son, Tom."

Anna took off her gloves and plastic apron. "Will you be okay for a minute? I want to go and speak to his friend. I've got a feeling he won't hang around for long."

* * *

Anna found Ronnie sitting on one of the hard plastic chairs outside the trauma room. He was shaking and he kept scratching his thin arms. Anna sat down next to him.

Ronnie's hands, clenched into tight fists, rested on his knees. "Is he going to be okay?"

"At the moment, he is stable. But his condition is extremely serious. We are trying to replace the blood he has lost with a transfusion."

Ronnie nodded. "Then he'll be okay?"

"I hope so, Ronnie," Anna said. "But you know, every time he takes drugs, he is taking a risk."

"It's never happened before."

"Ronnie, tell me, did Scott inject the heroin or smoke it?" Anna had already seen track marks, but she wanted to get as much information from Ronnie as she could.

"He injected."

Ronnie's lower lip trembled so much that Anna knew tears weren't far away. "That's good. Really helpful. Now I need to find Scott's next of kin. His parents? Do you know how I can contact them?"

Ronnie shook his head. "Scott told me he hasn't seen his parents in years."

"You have no way of contacting them, at all?"

"No. I mean he's a... friend... someone I hang out with, but I mean..." Ronnie buried his head in his hands. "I don't even know his last name."

Anna waited for a moment, to give Ronnie time to collect himself. She put a hand on his shoulder. "There's something else I have to ask you, Ronnie."

Ronnie looked up at her through bloodshot eyes.

"Did you use the same heroin?" Anna asked.

Anna knew the answer before Ronnie opened his mouth. The horror was etched on his face. "You mean that's going to happen to me?"

CHAPTER FOUR

ANNA KNOCKED ON THE door of the pathology lab. "Hello?"

She stuck her head around the door and caught Rita Stafford, the on-call biomedical scientist, mid-yawn.

"Sorry, it's been a long night." Rita put down the sample of blood she had been carrying. "Can I help you?"

"I wondered if you had started analysing those urgent samples yet? The ones I sent down from A and E?" Anna looked around the laboratory. Machines were humming and beeping in full operation.

"They're running right now. Should get the results in a couple of minutes. Cross-matching will take a bit longer. How's the patient holding up? Do you need more O-negative blood?"

"I think he's stable enough to wait for the cross-matched blood. I was most interested in the coagulation tests."

"They won't be long. Do you mind if I carry on working while we talk?"

"Not at all," Anna said, following Rita into a smaller laboratory.

Rita picked up three, purple-topped vials of blood, and compared the numbers on the vials with the numbers on the forms. Then she slipped the vials into a clip, which she attached to a moving conveyor belt. The belt moved the blood samples into the belly of a large machine. It had a needle at its centre, which plunged into the sample and sucked up a small amount of blood.

The blood was mixed with a set of solutions, to make the blood clot. The time lapse until the machine detected a blot clot was then recorded by the machine.

"Do you remember the case we had, about a fortnight ago? The heroin addict with the gastrointestinal bleed?" Anna asked as Rita logged on to her computer screen.

Rita grimaced. "How could I forget? I was up all night cross-matching units of blood for him."

"The addict we just admitted has very similar symptoms."

Rita turned to face her. "How similar?"

"Vomiting blood."

Rita paled.

She had dark rings under her eyes, a testament to her twenty-four hour shift. Scientific officers worked a full day in the lab, and were required to be on-call all night at least once a week. A decade ago, this hadn't been a problem. There were few emergencies and routine blood tests wouldn't be required until after nine in the morning. But recently, the workload had increased.

Now routine work came in late at night and early in the morning, which usually meant the scientific officer would be up all night, despite having worked all day too. It was surprising that mistakes weren't made more often.

Rita got to her feet with a sigh. "That doesn't sound good at all. While I've got these samples running, I'm going to make a start on the cross-matching. Sounds like you're going to need it."

Anna followed Rita into the blood transfusion laboratory. There were even more machines here. Most of the routine work was automated these days, but when a result was needed urgently, the test was performed by hand so the sample didn't have to wait in line.

Rita picked up Scott's red-topped blood sample, read the hospital number off the side, and typed it into the computer. "We have a blood group. He's A-positive."

Rita grabbed four units of A-positive blood from the tall, glass-doored fridge at the end of the lab. "You said you wanted four on the request form."

"Yes. I hope that's enough."

Rita shut the fridge door. "It wasn't enough last time."

Last time, despite pumping unit after unit into the teenage girl, it wasn't enough. They couldn't stop the bleeding. She bled out faster than they were able to push new blood in.

Anna closed her eyes, remembering.

"Let's hope we have better luck this time," Rita said.

Rita carried the units of blood over to the workbench. Each unit was in a plastic sheath, containing about half a litre of blood. Tubes attached to the plastic were filled with blood. Rita clamped off the end of the tube and then cut it. She squeezed the tube, forcing a small amount of blood into a glass test tube.

It wouldn't take long now. All Rita had to do was mix Scott's cells and plasma with the cells and plasma of the donor blood, and make sure there was no visible reaction. Hopefully, there would be no reaction, no clumping of cells, which would mean the units of blood were safe to use in the transfusion.

The computer beeped. Rita turned to face it. "Coagulation results are in." She nodded as she scrolled through the data on the screen.

She turned to face Anna. "Looks like you were right. We've got another one."

* * *

Dr. Anna Sorensen spent the next hour extracting a coin from the nose of a five-year-old and patching up a drunk who had fallen down the stairs. As soon as she had a break, she made her way to the ward where Ronnie had been admitted for observation.

He had changed into a blue-patterned hospital gown and sat on a trolley bed, which was set back against the wall. The wards were full to bursting at the moment. Ronnie was lucky he was in the ward, rather than in the corridor.

He chewed on his thumbnail and stared around the room. One hand clasped the bed sheet against his chest.

"Hello again, Ronnie," Anna said.

He blinked and then smiled. "Hi."

"How are you feeling?"

"I'm fine. I'm pretty sure I don't have, you know, what Scott's got. Is he okay?"

"He's still having his blood transfusion. I want you to stay under observation, Ronnie. It's possible that you might become ill later. It just might not be as fast as it was for Scott."

Ronnie nodded, and traced the edge of the blanket with his finger. "Right."

"I can't say for certain, but you know that whatever you and Scott took tonight-"

"I know, I know." Ronnie held his palms up. "The drugs are bad. They're going to kill me."

"Have you ever tried to quit? Or attend any counselling programs?"

Ronnie grinned, showing the yellow and black marks on his teeth. "Oh, yeah. I've been there, done that." He gave an emphatic nod. "A lot."

"You don't want to quit?"

A flash of irritation crossed Ronnie's face. "Of course, I do. It's just not easy, that's all."

"What about family and friends? Do you have anyone to call? To help you with this?"

"I did." Ronnie shrugged. "I had family and friends the first time I tried to get clean. And the second time, and the third. I think it was the fifth time I screwed up that they gave up on me."

Anna was quiet for a moment. There wasn't anything she could say or do. She couldn't force him. What could she do? It wasn't like she could chain him to the bed.

"You have children?" Ronnie asked.

Anna's eyes widened. "Children? No, I don't."

Ronnie smiled. "I do. I got a little girl. She's eight now." Ronnie's eyes shone. "Yep, eight years old and such a clever little thing. Doesn't take after her dad." He laughed, and a few of the other patients in the ward looked over.

When Anna turned back to him, the smile dropped from his face. "That's how I know," he said.

"That's how you know what?"

"That I'll never give up. I tried, you know. I really tried. And if I can't do it for my little girl... then I can't do it at all."

He needed sympathy, maybe someone to chat to, but Anna couldn't offer him that. She had to check on Scott and finish off her shift at A and E.

"Look Ronnie. I have to get back and make sure Scott is okay. But before I go, I want you to promise that if you can't get clean, you'll at least stay away from that supply of heroin. Get a new dealer."

Ronnie nodded. "Sure."

Anna stood up to leave. She didn't know if he'd keep a promise like that. Or even if he did, who's to say the next dealer he chose wouldn't be selling the same supply?

She left Ronnie in the ward, and cut across to her office before going to check on Scott. She needed to make a phone call.

They couldn't ignore her this time.

She wouldn't let them.

CHAPTER FIVE

JACK MACKINNON HAD ONLY been at work for five minutes when a file landed with a thump on his desk.

He looked up. "What's this?"

"Job for you," said Detective Superintendent Wright, not breaking his stride. "Come and see me in five minutes and I'll fill you in."

Mackinnon smiled. Great. A proper case.

Mackinnon opened the file, eager to get started. He flicked through the pages. Three deaths in the past month, all heroin cases. Where was the case in that? He slumped down in his chair.

Three addict deaths. What on earth was he supposed to do with that?

Six months ago, he was working in the Major Investigation Team, on a high profile murder inquiry. It was challenging, and at times, dangerous, but it was the type of case that made Mackinnon feel like he was making a difference.

After that case was over, Mackinnon had been unceremoniously dumped back into the main pool of the City of London police; and he'd clearly just been given the job that no one else wanted. Brilliant.

He spent another couple of minutes leafing through the file, then walked to the superintendent's office.

The door was open and Detective Superintendent Wright sat at his desk, nursing a steaming cup of coffee. He looked up when Mackinnon entered.

Mackinnon sat down and put the file on Wright's desk. "I don't understand."

"What don't you understand?"

"I have been finishing up that paperwork on the muggings. I haven't complained about being chained to my desk, shuffling paper. I haven't complained that my request to transfer to MIT has been ignored. And now this." Mackinnon held up the file. "Have I messed up? Annoyed you? Because I am starting to think I'm being punished for something here."

"Nothing so dramatic, Jack. I need someone to look into this. Someone who isn't going to shrug it off, or think it isn't important because the victims are drug addicts."

Mackinnon leaned forward, picked up the file and opened it. "They died of drug overdoses. Where's the crime?"

Wright took the file from him and leafed through it. He pulled out a sheet of paper and pointed at a name printed on it. "You need to speak to Dr. Anna Sorensen at St. Bart's. She is the doctor who reported these deaths and she is convinced that these are not straightforward overdoses."

"Why not?"

"Ask her."

With glum resignation, Mackinnon stood up. "Right. I'll give her a call, arrange to meet her."

Wright nodded. "There is a case in this, Jack. I'd stake my reputation on it."

* * *

Dr. Anna Sorensen ran a hand through her hair. Her shift was over, and she was shattered. She had handed over all her cases, including Scott to the incoming doctor. Currently, Scott was stable. The ultrasound showed that his internal bleeding hadn't stopped, but it had slowed down enough for the blood transfusion to do its work.

She was dreaming of having a long, hot soak in the bath, and then letting her head fall back onto plump pillows and curling up in bed. But before she left, she wanted to check on Ronnie.

She walked into Ronnie's ward, yawning, and looked around for the ward sister. There were no nursing staff in the ward, and she couldn't see Ronnie.

That wasn't unusual. Ronnie may have been moved, if by some miracle, a bed had become available, and the nursing staff may have been attending an emergency. This ward seemed peaceful enough, apart from a deep rumbling snore emerging from a patient at the far end of the ward.

Anna took a seat at the nurses' station and waited.

After a couple of minutes passed, Anna's eyes started to close. She shook herself awake. If she sat there any longer, she would nod off. She took a couple of deep breaths, then stood, to go in search of the nurse in charge.

At the doorway, Anna was almost knocked off her feet by a nurse rushing into the ward.

"Sorry." The nurse slipped by Anna and picked up the

phone at the reception desk. Anna listened to the one-sided conversation.

"There's no sign of him... I've looked everywhere... He's disappeared...What? You want *me* to tell the doctor?... Oh, thanks very much."

The nurse put down the telephone and sighed.

She eyed Anna, who hadn't moved from the spot by the door.

"Are you Dr. Sorensen?"

Anna nodded.

The nurse put her hands on her hips. "Well, I have some bad news for you. Your patient has gone on walkabout."

Anna didn't need to ask which patient.

Ronnie was missing.

"Where is his file?" Anna asked.

The nurse rummaged through her file system, which seemed to consist of files scattered about her desk. "It isn't my fault, you know. I can't keep my eye on all these patients every second."

"The file?"

The nurse scowled and handed her a thin file. Anna flicked through her own notes from earlier.

"Have his details been entered on the computer?"

The nurse nodded and scooted back on her chair, so Anna could access the computer, but she would have to stand. Anna quickly searched for Ronnie's address using the postcode. It didn't exist.

She used the phone at the nurses' station to dial the mobile number he had given her.

She got a recorded message. *"The number you have dialled has not been recognised..."*

Anna put down the phone, nodded to the nurse and headed out of the ward.

She remembered Ronnie smiling when he talked about his little girl. Why couldn't he have waited just a little longer?

What were the chances of him using the same drug as his friend and not getting sick?

She answered her own question: His chances were very poor indeed.

CHAPTER SIX

DI TYLER APPROACHED MACKINNON'S desk with a face like thunder.

"The super tells me you could use my help on a case," Tyler said, pulling up a chair. "Sounds like a waste of time to me."

Mackinnon shrugged. "A doctor at Bart's has reported the unusual deaths of three heroin addicts under her care. All three of them bled to death."

DI Tyler screwed up his face. "Heroin addicts overdosed and died? That's hardly unusual. What is she, fresh out of medical school?"

"I don't know," Mackinnon said. "I've arranged to meet her."

DI Tyler rolled his eyes and pointed to the file, which was open on Mackinnon's desk. "Can I have a look then?"

Mackinnon handed him the file. "Be my guest."

"Seeing as the super called me away from MIT for this, I may as well give you the benefit of my expertise," Tyler said.

Mackinnon was silent for a few minutes while Tyler flicked through the pages. Tyler made a couple of disapproving grunts, then put it back on Mackinnon's desk.

"My professional opinion," Tyler announced, "a complete waste of time."

Mackinnon found it hard to argue. "I thought I'd go and see the doctor and find out what she has to say."

"Rather you than me, mate. Look, I'll tell you what..." DI Tyler looked around the open plan office, then moved a little closer to Mackinnon as he lowered his voice. "I know someone in the drugs squad. He's got loads of contacts. If there's anything to this, he'll get to the bottom of it."

"Right. Thanks," Mackinnon said. "I appreciate it."

"Leave it with me. Why do it yourself when you can get another department to do it for you?" DI Tyler winked and stood to leave. "It'll be enough to keep the super happy."

"I'll let you know what the doctor says," Mackinnon said.

Tyler raised an eyebrow. "You're still going to go? Suit yourself. Waste of time, though."

Mackinnon shrugged. "Yeah, well not much else going on right now. What's happening in MIT at the moment?"

Tyler grinned. "Big robbery case. We've got their mobile phone data, so we can see who phoned who, and when. Like working for the telephone exchange. We've got I2 charts plastered on all the walls at the moment. It's enough to send you boss-eyed."

"Big job, is it?"

Tyler nodded. "Really big. Going to be a brilliant result for Brookbank when we bring them in."

"Good for Brookbank," Mackinnon said.

"I forgot. You two don't get along, do you?" Tyler, who clearly hadn't forgotten at all, grinned.

Mackinnon reached for the file and started to shuffle the paperwork, hoping DI Tyler would take the hint and head back to MIT.

But Tyler wasn't going anywhere. He grinned. "So Brookbank's still not forgiven you for knocking out his son?"

"I didn't knock him out!"

"Not what I heard."

"Well, you weren't there. And, anyway, it was ages ago."

"Yeah well Brookbank's like an elephant. He doesn't forget, and as long as he is the DCI in charge of MIT, you won't get a look in."

"Thanks for your insight."

"You're welcome," DI Tyler said as he sauntered off, humming the tune to Rocky.

CHAPTER SEVEN

JT USHERED THE BOY into the back room of the bar that he used as an office. He stuck his head round the door to make sure his wife, Siobhan, wasn't nearby, and then he shut the door.

JT nodded to an empty chair. "Sit."

The boy shrugged, and with a lazy saunter, walked over to the chair. He hitched up his low-riding jeans a little and sat down on the padded computer chair. He smirked.

He didn't look worried, JT thought. And that was the problem.

He believed his own hype. This was all a game to him. The boy was a fool.

JT walked around and sat down behind his desk.

JT liked the desk. Solid red wood, polished to a nice shine, the type a real businessman would have. Details like that were important to JT. He flicked a speck of dusk off the surface.

The boy looked back at him, waiting for JT to speak. The

boy's smooth brown skin was unlined. He wouldn't get a chance to see his face wrinkle with age if he weren't careful.

The boy smirked.

"My deputy and I need a word with you," JT said.

The boy started and turned around to see JT's deputy sitting in a hardback chair by the door. It was clearly the first time he noticed there was someone else in the room. JT was gratified to see the worry in the boy's eyes when they flickered back to him.

"We've been hearing that some of our product has been making its way to the street," JT said.

"JT, I-"

JT put a hand up. "I'm not done." He leaned forward over his desk, staring hard at the boy. "We've heard you've been doing a little business on the side."

"No, JT, you got it wrong. I-"

JT put up a hand again. "I said, I'm not done. We've also heard that you have been mouthing off to the Tower Boys."

The boy shot a nervous look at the deputy sitting behind him.

JT waited a couple of seconds, then said, "Okay, boy, now you can talk."

"I've not been doing nothing on the side. Honest, JT. I swear it. And I ain't scared of the Tower Boys. I can handle them." Sweat glistened on his upper lip.

JT sat back in his chair, tilting his head to one side, to give the impression he was mulling things over.

Truth was, he had already made his decision.

He'd had the boy watched for a couple of weeks and there was no evidence he was selling on the side. Everything he sold went through the bar. But he had been crossing swords with another crew, and that was serious.

At the moment, it was all bravado, a load of talk - nothing more, but it could boil over into something more. JT didn't want that.

He couldn't afford that.

JT was under no illusions. He was small fry. At the moment, the Tower Boys allowed JT to operate purely because he only sold from the club, and he kept out of matters on the street. If this situation was allowed to develop into a turf war, he would lose. No question.

JT nodded to his deputy.

The big man stood up, walked over to the boy and rested a large, meaty hand on the boy's shoulder.

The boy looked straight ahead, with eyes wide.

"I'm going to tell you something, now," JT said. "And you better listen."

The boy nodded.

"You tell me that you're not scared of the Tower Boys. You think that makes you brave. You're the big man, afraid of no one. You really think that makes you brave? No, it makes you stupid. You think anyone will remember you if they take you out? If the Tower Boys blow your brains out in this bar? You think people will talk about how brave you were?

"No, boy, they'll talk about the colour of your brains on the pavement for a week or two, then you'll be forgotten.

"The only thing you'll be remembered for is how you looked face down on the floor."

* * *

The deputy escorted the boy out. JT hoped to God, he would keep his mouth shut now. Otherwise, he would have to get rid of him permanently.

He glanced at his watch. Time to open up. He left his office and walked down the hallway to the bar.

His wife, Siobhan, was in the kitchen, working on the lunches. She didn't notice him in the doorway, and he stood for a moment watching her. She'd been beautiful once. Stunning. All long, wavy, red hair and the greenest eyes he had ever seen.

But that was years ago. Siobhan's hair had faded, her pale skin was now drab and lifeless, and her body lumpy and ugly.

She sensed him behind her and turned, raising a ginger eyebrow. "Justin?"

JT ignored her and walked on towards the bar.

At seven-thirty, JT left John in charge of the bar and went through to the back for dinner. He was in a bad mood. He didn't fancy this family dinner, at all.

Not that he was against family. The Junction was a family business. JT managed the bar, Siobhan managed the kitchen staff, and even Emily, their daughter, helped out at weekends. His own family he could put up with. It was Siobhan's family he couldn't stand.

Tonight, she had invited her half-brother, Billy, who was a layabout failure of a man. He'd gone crawling to Siobhan, pleading for a handout, and Siobhan in turn, had nagged JT until he gave in and agreed to give Billy a job.

That was a joke. The man couldn't stack supermarket shelves without supervision. There were two sorts of people in this world: winners and losers, and Billy was definitely a loser.

The family were already gathered round the big pine table

in the kitchen when JT walked in. He took a seat next to his daughter.

"Hello, Daddy," she said, leaning over to kiss him on his cheek.

"Hello, sweetheart. How was college?'

"Oh, you know," she said, distracted by a beep from her mobile phone. "It was okay."

Siobhan brought a steaming bowl of boiled potatoes to the table. "Put that phone away, Emily. We're about to eat."

Emily rolled her eyes, but stuffed her phone into the pocket of her jeans.

"Uh, it's… it's good to see you, Justin," Billy stammered.

God, the man was pathetic.

"Yeah, you too, Bill. Keeping well?"

Billy shrugged. "Not bad."

Siobhan set down another serving bowl. This time full of beef stew. The steam rose up around her face, making her hair frizzy and her face red and blotchy.

He turned to his daughter. What a contrast. Her skin was a lovely, golden colour, a mixture of Siobhan's pale and his dark.

JT's mother's family originated from Jamaica. His father was some white bastard who left them when JT was three years old. But together, they managed to produce Emily, and she appeared to have gotten the best of both of them.

Luckily for her, she'd inherited his brains, and was doing well at college. She might even go on to university. He'd like that. His little girl working as a doctor or a lawyer. He didn't want her to get too involved in the bar. She was better than that. And he sure as hell didn't want her to know about his other business on the side. As far as JT was concerned, Siobhan and Emily would never have anything to do with that.

They all started eating and there was silence for a few minutes before JT asked Billy how he was getting on with his new job. "I'm sorry I couldn't give you any more hours, Bill, but things aren't exactly flush at the moment."

"Oh, I understand, Justin. I appreciate you helping me out."

"That's what families are for," Siobhan said, smiling at her brother.

Emily started talking about college and Siobhan and Billy listened attentively. He didn't like the way Billy held onto every word Emily said. He didn't like the way he looked at her. It gave him the creeps. Emily didn't seem to mind. She'd always loved an audience, even from when she was tiny.

JT let his mind wander.

Perhaps he'd made a mistake taking Billy on. Siobhan was very close to her brother. Of course, he'd made Billy promise never to mention a word about his little sideline. But would Billy keep that promise?

JT watched Billy laugh at something Emily said and scowled. Maybe he would have to think of something to make his point. To make sure Billy realised just how important it was to keep his mouth shut.

CHAPTER EIGHT

JACK MACKINNON PULLED UP outside Chloe's house on the Woodstock road. He was shattered. The commute from London to Oxford wasn't an easy one, and all he wanted to do now was have a couple of beers and crash out on the sofa. It hadn't been that busy at work, but the never-ending paperwork seemed to send his brain to sleep.

As soon as Mackinnon opened the door, he knew he wasn't going to get the quiet night he'd hoped for. Angry screams came from the kitchen, and Katy sat at the bottom of the stairs, her head resting on the banister.

"What's going on?" Mackinnon asked.

"Not sure," Katy said, "But Sarah's just got home and Mum's furious."

Mackinnon glanced at his watch. It was only eight pm, much earlier than Sarah's curfew, so they couldn't be fighting about that. He took a deep breath and considered heading upstairs for a shower, to keep out of the way. Then he looked at Katy chewing her lip and thought he had better go and see if he could calm things down.

As soon as he walked into the kitchen, he understood why Chloe was so upset.

He could smell the marijuana on Sarah's clothes.

Sarah's tight, furious expression disappeared when she saw Mackinnon, and she collapsed into giggles.

"Hello, Jack. Have you come to arrest me?" She held out her wrists and looked at him, her eyes wide and unfocused. "It's okay, officer. I promise to come quietly."

Mackinnon ignored her and turned to Chloe, who seemed close to tears. She ran her hands through her hair.

"I don't know what she's taken."

"Smells like marijuana," Mackinnon said.

Chloe moved forward and put her hands on either side of Sarah's face, tilting her head back so she could see into Sarah's eyes.

Sarah's jovial mood disappeared in an instant. "Gerroff!" She flung out her arms, and the back of her right hand connected with Chloe's jaw with a crack.

In the silence that followed, Sarah stood, swaying, eyes wide with shock, and Chloe faced her, fists clenched at her sides.

They stared at each other for a moment, before Chloe stormed out of the kitchen.

Sarah looked down at the floor.

"Why do you do it to her?" Mackinnon asked.

"Why does she do it to me? I'm the child!"

Mackinnon could smell the alcohol on her breath. He shook his head. "You're nearly eighteen."

"Screw you," Sarah said over her shoulder as she left the kitchen. "It's none of your business."

Alone in the kitchen, Mackinnon got a bottle of Beck's from the fridge, leaned back against the counter, and swallowed half the beer in one go.

Maybe Sarah just needed to get it out of her system. If he tried to help, he'd be accused of interfering. If he said nothing, he'd be accused of not caring.

He drained the rest of the beer and wondered if he ever gave his parents this much grief.

Chloe thought Sarah just needed time to sort herself out. She thought it was some kind of delayed reaction to her father leaving for New Zealand. Maybe Chloe was right. Maybe time would help, but Mackinnon had a horrible feeling things were going to get worse before they got better.

A few minutes later, Chloe returned to the kitchen. Worry lines were etched on her forehead.

"What am I going to do with her?"

Mackinnon knew this was a rhetorical question; Chloe didn't want an answer. Although he was very tempted to reply, he knew it was better to wait until tomorrow morning when she'd be nursing a hangover and start vacuuming outside her bedroom door. That's how Mackinnon's mother had expressed her disapproval at him getting drunk when he was Sarah's age.

"Do you want me to start dinner?"

Chloe walked over to the fridge and opened it. "I'll do it. I got some prawns. I thought I'd do a stir-fry; okay with you?"

"Sure. You want me to chop some veg?"

Chloe pulled out a packet of premixed stir-fry veg. "I cheated." She nodded at a bottle of white wine in the fridge. "You can pour the drinks, though."

Mackinnon fixed the drinks and set the table. He paused

over the fourth place setting. "Will Sarah eat with us, do you think?"

Chloe vigorously shook the wok. "Probably not, but set it anyway."

Mackinnon finished up, then sat down at the table and took a welcome sip of the wine. "I thought I'd stay at Derek's tomorrow."

Chloe nodded and started to spoon the stir-fry onto plates. "Yeah, makes sense, staying with Derek means you'll be much closer to work during the week. I'll miss you though." She looked up at him and winked. "Bet you won't miss us much, though. You'll probably be glad to escape from the madhouse."

"I'll be here at the weekends. You'll hardly notice I'm gone. I'll call the girls for dinner."

Mackinnon climbed the stairs and knocked softly on Sarah's door. No answer. He knocked a little louder. Still nothing, he guessed she was giving him the silent treatment. Katy came out of her room and frowned at him.

"I guess Sarah's not hungry," Mackinnon said.

Katy shrugged. "I doubt she's even in there."

"What?"

"This is Sarah we are talking about," Katy said and raised her eyebrows. "I can't hear her music, she's not on the phone, so..."

Mackinnon gave the door two loud knocks with the side of his fist. Katy squeezed past him and walked down the stairs. When Sarah didn't respond, he opened the door.

The bedroom was empty.

He felt a chill in the air and crossed to the window. It had been left open a fraction. She wouldn't have, Mackinnon thought, opening the window wider and looking down. Underneath Sarah's bedroom window was the flat roof of the extension. She must have climbed down.

The girl was crazy.

CHAPTER NINE

THE FOLLOWING MORNING, AT Wood Street station, Mackinnon was unsuccessfully trying to track down DI Tyler. It seemed that most of the members of MIT were attending a briefing.

"Is Tyler in that meeting?" Mackinnon asked DC Collins.

DC Collins looked up from his computer screen. "Yeah, along with half the station."

Mackinnon filled a bit of time, chatting to Collins.

The I2 charts on the wall caught Mackinnon's eye. "Is this what Brookbank is working on?"

Collins nodded. "Yeah, the team has been tracking mobile phone calls for weeks now. Going to be a big one if he pulls it off. He's got everyone working on it... er... well, that is to say, not everyone." Collins flushed. "Look, Jack, I just wanted to say, I don't think Brookbank's being very fair..."

"It's all right, don't worry about it. It's not a big deal."

Everyone at the station knew Mackinnon didn't get along with Brookbank, not since Mackinnon had gotten into a fight with Brookbank's son. If there was a chance Brookbank could avoid working with Mackinnon, he would, which was why Mackinnon worked his way through a stack of paperwork every day, while everyone else was involved in the big case.

"Robbery is it?" Mackinnon asked.'

"Target's a bank, and they're pretty well organised about it."

Mackinnon looked up again, studying the I2 charts, then stood up. "Could you tell Tyler I was looking for him?"

Mackinnon wandered back to his pile of paperwork, dragging his feet as he went.

It was eleven am before Tyler appeared at Mackinnon's desk.

"All right? Collins said you were looking for me?"

"I was." Mackinnon picked up his mug of coffee. "You want one?"

"Nah, I'm swimming in the stuff. I had four cups in Brookbank's briefing to try and stay awake." He perched on the edge of Mackinnon's desk, just about finding room in between the piles of paper.

"Robbery case going okay, is it?" Mackinnon asked.

Tyler smiled. "Like clockwork. It's a belter of a case. Shame you're not on it too, really. Going to be big kudos for everyone on the team when Brookbank nails it." Tyler said. "So what did you need me for?"

"About the death of those addicts-"

"Oh, that. Don't worry about that. I talked to a DI I know in drugs, and he's happy to do the leg work. Give him a couple of days and he'll give us something to bung in the report."

"Can I have his number?"

"What?"

"The DI from drugs. I'd like to talk to him myself."

"What for?"

"Because the super gave me a job to do, and-"

"Oh, for God's sake, Mackinnon, you don't have to keep up the whiter-than-white act with me. It's just a bunch of addicts. Relax, the super will be happy with the report," Tyler said. "You know, if you were a bit easier to work with, you might find yourself back on the team. Stop getting wound up. I'll get back to you in a couple of days."

"And what do I say to the super if he asks?"

Tyler eased himself off the desk and looked down at Mackinnon. "You're a smart chap. I'm sure you'll think of something."

After Tyler left, Mackinnon managed to focus on the paperwork for about twenty minutes, before DC Charlotte Brown wheeled a chair over to his desk.

She flopped into the chair. "God, that was a long meeting."

Mackinnon pulled a face. "I wouldn't know about that."

"Feeling sorry for yourself, Mac?"

"You'd be feeling pretty sorry for yourself, too, if you'd been stuck doing endless bloody paperwork, when everyone else is working on the most interesting case of the year," Mackinnon said, picking up some of the sheets of paper. "I'm getting lost in duplicates."

"I wouldn't feel too put out if I were you. I've been going cross-eyed after looking at the charts all week. To be honest, it's not much better than bog standard paperwork."

"DI Tyler said it's a big case, filled with kudos for Brookbank."

"Tyler is winding you up, you plank. Brookbank has got us all tracking calls. A called B, then B called C at x time and so on and on and on...

D. S. BUTLER

"Anyway." Charlotte looked down at the scattered files on Mackinnon's desk. "Why are you here doing paperwork, rather than working on the suspicious deaths?"

"Nothing is really happening with that. I've got to wait for Tyler to get back to me."

"What for?"

"He's getting some information from a guy he knows, who works in the Met's central task force."

Charlotte frowned. "Right. What information did you get from the doctor who reported the deaths? Do you think there is anything in it?"

Mackinnon shrugged. "I've not seen her yet."

"Why don't you go and see her now? Rather than stay buried under all that paperwork." She tapped one of the stacks of paper with her finger. "I know what I'd rather be doing."

Mackinnon dropped his pen on the desk. "You're right."

"As always." Charlotte grinned.

"Well, I wouldn't go that far."

CHAPTER TEN

MACKINNON WALKED THE SHORT distance to St. Bart's from Wood Street station. He had called ahead and arranged to meet Dr. Anna Sorensen at the pathology department at two. First, he had to find the place.

Sections of the hospital were cut off. According to a helpful, elderly gentleman, some of the hospital departments were currently being relocated to the new Royal London Hospital. After going the wrong way and ending up in a dimly lit corridor lined with wheelchairs and empty stretchers, Mackinnon found a hospital porter, who kindly pointed him in the right direction.

When he finally arrived at the pathology reception, there were two women who looked up as he approached the desk. One was short with dark hair, cut in spikes; the other woman was tall, and had blonde hair swept back in a ponytail.

He gave his name and told them he had an appointment to see Dr. Sorensen.

The blonde woman extended her hand. "DS Mackinnon, I'm Dr. Sorensen, I reported the suspicious deaths."

Mackinnon shook her hand, surprised at how young she looked.

"Good of you to come, eventually," she said.

Mackinnon noted the dig, but took it in his stride. "Is there somewhere we can talk?"

She nodded. "I'll take you to the lab, this way," She led him past the reception desk, through a set of blue double doors and into a narrow corridor that smelled of disinfectant even more strongly than the rest of the hospital.

As they walked, she pointed out the different labs, then said, "We're heading for haematology."

They passed through the blood transfusion lab. A middle-aged woman, with her grey hair in a bun, sat in front of a plastic pouch of blood. She took hold of a long tube connected to the pouch and snipped off a section of the tube, about five centimetres long. She then squeezed the blood out of the tube into a glass vial in front of her.

Mackinnon felt his stomach flip over and turned away. "What's she doing?"

Dr. Sorensen looked back, unconcerned. "Cross-matching blood."

"Right," said Mackinnon. He couldn't think of a more intelligent response and concentrated on keeping his eyes averted from the blood. It was ridiculous. He had attended accidents and crime scenes where there were obscene amounts of blood, but in this setting, it just made him nauseous. All that blood in packets, being squeezed out of tubes. He shuddered.

They arrived at a door labelled COAGULATION LABO-RATORY. Dr. Sorensen rapped on the door and then entered.

There was only one woman in the room. Dressed in a white lab coat, she sat in front of a machine that looked like something out of a factory.

"Ah Rita, I'm glad you are here. This is DS Mackinnon. He has come about the bleeders."

"Ah," Rita said, turning her eyes to Mackinnon, expectantly.

At that moment, Dr. Sorensen's pager sounded. She pulled it from her belt and glanced at the screen. "Damn. I won't be long. I just need to use the phone." She backed out of the lab and left Mackinnon with Rita.

Mackinnon looked at the strange machine on top of the lab bench. A row of blood samples were lined up on a small conveyor belt, heading towards the centre of the machine.

"What does this fancy bit of kit do?"

Rita tapped a couple of quick key strokes, then turned to face Mackinnon. "It's an automated way of measuring how quickly blood clots. We have an outpatient clinic today, and we need to make sure people are on the right dose of anti-coagulant. If they take too much, they are at risk of a bleed; not enough, then they could develop blood clots, thrombosis."

She opened one of the metal panels on the machine and picked a blood sample from the conveyor belt.

The blood looked dark in its clear glass tube with a purple lid.

"Now if you look at the top of the lid, here," she said as she pointed to a black circular area on the sample's lid. "This is a seal, the blood can't come out." Rita held the sample tube upside-down to prove her point. "But the machine's needle can penetrate the seal and take a sample of the blood. Here, I'll show you."

She put the blood sample back on the conveyor belt and

then opened up a metal panel on the machine, so they could see right into the heart of the machine.

"The blood samples are taken towards the sampling needle." She pointed at a five-centimetre-long, steel needle. She paused while a sample was clamped into position, and with a hiss, the vicious-looking needle stabbed the centre of the lid and shot down into the blood inside.

"The blood gets sucked up and mixed with chemicals, back here." She patted the back of the machine, whose workings were hidden by more metal panels.

"The chemicals trigger the blood to coagulate, or clot, and the time it takes is recorded by the computer."

"I see," Mackinnon said, watching as the machine clamped onto its next sample.

"If the blood coagulates too quickly, that's bad, because the patient might be at risk of developing a blood clot, and like I said earlier, if it coagulates too slowly-"

"Then they could bleed to death." Dr. Sorensen finished Rita's sentence as she came back into the lab. "And that's what happened in the cases I reported, DS Mackinnon, the patients bled to death."

While Rita got back to work, loading more samples onto the machine, Dr. Sorensen took Mackinnon through the three case histories, one by one. She finished up by saying, "So it is obvious that these deaths are linked."

"I'm sorry, but I don't follow," Mackinnon said. "None of the causes of death are the same. You said one died from a brain haemorrhage, one from a gastrointestinal bleed and one died on the operating table. The only real thing they have in common is that they were addicts. Heroin isn't exactly a healthy habit, is it? Isn't it possible they just got sick? The heroin weakened their immune system, and so they-"

Dr. Sorensen interrupted. "In each case, the haemorrhage, the GI bleed, the death on the operating table, the deaths occurred because the patients' blood was unable to clot properly. That's what links all these cases. Heroin itself does possess a small amount of anti-coagulant activity, but nothing like what we saw in these patients. There were different organs involved in the different cases, but ultimately, all these addicts bled to death."

"If it isn't the heroin causing them to bleed to death, what is?"

I think there is something else in the heroin they took," Dr. Sorensen said. "I think it must be contaminated by another drug."

"Can you be sure it's not caused by an infection?"

"I can't be sure. We ran blood cultures and various tests. But so far, we haven't detected any infections. If anything, their white cell counts were on the low side of normal, so nothing indicated an infection."

"Dr. Sorensen..."

"Please, just call me Anna."

Mackinnon nodded. "Right, Anna, I'll report back to my superiors. We can probably get a public health warning issued pretty quickly, which will let people know there is contaminated heroin on the streets."

Anna sighed. "What do you think addicts will do? Stop taking it? If it were that easy, they wouldn't be addicted."

"Without knowing where this contaminate drug is coming from, there's not a lot else we can do. Unless you know where they are getting their heroin from? Are all three from the same area of London?"

"Funnily enough, they weren't exactly fit to answer my

questions while they were coughing up blood, or had blood flooding their brains."

Mackinnon raised an eyebrow.

"I'm sorry." Anna pinched the bridge of her nose. "I've been trying to get people to pay attention to this after I saw the other three cases. Now I have another one in ICU. I feel like no one is listening to me, like I am trying to stop this all on my own."

"I'm going to do all I can to try and help," Mackinnon said. "We can contact other NHS trusts and see if any other trusts have seen similar cases, and of course, we'll report it to the Health Protection Authority."

Anna nodded. "I have informed the Health Protection Agency already."

Mackinnon stared down at the patient notes on the table and started to mentally plan the things he would need to do when he got back to the station.

Anna's voice cut through his thoughts. "The patient I have in ICU at the moment was brought in with a friend. I was sure his friend had taken the same stuff, and I tried to persuade him to stay and get treatment, but he left, and I'm worried that..."

"Did you get a name? An address? I could try and trace him."

Anna shook her head. "He gave us false information."

"Maybe he didn't take it. Maybe he's fine."

"Maybe."

"Have you heard of any similar cases? In other hospitals? Other trusts?

"No, I haven't."

"Hopefully, that means it is localised to this area."

Mackinnon jotted down a note to remind himself to

mention other hospitals to the superintendent. "Do you have any idea what the heroin could be contaminated with?"

Mackinnon knew heroin was commonly cut with other substances, usually things like sugar or caffeine. But sometimes it could be cut with other prescription drugs, which could be fatal for a user. Bulking out the heroin with other cheaper drugs means more profit for the dealer, and as the drug trickles down the supply chain, it gets less and less pure.

"My best bet would be the heroin was cut with another drug, either here or abroad. As for what I think that drug could be, I'm sorry, but I really don't have a clue. All sorts of things have been found mixed with heroin."

Mackinnon wished there was something more he could do, something to reassure the doctor that she wouldn't have any more addicts bleeding to death in her wards. He could make sure alerts were issued to hospitals and other police forces nationwide, warning people of the potentially contaminated heroin supply. Still, it was unlikely to convince addicts to stay away from the drug.

Mackinnon handed Dr. Sorensen his card. "If you need to get hold of me, my mobile number is on the card, too. If you hear of any more cases, let me know."

Anna took Mackinnon's card and led him back out, through the labs and the narrow corridor.

When they reached the reception, Mackinnon slowed and said, "Just one more thing, rather than using this contaminating drug as a bulking agent, do you think this contamination could be deliberate?"

"A deliberate poisoning?" Dr. Sorensen frowned, then said, "Your guess is as good as mine."

CHAPTER ELEVEN

2001

TEN YEARS AGO...

Inside the ICU ward, Grace lay on her hospital bed, floating on the painkillers the doctors had given her.

When Grace came around, she wasn't afraid. She knew she was in hospital. It felt like a familiar place to her, her home away from home.

She listened to the steady beep of the machine by her bed and tried to focus her thoughts. What was she doing back in hospital? Another infection? She couldn't remember.

She searched her mind for memories. There was an ambulance, she remembered the blue flashing lights, but nothing else. How strange.

She started to drift off again, enjoying the soft blanket of painkillers, when there was a clatter as something fell to the floor.

It was probably just a nurse dropping something as small as a pen, but the noise triggered Grace's brain to remember.

She remembered that man's grasping hands, and his leering face filled her mind. She had tried to run, tried to get away. Then he hit her.

She tried to shake her head.

Despite the painkillers, the movement felt like nails were being hammered into her skull. She winced and caught her breath.

She blinked her eyes open, and saw her father sitting beside the bed, his face etched with worry. She struggled to speak, to reassure him, forgetting at first that she had a tube in her throat. All she could do was grunt out a noise.

The tube didn't really bother her. It was uncomfortable, and she felt like she wanted to keep swallowing, but she was used to the tubes. She had been in and out of hospital since she was a baby, and eighteen months ago, she'd had a heart and lung transplant.

Compared to that, this was nothing.

She moved her fingers to cover her father's hand.

He took her hand in both of his. "It's all right, Grace. Everything is going to be okay, sweetheart. The doctors know all about your cystic fibrosis. I've told them which medications you are on. Your surgeon, Dr. Meyer came down earlier. He was really upset about what happened to you, said he'd come back later." Her father's eyes shone with tears. "So don't you worry about anything. I've got it all under control. You just relax and concentrate on getting better."

She heard the tremor in his voice, and unable to comfort him with words, she squeezed his hand tightly.

CHAPTER TWELVE

2011

PRESENT DAY...

MACKINNON found DI Tyler in the canteen. He was chatting away to a pretty DC, touching her on the arm as he spoke, leaning into her, like he was sharing secrets. Mackinnon recognised the DC's face, but couldn't remember her name.

Mackinnon queued up and collected his coffee, then walked behind the two of them, unnoticed, and laid a hand on Tyler's shoulder.

Tyler whirled around, saw it was Mackinnon, then exhaled dramatically, putting a hand to his chest.

"Don't do that, you daft sod. I thought it was Brookbank."

"I need a word," Mackinnon said. They both looked up at the DC.

She took the hint and stood up. "I'll leave you to it, shall I?" she said and stalked out of the canteen.

"Sorry to break up your little tete-a-tete," Mackinnon said, looking at Tyler's wedding ring.

"No you're not. So, what is it?" Tyler said and drained the rest of his coffee. "I should be downstairs by now. Brookbank will be on the warpath if I'm not down there soon."

"I want to see this DI of yours, the one in drugs. I want to speak to him."

Tyler gave a frustrated sigh. "Why? Why are you so determined to make more work for yourself? Bruce knows what he's doing. I know you are the super's blue-eyed boy, Mackinnon, but you don't have to keep up the act with me. I won't grass you up."

"I just want to do this the right way. Why is that so hard to understand?"

"Christ," Tyler slammed his coffee cup down on the table. "Fine. I'll ask if he has got time to see us today. Satisfied?"

* * *

Sarah woke up with a pounding headache. The curtains were open, flooding her bedroom with daylight, which only made it worse.

She pushed back the duvet and sat up. She felt clammy and really ill, like she was going to throw up. Her mouth was so dry, it was difficult to swallow. Why was she so thirsty?

She reached for a half-finished can of Coke on her bedside table, took a sip and almost gagged. It was warm and flat.

A cup of tea. That's what she needed to make her feel better. She got out of bed, put on her dressing gown, stepped over the clothes on the floor, which absolutely stunk of smoke, and headed downstairs.

As she walked through the living room, she glanced out of the front bay window and saw that her mother's car was still parked in the drive. Brilliant. Just what she didn't need: Another bloody lecture.

She felt a shiver of shame, remembering last night.

She rubbed the red mark on the back of her hand. It wasn't her fault. It wasn't as if she hit her mother deliberately. Sarah bit down on her lip. Maybe she should apologise. It might not have been her fault, but things did get out of hand last night and...

Sarah froze.

Her bag sat in the centre of the kitchen table, its contents stacked in a heap next to it. Chloe was sifting through it.

"What the hell do you think you're doing?" Sarah yelled.

Chloe jumped and dropped the packet of cigarettes she was holding. Then she thrust her chin in the air.

"I'm looking for whatever it was you took last night." Chloe picked up a compact mirror, held it up to the light, then put it back down on the table.

"You've got no right to go through my stuff!"

"I've got every right. I'm your mother, and this is my house."

"You're a nosy, old cow, that's what you are." Sarah grabbed her bag and started shoving her things back inside it.

Chloe sat down and put her head in her hands. "I don't want another argument, Sarah. I want to help you."

Sarah ignored her and dumped the compact mirror and a lipstick back in her bag.

"If you can't talk to me, why don't you try to talk to Jack..."

"Ha! Jack?"

"Well, he could-"

Sarah put her hands on her hips. "He could what? He's not exactly..." She made speech marks with her hands and put on a silly, high-pitched voice, "...down with us kids, is he? He is young, mother, but not that young."

"He would like to help. He would do his best to-"

"Oh, I am sure he would," Sarah said. "Loves a good cause, doesn't he? We're just like a project to him. He regrets moving in now, you know. You do realise he only sticks around because he feels sorry for you."

In a flash, Chloe reached across the table and slapped Sarah's cheek. It wasn't a hard slap, only her finger tips made contact, but Chloe snatched back her hand as if she'd been burned.

Sarah put a hand up to her cheek. "One all," she said, picking up her bag. "Don't expect me back tonight."

She made to leave, but before she reached the door, she turned. "Did you know Katy gets teased at school because of your toy boy?" Sarah smiled at the obvious hurt on her mother's face. "Don't wait up, Mother."

CHAPTER THIRTEEN

CHARLOTTE STIFLED A YAWN. If this briefing went on for much longer, she'd be asleep. It wasn't through lack of coffee, she had two cups in quick succession, but even coffee had its limits. She couldn't survive without a proper night's sleep. All this week, she'd been up at night, checking the door was locked and all the windows were shut, and jumping at every little sound.

She was tempted to stay over at her nan's place tonight, just one night. A full night's sleep was so appealing. But that would be giving in, letting the bastard win, and she couldn't do that.

She rubbed her eyes. The state she was in now, he was winning anyway.

Brookbank finally drew the meeting to a close, and Charlotte followed the rest of the team filing out of the briefing room.

"Are you feeling all right, DC Brown?" Brookbank asked as she neared the front of the room.

"Oh, I am fine," Charlotte said, just as she walked into a chair. She winced and rubbed her bruised shin.

"I'm fine, really," she said, forcing a grin. "Just a bit tired."

"Perhaps an early night would be a good idea."

There were a few barely suppressed sniggers from the rest of the group. Charlotte ignored them.

"Yes, sir."

She headed off to the vending machine. Caffeine alone might not be up to the job, but sugar and caffeine made a winning combination.

Charlotte took a large bite of the Dairy Milk bar just as Mackinnon walked around the corner.

"Chocolate, this early in the day? Must be bad."

Charlotte swallowed the chocolate. "How are you enjoying working with DI Tyler on your drugs case?"

Mackinnon pulled a face that told her how he found working with DI Tyler better than any words. "Not sure you could call it work. He just wants to pass everything on to the guy he knows in the Met."

Charlotte broke off the next segment of chocolate. "How did it go with the doctor?"

"Interesting. She is really concerned. I met her in the labs and got a bit of a science lesson, all about blood clotting." Mackinnon paused, wondering if Charlotte really wanted to hear this while she was eating, but Charlotte munched away happily. She nodded for him to continue.

"So far, she's had three patients bleed to death in different ways. With no real explanation, and nothing linking them other than the fact they were all addicted to heroin."

"Not the usual cause of death after an overdose."

"Exactly, you might expect a heart attack, or choking on

vomit, but this is very unusual. She thinks the heroin might be contaminated by another drug."

"Which drug?"

"No idea."

"I remember the anthrax scare a while back," Charlotte said. "It was suggested that anthrax spores had somehow managed to contaminate the drugs when they were stored with animal skins."

Mackinnon nodded. "Yes, the anthrax was thought to be accidental."

"And this isn't?"

"Well... it could be."

Charlotte looked up at him, the final piece of chocolate melting in her hand. "But you think it's deliberate, don't you?"

CHAPTER FOURTEEN

DI TYLER IGNORED MACKINNON as they walked side-by-side to the coffee shop on Gresham Street. Mackinnon didn't mind. He preferred watching people bustling along the street to talking to Tyler.

A man darted in front of Mackinnon and Tyler, ran across the road, and narrowly missed getting crushed under the wheels of a red, double-decker bus.

"Bloody fool," Tyler muttered. He was in a real stinker of a mood.

When they reached the coffee shop, Tyler entered first, looked around, then headed to a table at the back of the room.

The man sitting at the table stood to greet them.

"This is DI Evans," Tyler said, then jerked his thumb at Mackinnon. "This is Jack Mackinnon, the DS I told you about."

Bruce Evans held out his hand. "Good to meet you, Jack. You can call me Bruce."

Mackinnon and Bruce Evans shook hands, then Tyler

looked pointedly at Mackinnon. "I'll have an Americano, thanks."

"I've got mine already," Bruce said before Mackinnon asked him if he wanted one.

Mackinnon joined the end of the line and watched Tyler and DI Evans. They chatted away like old friends. He couldn't catch what they were saying, but the emphatic hand gestures and laughter made him think they got on well. That immediately made Mackinnon wary. In Mackinnon's opinion, anyone who got on with DI Tyler couldn't have sound judgement.

Bruce Evans had an open and expressive face. Mackinnon put him around mid-forties. Sandy hair, blue eyes, average looking, not the sort of bloke you'd remember, nothing distinctive about him. He just blended into the background, which was probably a useful attribute in his job.

Mackinnon carried the coffees over to the table.

"Do you two go back a long way?" he asked, transferring the coffee cups from the tray to the sticky tabletop.

"We've known each other a while," Bruce said and smiled. "We worked together about ten years ago."

Tyler added three sachets of sugar to his coffee, then moaned because Mackinnon hadn't picked up any stirrers.

"They're over there," Mackinnon said and nodded at the corner of the room where the napkins, stirrers and packets of sugar were stored.

Making a fuss about it, Tyler got to his feet and went to get his stirrer, dodging a couple of hyper-active toddlers on his way.

"So what did you need to see me for?" Bruce Evans asked Mackinnon.

"Tyler said you might be able to help us. I'm not sure how much he has told you so far."

Bruce nodded. "Tyler filled me in, but he said you were adamant you wanted to see me yourself?"

"Yeah, sorry about that, Bruce," Tyler said, wandering back over with the stirrer in his hand. "I did tell Mackinnon it wasn't necessary, but he's keen, likes to dot all his i's and cross all his t's."

"Nothing wrong with that," Bruce said and smiled again.

Tyler grunted. "Unless you have to work with him."

Mackinnon decided to try and pretend Tyler wasn't there. "I don't know how much Tyler has told you, but there have been a series of suspicious deaths among heroin addicts in the City area. We were alerted to the deaths by a registrar at St. Bart's, who was very concerned. The deaths were nothing like you would expect in a normal overdose case. Her patients bled to death."

Bruce grimaced. "Nasty. I have to tell you, in my opinion, preventing more deaths isn't going to be easy. The big problem is that heroin gets mixed with all sorts. And that isn't necessarily a bad thing. Lots of overdoses actually happen because an addict got hold of an unusually pure fix."

"The doctor I spoke to thinks it has been mixed with some sort of anti-coagulant," Mackinnon said. "And that's why the victims are bleeding to death."

"I haven't heard of that one before. The more common ingredients for it to be mixed with are things like sugar or caffeine. That way, the dealer's supply stretches further, and that bumps up their profit." Evans took a sip of coffee. "The problem comes when they mix heroin with something dangerous. There was a horrible incident in the US a few years back when a stash of heroin was contaminated with clenbuterol."

"Oh, yeah, I heard about that," said Tyler, looking a bit peeved at being left out of the conversation so far.

"It was nasty. People died from taking that stuff. Our problem," Bruce said, leaning towards them, "is getting people to stop taking it.

Tyler took a long slurp of his coffee, then smacked his lips together. "Definitely something that is easier said than done."

"I take it you are organising ways of informing people who might be at risk," Bruce said.

Tyler nodded. "Yes. Our superintendent will be sending out information to forces nationwide, in case it isn't a localised problem, and he is arranging for the NHS trusts and some of the drugs charities to be informed, so they can be prepared if new cases turn up. There's going to be a press release tomorrow."

"Right. Our next problem is finding the source, and that won't be easy," Bruce said. "People aren't going to want to tell you where they got their drugs from."

"So you're saying there's nothing we can do?" Mackinnon said.

Bruce Evans shook his head. "I have been working in this area for a while, and I've got a couple of informants. One guy, from the Towers Estate, is a long-term addict, who knows a few of the suppliers around there. He might know something, or he might even be able to get us some samples." Bruce sat back in his chair and looked at Tyler and Mackinnon in turn. "Of course, if we get him to collect samples of heroin for us, they are not going to be much use as evidence for a prosecution, but it will give us a place to start. I mean, if we are lucky, it could tell us if the whole supply chain is contaminated, or just one source.

"It would really help if we could narrow it down."

"Right. I'll talk to my guy and get back to you both as soon as I can, all right?"

"I'd like to talk to him," Mackinnon said.

Bruce exchanged a look with Tyler. Tyler then snorted and shook his head. "That is not how it works, Mackinnon."

Bruce Evans smiled at Mackinnon. "The information I get is on a confidential basis. The informants don't want anyone to know that they are talking to the Old Bill, so that's why I meet them one-on-one."

"All the same, I would like to see him and hear what he has to say myself."

Bruce exhaled, puffing out his cheeks. "It really would be easier-"

"I don't care about easier," Mackinnon said. "I want to find out what he knows about this dodgy heroin."

There was a long pause, then Evans said, "All right, I'll set it up."

He smiled again, but his eyes were no longer so friendly.

CHAPTER FIFTEEN

RONNIE SLID INTO THE back of DI Bruce Evans' car. No one said anything, until Bruce drove away, edging into the slow moving traffic.

"Are you all right, Ronnie?" Evans asked, looking at him in the rearview mirror.

Ronnie nodded, his eyes fixed on Mackinnon, who sat in the front passenger seat.

Never one to do work when he could get out of it, Tyler had made his excuses earlier and left Mackinnon and Bruce to track down Ronnie, Bruce's informant.

"This is DS Mackinnon, Ronnie," Bruce said. "He is after some information, and I thought you might be able to help us out."

Mackinnon turned and smiled at Ronnie, trying to look reassuring.

Ronnie stared back at him, weighing him up, distrust in his brown eyes. Up close, Ronnie looked a hundred times worse than Mackinnon had expected, even though he knew Ronnie was a long-term addict.

Ronnie's springy afro was cut unevenly, suggesting he had cut it himself. Most of his hair stood on end, but on the right side of his scalp, he had a bald patch and below that, a section of matted hair that hung down over his ear.

He had a large, red and inflamed sore on his cheek, that would probably need a strong course of antibiotics to heal. Smudges of dirt covered his face, and his fingernails were black with grime. But Ronnie didn't seem the least bit concerned by his appearance.

Defiantly, he stared at Mackinnon. "I don't talk to strangers."

"I know that, Ronnie. But this is different. DS Mackinnon is someone you can trust, and we really need your help." DI Evans' voice was smooth and cajoling. "When DS Mackinnon came to me, I knew you were the only one for the job. The only one I could trust."

At this obvious flattery, Ronnie's eyes narrowed, and he shot Bruce a look that seemed to say, "I may be an addict, but I'm not stupid enough to fall for all that fluff."

Mackinnon thought DI Evans might have gone overboard with all the flattery and that any second, Ronnie would open the door and leave the car, taking advantage of the fact they'd slowed to a crawl in the traffic.

DI Evans carried on, oblivious to Ronnie's reaction so far. "There has been some really nasty stuff going on recently. People on heroin have been suffering awful deaths."

Ronnie grunted. "That is what happens when you get hooked on heroin, isn't it?" he said, sarcastically.

Evans looked at Mackinnon. "Tell Ronnie what happened to those addicts."

Mackinnon turned in his seat to face Ronnie. He needed to be his most persuasive. He couldn't afford to waste this opportunity.

"These deaths have been different, Ronnie," Mackinnon said. "We haven't seen anything like them before."

Ronnie put his hand on the door handle.

"These people have been bleeding to death, Ronnie," Mackinnon said. "Even when they get to hospital, the doctors haven't been able to save them. And it isn't the heroin."

"It's not the heroin?" Ronnie looked puzzled, but interested enough to keep talking. That was a positive sign.

"We think something has been added to the heroin supply... something toxic that is causing people to bleed to death."

"Like the anthrax." Ronnie sat back into his seat. "They had that scare a while back, but hardly anyone actually got sick, only a few..."

"This might be different. It looks like three people have already died."

"Yeah." Ronnie looked down at the footwell. "I heard something about the bleeding."

"You did? What?"

Ronnie didn't answer.

"We are going to put out warnings," DI Evans said. "But you know, Ronnie, people won't find it easy to stay away from their fix."

Ronnie shifted in his seat and looked out of the window, as Evans pulled into a parking space in front of a parade of shops.

At first, Ronnie seemed more interested in watching a woman, with four kids dancing around her, leave the laundrette. Then he said, "What do you want to know?"

"Tell us what you have heard," Mackinnon said. "Have you any idea where these dirty drugs might be coming from? Is it one particular dealer? Or…"

"I heard about some poor bastard bleeding," Ronnie said, avoiding eye contact. "Not sure where he got his gear from, but maybe I could find out…" Ronnie looked up and chewed on a dirty fingernail. "You know, maybe if I had a little something for my expenses…"

"If I give you expenses, Ronnie," DI Evans said, "how do I know you will come through for me?"

Ronnie looked hurt. "You can trust me. I always come through."

A smile played across DI Evans' mouth. "I've got a better idea. I'll give you money-"

"You won't regret it. I'll make sure-"

"Wait, there is a proviso. I'll give you the money, but you need to get samples for me from different dealers, okay?"

"Yeah, sure. I can do that."

"I don't want you getting them from different runners, all working for the same dealer. I want them from different dealers, different suppliers."

Ronnie's forehead puckered. "Well, I can do that. But for all I know, the dealers get their stuff from one place."

"You let me worry about that, you just get samples from different dealers. I want at least four."

"Who do you want? I can get it from the Tower Boys' crew, the 10-5s, The Junction and-"

"Don't bother with The Junction," DI Evans said. "They are too small time and they don't deal on the streets anyway. That'll be a waste of time. Try the dealer on the Jubilee Estate instead, all right?"

Ronnie nodded, his bushy hair bouncing and his eyes fixed on DI Evans as he pulled out his wallet.

* * *

"Are you happy now?" Bruce Evans said, after he and Mackinnon dropped Ronnie off at a bus stop on Whitechapel Road and drove away.

Mackinnon waited until Evans had overtaken a bicycle courier then said, "Thanks for setting it up and letting me meet him. I appreciate it."

Evans switched on the radio, found a station playing "Don't Stop Me Now" by Queen and started humming along as they slipped through the city traffic.

Questions were flooding Mackinnon's mind. How many people were going to die from this contaminated heroin? Would the alerts they sent out, do any good? And top of the list, even if they managed to get a sample of this tainted heroin from Ronnie, what good would it do them? Officially, would they be able to use it in a prosecution? Mackinnon doubted it.

Evans stopped at a pedestrian crossing and they both watched commuters bustling across the road. Night was drawing in on the city and people were heading home.

"Do you mind if I ask you something?" Mackinnon said.

Bruce shrugged. "Go ahead."

"Do you really think he's going to buy you samples with the money you gave him? You don't think he's just going to buy some samples for his *personal* use?"

Bruce smiled. "Oh, sure. He'll buy a little something for himself, but I gave him enough for that. I factored it in. Funny bloke, Ronnie. For an addict, he's pretty reliable."

They fell into silence for a few moments as Bruce turned

left and cut across a break in the oncoming traffic. Then Bruce turned to Mackinnon. "All right. Time for me to ask you something."

"Yeah?"

"Why did you want to meet him yourself? I mean, did you think I looked a bit shifty when we met?"

"No, nothing like that." Mackinnon didn't really know the answer. Was it because he was worried about Sarah? And what she might be taking? Or simply because, when someone he didn't know offered to take work off his hands, he couldn't help feeling suspicious?

Mackinnon shrugged and said, "I like to be thorough."

CHAPTER SIXTEEN

MACKINNON GOT TO DEREK'S place a little after eight. Derek answered the door with a beer in his hand and his Border Collie, Molly, dancing around his feet. "Hey, Jack, good to see you. Grab a beer. I'm watching last night's game."

Derek was watching American football. He was a total NFL nut, supporting the Patriots. Mackinnon was happy to watch it, and thanks to Derek, he was slowly learning the rules.

Mackinnon held up the plastic takeaway bag with one hand and scratched Molly behind the ears with the other. "I got us Chinese."

Derek turned from his position in front of the TV. "Great. I'm starved. I was going to suggest we call out for a delivery."

Mackinnon dumped his hold-all on the floor and took the food through to the kitchen area.

Derek drained his beer and walked across to the kitchen, keeping an eye on the TV. "I'll get some plates. You want a beer?"

"No, thanks," Mackinnon said. "I'm trying not to drink during the week."

Derek looked at him like he had suddenly grown two heads. "Good luck with that one."

As Derek started to dish out the beef in black bean sauce, Mackinnon headed to Derek's spare room, to put his bag in there and to hang up his shirt, so hopefully, it wouldn't look too creased tomorrow.

"You have got to be kidding me," Mackinnon said when he walked into the bedroom.

"What's the matter?" Derek said.

"What the hell are all these?" Mackinnon said, pointing to a collection of boxes, stacked up against the wall.

Derek stood in the doorway. "Ah, yes. I forgot to mention it. I didn't have space for them in my room."

Mackinnon picked up one of the boxes and inspected it. The writing was in Chinese, the picture on the box was recognisable in any language. "Irons?"

He looked around the room, taking it all in. "You must have fifty of them in here at least. What on earth are you going to do with fifty irons?"

Mackinnon didn't wait for Derek to reply. He'd just had a nasty thought. "These aren't dodgy, are they?"

Derek frowned. "What do you mean?"

"Have they fallen off the back of a lorry, Derek? Are they nicked?"

Derek looked horrified. He pressed his hand to his chest. "How could you ask me that? How could you think that?"

Mackinnon folded his arms. "How am I going to sleep in here? There's no room. I'll have to climb over the boxes to get into bed."

"We could stack them under the bed."

"Are you crazy? If we put all those boxes under the bed, when I go to sleep, my nose will be touching the ceiling!"

"I suppose you're right." Derek looked around at all the boxes. "There are quite a lot of them. Still, it is only for tonight. I'll clear them out tomorrow."

Great, Mackinnon thought. He would probably manage to climb into bed, but God help him if he needed to use the toilet in the middle of the night.

Mackinnon and Derek polished off the Chinese in record time and watched the rest of the game. Mackinnon was still pissed off and doing his best to give Derek the silent treatment. Derek didn't even notice.

Derek pointed at the TV with the neck of his beer bottle. "Did you see that? Illegal holding! Come on, Ref, put your glasses on!"

Molly lay on the floor by Mackinnon's feet. He reached down to stroke her soft fur. "Your owner is crazy, Molly, did you know that?"

Molly looked up at him with big brown eyes, then licked Mackinnon's hand.

CHAPTER SEVENTEEN

SARAH FOLLOWED HER FRIEND, Jessica, through the dingy hallway into what would once have been the sitting room. There were no sofas or TVs in here now, though. The carpet was dirty and littered with cigarette butts.

The people at the party didn't seem too bothered about the lack of furniture in the derelict house. They sat, or sprawled out on the floor, gathered together in small groups. The tinny beat from a small portable stereo dominated the noise in the room.

Jessica was edging her way to the back of the room. Sarah tried to get her attention. Surely Jessica would want to leave too. No one in their right mind could enjoy staying at a party like this. But Jessica ignored her and seemed determined to get to the back of the room. Perhaps she recognised someone. Sarah followed her, stepping over people's feet as she went.

She tripped.

"Watch it, bitch!" a skinny girl said. The girl had her hair pulled back in a tight, greasy ponytail.

"Sorry," Sarah mumbled, hurrying away.

Sarah looked around for Jessica again and felt a stab of panic when she couldn't see her straight away.

Her eyes scanned the room. She noticed a woman sitting in the corner, propped up against the wall, with a tiny baby held in the crook of her arm. What sort of person would bring a baby to a place like this? There were more men than women here too; a couple of them looked Sarah up and down, speculatively.

The place stunk of stale sweat and smoke from cigarettes and weed. Sarah pushed her fringe back out of her eyes. Where the hell had Jessica gone? Sarah stepped in a wet patch on the floor. Oh, that was disgusting, Sarah stepped back. It smelled of urine.

Finally, she caught sight of Jessica. Thank God. She was sitting cross-legged on the floor, talking to man with dreadlocks. Sarah didn't recognise him.

Sarah crouched down on the floor next to Jessica. "This place is a dive. We need to get out of here."

"Mm-hmm, sure," Jessica said. "Just need to score first. You want anything?"

"No. I just want to go."

Jessica crawled over the dirty carpet, on her hands and knees, to a man sitting a few feet away. He wore a jumper and a padded coat, despite the fact he looked uncomfortably hot and sweat glistened on his forehead. His sneer made Sarah look the other way.

Across the other side of the room, a dirty man, with a huge afro was staring at Sarah. Creepy-looking bloke. She had to get out of here, but she was supposed to be staying at Jessica's tonight, and there was no way she was going home after that row with her mother.

The creepy guy with the afro was still staring. Sarah scowled at him. "Asshole," she muttered. What was his problem?

Jessica came back to sit beside Sarah and handed her a reefer. "Are you sure you don't want anything else?"

"What are you going to take, Jess? It's not exactly hygienic around here."

Jessica giggled. "Oh relax. Come on, try something new."

"No. I'll stick with this, thanks." Sarah held up the spliff.

"Come on. It will be amazing."

"No!"

The guy with the afro slid past them, and Sarah shuddered. There was no way on earth she was going to get off her head with all these weirdos around.

CHAPTER EIGHTEEN

BILLY STOOD IN THE kitchen of the safe house on the Towers Estate, bagging up.

They called it a safe house, but really it was a dingy little flat, the same as all the others on the estate, except this one had a few more locks on the front door.

It was Billy's job to split the merchandise, weigh it into small portions, add a little icing and put it into small bags, ready for distribution. JT didn't trust him with anything more demanding.

The deputy delivered the small bags of heroin to his dealers, who worked out of JT's club, The Junction.

This meant that JT never actually had a stash of drugs in his club; and if any of the dealers were caught with drugs on them, JT could deny all knowledge.

Billy had to admit that was pretty smart.

None of the dealers were supposed to know where the safe house was either, which in theory, cut down the risk of someone stealing JT's stash. Only Billy and JT's trusted deputy were supposed to know the location of the safe house. At least, that was how it was supposed to work.

The sound of the door slamming echoed around the flat.

Billy froze, his hand clenched around the spoon he was using to measure out the drugs.

When Billy heard the high-pitched voice of the kid, he relaxed.

The kid was the deputy's runner, his name was James, but no one called him that. Everyone Billy knew just called him "the kid."

JT had no idea his trusted deputy was skimming the drugs and letting the kid sell them all over the estate.

As far as JT was concerned, he was dealing out of his club, off the street. JT thought his business was nice and safe. He didn't want to tread on the toes of any other dealers.

JT liked to act the hard man and play at being Mr. Big, but he'd wet himself if he thought one of the big boys might find out that members of his crew were dealing on their turf.

Billy carefully deposited more of the cream-coloured powder into a small plastic bag, then sealed it up. He could hear the murmur of voices in the corridor.

They didn't care that Billy knew what they were up to because they didn't think Billy had the balls to grass on them. Both the deputy and the kid knew that JT couldn't stand Billy, and the only reason he'd been given a job at all was because he was JT's brother-in-law.

Billy felt sorry for the kid at first. When the boy first turned up at the safe house, Billy was horrified, not because they were cheating JT, but because the boy looked so young. He couldn't be older than fourteen, and most days, turned up for work in his school uniform.

The kid's round, baby face and chubby cheeks made it

hard to believe he could steal sweets, let alone hand out drugs all over the estate.

But Billy soon realised there was nothing sweet and innocent about the kid. Foul-mouthed and vicious, he wasn't averse to trying to trip Billy up, and he stole stuff from the safe house, too. Silly things, but things that Billy would get in trouble for.

He was that sort of kid. Born bad, or turned evil by his environment, either way, the boy was beyond help, beyond redemption.

Billy dug a tiny spatula into the powder and heard laughter from the hallway. They were laughing at him.

But Billy didn't care.

He didn't mind the deputy's contempt, or even being bullied by a fourteen-year-old. Billy had a job to do and he wouldn't let scum bags like that spoil things.

Billy was prepared to put up with a lot to keep this job.

CHAPTER NINETEEN

SARAH COULDN'T BELIEVE HER eyes. This could not be happening.

Jessica had removed the belt from her jeans and wrapped it around her own arm, using it as a tourniquet.

The greasy guy in the tracksuit leaned over Jessica and started tapping her arm. Sarah shivered and watched as the veins appeared, blue and plump, in the crease of Jessica's arm.

She knew what they were going to do, but she couldn't watch this. She was going to be sick. But she didn't turn away.

Morbid curiosity? Fear? Whatever it was, Sarah's eyes were locked on Jessica, and she couldn't turn away.

The guy in the tracksuit, shifted his position slightly, then slid the tip of the needle into Jessica's vein.

Jessica's eyes opened wide, and Sarah's heart thudded in panic. Something was wrong. The stuff was bad... Jessica might have overdosed... If this was her first time, he might have given her too much.

But even as that thought entered her mind, she saw Jessica relax.

Jessica smiled lazily, sighed and leaned back against the wall. The tracksuit guy removed the syringe. Suddenly, Sarah realised that her friend had been hiding this from her. This was not the first time Jessica had injected heroin.

Sarah grabbed her bag. What the hell had she been thinking? She dumped the spliff on the floor and headed for the door, nausea building in her throat.

"Where you going, honey? I can give you a freebie if you give me one," said a deep male voice.

Sarah recoiled in horror and then ran, heading for the door.

She was almost there, almost safe, when she felt a hand clamp around her forearm.

She tried to wrench her arm free, but she yanked too hard, and unbalanced, she fell to the floor. She couldn't see properly in the dim light. There was no electricity wired here, and even if there had been, the smashed lightbulbs were no use anyway.

"Please." The word escaped with a sob.

She was hauled to her feet.

"You shouldn't be here." It was the guy with the afro. She shrank back against the wall.

"I just want to go home. Please."

He opened the front door. "I'm not gonna hurt you. You should go home. This isn't a safe place for a youngster like you."

Sarah didn't need to be told twice. She flew through the door and sprinted down the street. She didn't stop running until she was gasping for breath.

Winded, she stopped and leaned against a set of railings in front of a block of flats. She stayed there for a moment, images of Jessica flashing through her mind. How had things changed so much?

They used to be so close at school, always giggling so the teachers had to separate them in classes. But it had been innocent fun. Jessica's father was rolling in it. He lived in a huge house in Oxford. Jessica's mother had left him several years ago and moved to a flash apartment in the Docklands. Jessica hadn't gone off the rails then, so why now?

Slowly, Sarah caught her breath and began to calm down. She shouldn't have left Jessica alone in that place. Anything might happen to her, especially in the state she was in. Sarah remembered the greasy guy with the tracksuit and shivered. Jessica had clearly known some of the people at that party, so maybe she would be okay.

She heard a shout and saw a group of boys further up the road, kicking a football about.

Disorientated, she looked around. Where the hell was she? She had never been here before. She spotted a sign further ahead, but couldn't quite make it out from here. She walked closer. The street sign told her she was on Burgess Street. Sarah had never heard of it, but it was pretty quiet. She needed to get back on the main road and find a bus stop or tube station.

She followed the sound of traffic until she reached a road backed up with cars.

Her heart was still banging in her chest, but she felt a little safer with all these people around.

She walked on for a little way, past a kebab shop and a betting shop that was closed for the night. A red double-decker stopped a little ahead of her, and two girls, around Sarah's age, got off the bus.

"Where's the nearest tube?" Sarah asked them. She wrapped her arms tightly around her torso.

The two girls gave her a wide berth but pointed up the road. "Mile End. Five-minute walk."

"Cheers." Sarah set off for the station, then she remembered something that made her want to cry.

Jessica had the return portion of her train ticket.

She didn't want to get her wallet out here; she didn't need to. She knew she didn't have enough money for the train fare all the way back to Oxford.

She couldn't use the cash point either. She had six pounds and forty-five pence in her account, and the cash machine didn't give out fivers. Not that five pounds would be anywhere near enough to get back to Oxford anyway.

She couldn't call her mum. She'd go mental.

There was only one thing she could do.

She moved out of sight, stepping into a shop doorway, and when she was sure she couldn't be seen, she pulled out her mobile phone and dialled.

CHAPTER TWENTY

AFTER A HELLISH DAY at work, Michael King was unwinding at The Junction, a bar just around the corner from his office.

Listening to the buzz of conversation and the clink of glasses, he felt the tension between his shoulder blades melt away.

All week, work had been absolutely awful. He hated it. The whole situation kept whirring around in his brain. He tried to ignore it. He would worry about all that other stuff tomorrow. Tonight, he was going to enjoy himself.

He took a look around the bar. It was still pretty quiet, but things were picking up. City boys took up most of the occupied tables. Laughing and joking around, their voices were getting louder and louder. They had obviously come in straight after work, and they looked wasted.

There were a couple of stunners in here tonight, too, and he knew he'd be able to take his pick. He smiled at the blonde, over by the bar, who had been eyeing him up for the last five minutes. No doubt, she had noticed his Rolex, his Armani suit and his solid gold cufflinks.

Women went for money, and Michael didn't mind that at all.

Hell, he might as well make the most of it before... But no, he wasn't going to think about that tonight. It wasn't even his fault. It could have happened to anyone.

It was horrifying how quickly things could go bad in his business. Avery Investments might pay well, but they were not known for their understanding when their staff underperformed. And that's just what Michael had been doing. Under-performing. Spectacularly.

Christ, he was in trouble.

He drained his gin and tonic in one large gulp, and tried to catch the barman's eye to order another. He waved at him, money in hand, but the barman didn't pay him any attention, he turned to serve another customer.

He had better get used to it. It was a sign of things to come, a sign of how things would be from now on. People would ignore him. He would be a nobody. A failure.

He turned around on his bar stool, wobbled a little and clung onto the bar to stop himself slipping to the floor. He noticed the blonde, who had been giving him the eye earlier, had picked a better prospect. She was all over another bloke, practically draped across him.

Sod her. It's not like he was really interested anyway. Women only complicated things.

Still unable to catch the barman's eye, Michael decided alcohol wasn't really helping him anyway. He needed something stronger, something that never failed him.

He headed to the gents'. Once inside, he entered a cubicle

and closed the door. He could hear the steady thud of the music from the bar.

It wasn't exactly hygienic, but a lot of city boys drank at this bar, and Michael didn't want to be recognised. Of course, quite a few of them did it too, but it was career suicide to advertise it. Not that he needed to worry about that for much longer. He'd be out of a job soon enough. When people started to realise how much money he'd lost this week, Michael would be out on his ear.

Michael pulled out his wallet and removed a small wrap. His hands shook as he unfolded it.

His fingers felt thick and clumsy, and he spilled a little of the powder. In his panic to save the rest, he overcompensated, and the wrap slipped through his fingers to the floor.

Christ. He stared down at the white powder on the floor, and for one horrifying moment, he considered scrapping it off the urine-splattered tiles.

He took a deep breath. He needed to calm down. It wasn't a catastrophe. He had seen his dealer, just five minutes ago, hanging around by the bar. He would just buy some more.

Luckily, Michael didn't have to go far. The man Michael usually got his drugs from was standing close to the door, cradling his prop: a bottle of imported beer that he never seemed to drink.

The dealer nodded his head in time with the music and tapped his fingers on the side of the bottle. His eyes scanned the room constantly, on the lookout for trouble, or potential customers.

Michael stared at the dealer until he looked his way. When the dealer noticed him, an almost imperceptible smile played on his lips and he headed towards the gents'. Michael followed.

"I need more," Michael said even before the door closed behind them.

The dealer looked over the room, checking the bottoms of the toilet cubicles before he spoke. Satisfied, he turned back to Michael and shrugged.

"No can do. I'm all out."

"What? You can't be."

The dealer shrugged again and turned to walk out of the toilets.

"Wait!" Michael grabbed the man's arm, then quickly released it when he saw the look on the dealer's face.

"I'm sorry, but you must have something." Michael tried to keep control of his temper.

If the man had really run out, why was he still hanging around the bar? It didn't make sense if he had nothing to sell. He wanted to increase the price, that was the only explanation. He wanted to see how much Michael was prepared to pay for it.

"Please," Michael said. "I really need it tonight. I have had such a shit week..." Michael's voice trailed away. The dealer's face hardened. He wasn't the least bit interested in Michael's troubles.

Desperate now, Michael ran his hands through his hair. "Look, I can pay you a bit extra."

Something shifted in the dealer's expression. He smiled. "I'm not unreasonable. I can see you really need something. Something to take the edge off."

Michael could have laughed with relief. "Yes, that is exactly what I need."

"I'm outta coke, but I've got something else... Something better. Something that will make you feel on top of the world. You want that?"

Michael hesitated. Usually, he stuck to cocaine. He liked it. He had dabbled in the past, but he didn't like anything too heavy.

"It's not too strong, is it?" Michael asked. "I...er... I don't want anything that will make me feel bad tomorrow. I have to work."

The man shrugged. "It's not that heavy. Look, if you don't want it, there are others who do. It doesn't bother me if you take it or not."

"But will it make me feel good? Like the coke?"

"Better. It will make you feel on top of the world. You want it, or not?"

Michael nodded. Yes, he wanted it. He wanted it more than anything.

CHAPTER TWENTY-ONE

MICHAEL TOOK THE SMALL bag the dealer gave him and stashed it deep in his jacket pocket. He walked out of the gents' and past the bar. He intended to leave and go straight home, but now he thought perhaps one more drink would help him mull things over.

He wasn't sure about this. He was used to cocaine. He knew loads of other people who took it. But heroin was a different matter entirely. He had tried it before and liked it, but it scared him. To him, it seemed so much more serious than cocaine.

Michael was wrenched from his thoughts by a heavy hand smacking him on the back. "Hello, boyo. How is it going?"

Michael turned to see Harry Partridge beaming at his shoulder. Harry was thirty-five, balding and overweight. He tried so hard to fit the stereotype of a trader, it was embarrassing. He wore a blue, striped shirt, with white collars and cuffs, and a pair of red braces. Michael couldn't believe it. Surely the braces were a step too far, even for Harry?

But Harry seemed very proud of his braces, and plucked at them with his fingers, as if he wanted to make sure Michael noticed them. Michael shook his head, as if it were possible to miss those. He'd like to give them a good tug, then let them snap back hard.

"Hello, Harry," Michael said, attempting to smile.

"Can I get you a drink, Mickey? I'm celebrating."

Michael hated people shortening his name, and he especially hated people calling him Mickey.

"Go on then. I'll have a beer," Michael said. "What are you celebrating?"

Harry barked his drinks order to the bartender, who Michael noticed, walked straight over to serve Harry, even though Michael had already been waiting to order for five minutes.

Harry grinned at Michael, showing off a gold filling towards the back of his mouth. "Big result today, Mickey. Loads-a-money."

Loads-a-money? Michael stared at Harry. Did he really just say that? The man really was stuck in the eighties.

"Good for you," Michael said as he picked up the beer the bartender had just set in front of him. "Some guys have all the luck."

"Speaking of luck," Harry said, moving a little closer to Michael. "I've had a bloody brilliant week. There are rumours going around." Harry tapped the side of his nose with his finger. "Rumours that I am up for a promotion, a big one."

Until this moment, Michael hadn't realised how much it was possible to hate someone. He felt the loathing blossom in his chest, and he imagined smashing his beer bottle over Harry's head. That would wipe the infuriating smile off his smug, fat face.

"Will you join us?" Harry asked, nodded towards his friends sitting at a table a few feet away.

Michael shook his head, dispersing his daydream. "No, thanks."

"Ah, come on. We're going clubbing afterwards."

Clubbing? For God's sake. No one went clubbing at their age anymore. That was just embarrassing.

Harry leaned towards Michael, and once more, tapped the side of his nose. "I'll be honest with you, the only reason I'm going is to get some magic powder." He winked. "A celebration is just not the same without it."

Michael slid off his bar stool. "You know someone at this club who can sort us out?"

Harry grinned. "I know a man who can get us anything."

"Why didn't you say so before?" Michael slapped Harry on the back. "Let's go and join your friends and start celebrating."

CHAPTER TWENTY-TWO

THE BOY'S SHARP, LITTLE eyes followed Billy's every move.

Billy was in the kitchen of the safe house, weighing out the gear, while the boy sat at the table, watching him.

"Haven't you got anything better to do, kid?" Billy asked.

The boy smiled. "Why? Don't you like me watching you? Do I make you nervous?"

"I don't like you getting under my feet, that's all," Billy said. "I've got a job to do."

The boy sneered. "It's a pathetic job. I'm only fourteen, and I've got a better job than you."

"Good for you."

The boy's eyes narrowed. "Yeah, good for me. I think I'd top myself if I ended up like you, old man. You can't even get a job without your sister greasing your way."

Billy ignored him and set the kitchen scales to zero. He took out one of the large bags of heroin, then looked around. "Have you seen the spatula? I had it just now."

"You mean this?" The boy twirled the spatula through his fingers.

Billy gripped the edge of the kitchen counter. "Yeah, that's it. Can I have it?"

The kid stood up, smiling. "Well, sure, but I think you should say please."

"Give me the spatula," Billy said through gritted teeth.

Billy made a grab for it, but the boy danced away from him, cackling with delight. His laugh sounded like an untuned radio.

Billy moved towards him again, but the kid skirted away, using the table to keep distance between them.

At the sound of the front door opening, they both froze.

Heavy footsteps sounded in the hall, then the deputy appeared in the doorway.

"What's going on?" The deputy shrugged off his padded jacket.

"He's nicked the spatula," Billy said, nodding at the boy.

"God, you're pathetic," the deputy said, shaking his head "Can't you cope with a fourteen-year-old kid?"

The deputy turned to the boy. "Give it back." He cuffed the boy around the head. "And stop pissing about. You've got work to do."

Once the deputy handed over the kid's supply, the kid went off to distribute the drugs. So Billy could finally get on. He was almost done for the day, just a couple more baggies to fill.

The deputy was in the sitting room, watching TV, an episode of "Family Guy." Every so often, Billy would hear a snort of laughter.

The deputy would be here all night. There had to be someone in the safe house at all times to guard the stash.

Billy thought the thing with the names was stupid. He didn't know the deputy's real name. He knew the kid's real name was James, but no one called him that. The deputy was just called Deputy, no Christian name, or family name. Everyone referred to the kid as the runner, or just the kid.

They didn't mind using Billy's real name, though. Billy guessed they didn't think he was important enough to warrant a code name.

Billy sealed up the last little bag and walked over to the kitchen window. From here, he could see St. Paul's Way over to his left, and straight ahead, a scaffolding yard. Billy had grown up in this area. He and his sister, Siobhan, had attended Cardinal Griffins' school, not far from here.

He could see the spire of St. Mary's, the church where he had married his childhood sweetheart all those years ago. They had a few happy years before she up and left him to look after a three-year-old with cystic fibrosis.

All that was history now. Ancient history.

Billy washed his hands thoroughly, then wiped them dry and hung the tea towel on the back of a chair.

On his way out of the safe house, he stuck his head in the sitting room to say goodbye.

The deputy was sprawled on the sofa, his chin lolled down to his chest, breathing deeply. His feet were propped up on the coffee table, and next to them, clearly visible, was a handgun. Billy knew about guns, but he didn't like them. He didn't want anything to do with them.

"I'll be off now," Billy said.

The deputy's head jerked up. He blinked. "Oh, right. See you tomorrow, Billy."

Billy nodded and left, glad to leave the flat and the taint of drugs behind him.

CHAPTER TWENTY-THREE

RONNIE WAS ALMOST FINISHED. He only had one more collection to make. The small bags of heroin sat in his trouser pocket, next to the black marker pen he used to label them.

He had used a numbering system. So if he was caught, no one would guess what he was doing. He didn't fancy being picked up by the police with all this gear on him, but he was even less keen for the dealers to cotton onto his plan.

A couple of the suppliers were a little wary at first. Ronnie usually stuck to the Tower Boys or JT's runner for his supplies, but today, he had needed to widen the net to get hold of the samples for DI Evans.

The other runners didn't recognise him as one of their regulars and stared at him with suspicion at first. Ronnie mumbled something about getting a bad fix, so he was looking for a new dealer.

Despite their wariness, the runners were quite happy to hand over the drugs when they saw Ronnie had the cash.

Ronnie looked the part. It was quite obvious to anyone who saw him, Ronnie was a long-term addict.

He started buying the heroin from JT's runner because it was that little bit cheaper. He liked getting a little bit more for his money. Now, he wouldn't touch the stuff. Not after what had happened with Scott.

Even though Bruce told him not to worry about getting a sample of JT's drugs, Ronnie was going to get one because he was sure that it was JT's stuff making people sick. He didn't want to come right out and accuse anybody because then the police would want him to make a statement and do it all officially. And Ronnie didn't fancy testifying against the dealers. He'd seen enough to know that was a very bad idea.

The way Ronnie saw it, the police would find out it was JT's sample that was messed up, and they wouldn't need any evidence from Ronnie. The samples would be enough.

His skin crawled and he scratched his arm, hard, leaving red marks. He shivered. Ronnie put his hand in his pocket and felt the smooth plastic wrapped around the heroin. A warm feeling crept over him. One of those was his, his payment for getting all these samples. One more collection, and he could find somewhere safe and get high.

But first, he needed to get to the part of the Towers Estate where JT's runner had his little empire. It wasn't a long walk, but Ronnie's body shook in protest. He felt like an old man whose body was giving up. He knew he needed to quit the drugs soon. If he didn't manage it in the next year or so, he'd be dead. Another statistic. He'd seen it happen to friends. There was a limit to how much your body could take, and Ronnie reckoned he was getting close to that limit.

Ronnie headed for a small courtyard. He passed an abandoned shopping trolley and a girl, sitting on a wall, jiggling a baby on her knee.

When he reached the courtyard, he couldn't see the runner, so he leaned back against the wall to wait. A group of three men swaggered out of one of the blocks of flats. Ronnie kept his head down, and they walked past him without even looking at him.

He'd become invisible. Not a threat. Not even someone to push around and bully. Just an addict, who was not even worth a glance.

He waited for half an hour before the runner showed. The kid slipped out of the flats opposite, and slung his grey record bag over his shoulder. He was still wearing his school uniform.

Ronnie made eye contact, and a smile slowly stretched across the boy's face. He walked over, and leaned back on the wall next to Ronnie, just like they were two friends having a chat. A school kid, and a messed-up addict, Ronnie could imagine how ridiculous they looked. It wouldn't fool anybody.

The boy licked his lips. "You're lucky you caught me. I'm just about to go on my rounds. What's it to be, today? Twenty-pound bag?"

Ronnie nodded, sniffed and handed the boy a folded-up twenty-pound note.

The boy took it and opened up his bag. Ronnie thought about telling the kid about Scott, telling him that there was something bad in the drugs he was handing out.

The boy must have seen something in Ronnie's expression because his eyes narrowed and he said, "What?"

"Nothing man. Nothing," Ronnie said.

Ronnie took the tiny, cellophane-wrapped package and shoved it into his pocket.

Ronnie felt amazing. His whole body was warm and buzzing. The heroin had done it again. He felt fantastic. Why couldn't he always feel like this?

He was in the sitting room of a friend's flat, leaning back against the cold radiator, but Ronnie didn't notice the cold. He didn't know where his friend had disappeared to, and he didn't really care. He just wanted to hang onto this feeling for as long as possible.

The heroin samples were still in Ronnie's pockets. He wouldn't dare take them out here, someone would nick them in a second. That was the problem with his friend's flat, there was always someone dropping in, using it as a doss house.

Ronnie felt his eyelids droop. His chin dropped down to his chest. He had done well today. He had managed to get hold of all those samples. DI Evans would be pleased. He was helping to get that dirty stuff off the streets.

Ronnie imagined telling Scott all about it when he got better. Telling him what an important part he played. And Scott would be grateful because he would know Ronnie had done it for him.

Yeah, Ronnie would just stay here for a little while longer, then he would get in touch with DI Evans and give him his samples. Everything was going to work out just fine.

CHAPTER TWENTY-FOUR

CHARLOTTE TRIED TO SLOW her breathing. She lay on her bed, taking one deep breath after another.

Her heart was racing.

It's okay, she told herself. Everything was locked up securely. There was nothing to be scared of. Even if someone were lurking around outside, there was no way they could get inside.

A muffled creak sounded from somewhere in the flat.

Charlotte sat bolt upright. She gripped the duvet. What was that? Was someone there? Had he managed to get in? To get through all those locks?

She sat motionless on the bed as the seconds passed, but all was quiet.

It was nothing, nothing at all. Maybe someone had dropped something in the flat below hers. It was nothing to get worked up about.

She swung her legs out of bed and shivered as the cold air hit her bare skin. She took a few shaky steps towards her bedroom door, repeating, "There's nothing there, there's nothing there," over and over in her mind.

She put her hand on the light switch, then hesitated. No, better to leave the lights off, make it harder for him to see her.

She left the bedroom and walked, barefoot, through the flat, checking everything was just as she had left it.

Her eyes filled with tears, and she blinked them away. What was happening to her? She was losing it. She hardly slept these days, and when she did, she was haunted by dreams of him coming after her.

Maybe she should move away, go somewhere where she could put it all behind her.

But that wouldn't work.

He'd know where to find her.

He hadn't done anything. Yet. There had only been the phone calls. She could report him, but that hadn't exactly worked out well the last time she tried it. And it wasn't as if he were stupid enough to use his own mobile.

No, he definitely wasn't stupid. He knew exactly how she would react to the calls. He knew how scared she would be.

Charlotte stood by the window, behind the curtain and looked out at the East London skyline. The tower at Canary Wharf blinked in the distance. She looked at the lights shining from other flats, the cars on the street below. He could be anywhere.

She took a deep breath and headed back to the bedroom. She needed sleep. She had turned in early tonight in the hope of catching up on some sleep. She wouldn't be able to function tomorrow if she didn't get her head down for a few hours at least.

Just as she was about to climb back into bed, a thought struck her. Did she make sure that the dead bolt was all the way across? What if it was only partially across? She needed to make sure.

She checked the lock on the front door. Yes, it was fully bolted, secure. But seeing as she had checked that, she thought she may as well check all the other locks, just in case.

She bent down to check the main lock. Secure. The key was on her bedside cabinet. She ran her hand along the edge of the door, just to make sure it was properly closed, no gaps. She moved to the windows.

She was on the sixth floor, so she knew intruders wouldn't be able to get in through the windows, but she checked anyway, running her fingers along the windowsill. Making sure the locks were secure.

She was on the third window when the phone rang.

For a few seconds, she was unable to move. She stared at the phone, willing it to stop ringing.

It didn't.

She reached out a trembling hand and picked up the receiver.

"Hello?"

At the sound of her mother's voice, Charlotte let out the breath she'd been holding. The tightness in her chest melted away. It was so good to hear her voice.

Charlotte curled up on the sofa, cradling the receiver.

"When are you coming to visit us, sweetheart?" Charlotte's mother asked.

"Soon. Hopefully. Maybe next month if I can arrange the leave."

She chatted to her mum, told her how Nan was coping

with her arthritis and listened to her mother's stories about expat life in Spain.

The background noise got a little louder, making it hard to hear what her mother was saying.

"Where are you?" Charlotte asked. "It's so noisy."

"Charlie's bar, on the beach. It's smashing. You'd love it, sweetheart. Look, I better go. I can hardly hear you over this lot. I'll give you a ring next week."

"All right. Love you. Speak soon."

"Love you too, sweetheart."

Charlotte put down the handset, clutched a cushion to her chest and buried her face in it.

She couldn't go on like this.

CHAPTER TWENTY-FIVE

THE AMERICAN FOOTBALL GAME had only just finished, and Mackinnon was carrying the plates out to the kitchen when his mobile rang.

Who was that at this time of night? His stomach filled with dread. Late night phone calls meant two things: bad news, or he was needed at work.

Derek nodded to Mackinnon's phone, vibrating its way along the coffee table. "Work?"

"Probably," Mackinnon said, picking up his mobile and then glancing at the screen. He frowned. "It's Sarah."

Derek glanced at his watch.

After speaking to Sarah, Mackinnon hung up and turned to Derek. "Looks like I won't be staying here tonight, after all. I've got to go and pick up Sarah."

"I suppose it is a good job you didn't have a few beers then," Derek said, then yawned. "I'll say goodnight then. See you tomorrow?"

"Yeah."

"Oh and about those irons," Derek said. "I'll sort them tomorrow."

As Derek went off to bed, Mackinnon headed out into the night. Derek didn't have a car, so he had given Mackinnon his parking permit. Mackinnon was very glad he had driven up from Oxford, rather than taking the train, otherwise he would be forking out for a taxi to collect Sarah and take her all the way back to Oxford.

He gave Chloe a quick ring as he walked to the car. She had been asleep, and didn't sound too happy when Mackinnon broke the news.

"London? What the hell is she doing there? She is supposed to be staying at Jessica's dad's house, in Oxford!"

* * *

Mackinnon parked up next to the tube station on Mile End Road, and looked at the people walking by. Where was she?

There were a few people hanging around by the bus stop, and outside the tube station, but he couldn't see her. He switched off the engine and was about to get out and look for her when he spotted Sarah walking towards the car and let out a sigh of relief.

She wore a short, tight skirt and a little cropped jacket. She must be freezing. Her arms circled her abdomen, clutching herself tightly. He wondered if she was hurt. She opened the door and clambered into the passenger seat.

Mackinnon turned on the interior light, to see what was wrong. Her cheeks were pink from the cold, and her legs were covered with goosebumps, but he couldn't see any injuries.

He wasn't sure what he was expecting, maybe a thank you, or even a smile. He didn't get either.

"Don't look at me like that," she said, through chattering teeth.

"Like what?" Mackinnon said, turning on the heater full blast to try and warm her up.

"Like you're all disappointed, or something." She put her bag in the footwell. "You're not my father."

Thank God, Mackinnon thought. "Are you, okay?"

"Of course," Sarah said. "Why wouldn't I be?"

Mackinnon started the engine. "Oh, I don't know. Perhaps because you called to ask me to pick you up in East London at eleven o'clock at night."

Sarah sniffed and rubbed her nose with the back of her hand. "I just ran out of money. No big deal."

His hands tightened on the steering wheel as he stared at her profile. He felt a surge of dislike for this young girl sitting beside him, and he didn't much like himself for it.

She's young, he told himself. People do stupid things when they're young.

At eighteen, Mackinnon had been about to go to university. There had been many nights when he had drunk too much and made a fool out of himself, and many occasions when he'd rowed with his mum and dad. But he was sure he had never been as awful as Sarah. She acted as if he and Chloe were around simply to wait on her.

He waited before pulling away, giving her a chance to offer an explanation, but she avoided looking at him and just sat staring out of the passenger window.

There was something she wasn't telling him. Maybe something that happened tonight, some secret she was guarding, but she wasn't going to tell him, not tonight anyway.

He pulled away from the kerb. At least she was safe now.

When he got her home, Chloe would be able to relax. At least for a little while.

When they got back to Oxford, it was almost one in the morning.

As soon as they entered the front door, Chloe dragged Sarah into the living room. "You have got some explaining to do."

Mackinnon left them to it and headed to the kitchen to make tea. He was still too annoyed with Sarah to go straight to sleep.

He made all three of them a cup, and decided to take his upstairs. He walked out of the kitchen into the hallway and caught Katy with her ear to the door.

"Eavesdroppers never hear anything nice, you know?" Mackinnon said.

Katy straightened up and flushed with embarrassment. "I just wanted to know what's going on. No one ever tells me anything."

Mackinnon shrugged. "It's nothing very interesting. I just brought Sarah home. You should get to bed. You have got school in the morning."

Before Katy had a chance to reply, the door to the sitting room slammed open, and Sarah came storming out of the room, then stomped up the stairs.

Chloe followed her out. She looked washed out. When she spotted Katy, she said, "What are you doing up? Get to bed."

"You woke me up," Katy said, pouting. "Now I can't sleep." She eyed Mackinnon's cup of tea. "I'm going to make a drink."

"You can have Sarah's tea, if you want it. I left it in the kitchen." Mackinnon turned to Chloe. "I made you one, too."

Chloe smiled and put a hand on his arm. "Thanks."

"Oh, Mum, is my kit ready for hockey tomorrow?"

Chloe ran a hand through her hair. "Tomorrow? I didn't know you had a game tomorrow."

"Yes you did. I told you," Katy said. "It's the semi-finals. They start at seven."

Chloe sighed. "I'd forgotten. I've got a meeting tomorrow night. I won't be able to take you. I'll have to ask one of the other parents."

Katy's face fell. "So you won't be coming to watch me?"

"I'm sorry, darling, I can't. This meeting is very important."

"I can do it," Mackinnon said.

Both Chloe and Katy turned to face Mackinnon.

"Jack, you don't have to. You're staying at Derek's tomorrow," Chloe said.

"It's okay, I can stay here tomorrow night instead. I'll get back by six-thirty."

Katy cocked her head to one side. "Do you like hockey?"

"Are you kidding?" Mackinnon said. "I love it."

CHAPTER TWENTY-SIX

MICHAEL KING DIDN'T GET home until two in the morning. He shrugged off his jacket, threw his keys down on the coffee table and kicked off his shoes. He needed to wind down and relax. He needed to get some sleep.

He sat on the sofa, then leaned back and put his feet up. He smiled. It had been a fantastic night. Harry's man had come through and provided them all with a little bit of magic powder, as Harry called it. Michael had even gotten up on the dance floor. It was the first time in years. He couldn't remember the last time he danced like that.

Harry turned out to be a good laugh. He had thrown some funny shapes on the dance floor and paid for all the drinks and the gear.

Michael sat up again. It was no good he was buzzing, absolutely wired. His thoughts turned to the packet of heroin he had acquired earlier. That would calm him down.

He walked over to his jacket and fumbled through his

pockets. He pulled out the small bag. Damn. There wasn't much there. Maybe there was a hole in the bag?

Michael raised the small plastic bag up to eye level to inspect it. There wasn't enough there to do anything anyway. He slapped it down on the coffee table in disgust.

Unless...

Michael chewed on his fingernail. Usually, he would smoke heroin, but you needed quite a bit to do that. He wouldn't need quite so much if he injected it...

Michael walked through his open-plan living area, to his bedroom. He opened the wardrobe and from the top shelf, pulled out an old, black briefcase.

He entered the combination and opened the case. He kept it locked so his cleaning lady didn't stumble over the contents. Inside the case, there was a silver box that Michael picked up and carefully carried into the living area.

He set the box on the table in front of him and opened it. He took out the foil, citric acid and a lighter. It had been a while since he had injected. He had promised himself never to do it again. So why had he kept the case?

He would just do it this once, to relax so he could get some sleep. Then tomorrow, he would get rid of the case and never touch the stuff again. Cocaine he would use occasionally, but he would stay away from heroin.

Just once more, Michael told himself as he reached for the spoon.

CHAPTER TWENTY-SEVEN

THE FOLLOWING MORNING, MICHAEL King woke up with the world's worst hangover.

Last night had been awesome, the best night he'd had in a long, long time. He remembered going on to a club with Harry and his friends, and the music had been amazing. After that... Well, he couldn't really remember much after that. To be honest, it was all a bit of a blur.

He belched and felt the acid burn his chest. He groaned and reached for his mobile to check the time. Seven thirty. If he didn't get up now, he was going to be late for work.

And with that thought, he groaned again. He was probably going to get the sack anyway, why bother to go in?

Michael put his hands on either side of his head and squeezed. How much had he had to drink last night? It must be the alcohol; coke didn't normally make him feel this bad.

Then he remembered. Oh why had he done that? Hadn't it taken him months last time to try to quit? He closed his eyes in shame.

His head was banging, pounding with pain. It was no less than he deserved. He pulled himself up into a sitting position. He was in his own bed, at least. That was something to be thankful for, and there was no strange woman lying next to him. Thank God. He couldn't have dealt with that this morning.

Michael turned over. Blood rushed in his ears and a wave of nausea rose up from his stomach.

He staggered to the bathroom. Every step he took made his head pound. All his muscles ached, too. What on earth had he done last night? He must have been dancing for hours. He felt like he had been trampled by an elephant.

Stepping over the clothes he had thrown on the floor, he entered his en-suite bathroom, leaned over the sink and took a couple of deep breaths, trying to fight the vomit rising in his throat. Then he caught sight of his face in the mirror.

What the hell had happened to him?

His eyes were not just bloodshot, they were more red than white.

Small blood vessels had burst, making him look like something out of a horror film. There were little spots on his face, too, like tiny pinpricks of blood.

There must have been something in that gear last night. Something bad. Or maybe it was an allergic reaction?

He could ring his GP, but then what would he say? They'd ask him about the drugs.

He raked a hand through his hair, leaning in closer to the mirror and examining the tiny spots. Christ, he couldn't turn up at work looking like this. He would have to stay home today. Maybe he would look a bit better tomorrow.

Why did he take that bloody stuff? He should have stuck with coke and he wouldn't be in this mess.

He turned on the tap and picked up his toothbrush, but before he put the toothbrush anywhere near his mouth, a wave of nausea flooded over him. He couldn't hold it back and vomited in the sink.

When he opened his eyes he could not believe what he saw. He didn't want to believe it. He blinked three times, hoping it was a mistake.

But it wasn't.

His cherry-red blood was splattered across the sink, mixing with the water and gurgling down the drain.

He was vomiting blood.

This was serious. He needed to phone for help, for an ambulance.

He staggered, dizzy from the sight of his own blood. All that red against the white porcelain. He tried to grip the side of the sink, tried to stay upright. But he heard blood rushing in his ears, and black spots filled his vision.

He dropped to one knee, and spread his arms, trying to break his fall. But as he fell, his head cracked against the side of the bath.

Lying on the floor of his bathroom, too weak to move, Michael watched as blood seeped from the wound on his head and slowly spread across the black and white tiles.

CHAPTER TWENTY-EIGHT

AT NINE O'CLOCK THE following morning, Eileen MacDonald, Michael King's cleaning lady, started work.

She started on the kitchen first, wiping down the worktops as she hummed along to the radio. She always liked to do the kitchens first in the houses and apartments she cleaned. Some people didn't like cleaning, but Eileen enjoyed it. Well, most of it anyway. She wasn't sure anyone could actually like cleaning toilets.

Michael King's flat was one of her easiest jobs. It was only a one-bedroom apartment, but Eileen was sure it cost a packet. The building had a gym and a swimming pool, which didn't come cheap in central London.

Eileen got the impression Mr. King didn't spend much time at home. He certainly never used his oven; it was spotless.

When she finished up in the kitchen, she entered the bedroom with her Pledge spray and duster. She paused by the door.

That was odd.

In the three years she had been cleaning for Michael King, not once had he left his bed unmade. Granted, it wasn't as if he did it properly, with all the corners tucked under, as Eileen did, but he always smoothed the duvet over.

He must have left in a hurry this morning, Eileen thought as she squirted the dresser with polish.

As she leaned forward to put some elbow grease into her polishing, something caught her eye. There was a brown-coloured stain on the bedroom carpet, next to the door to the en-suite bathroom.

She moved across to open the door of the en-suite bathroom, to investigate. She pushed the door, but it wouldn't budge. There must be something wedged behind it. Her first thought was that a towel had fallen off the hook on the back of the bedroom door, but whatever it was, it was much heavier than that.

She pushed harder. The door gave way a little, enough for her to poke her head into the bathroom.

Eileen screamed. Covered in blood and quite clearly dead, Michael King lay sprawled on the floor of his bathroom.

By eleven o'clock, Eileen was talking to two police officers. Cradling her cup of tea, she explained in a tearful voice how she discovered the body.

The officers took their time questioning Eileen, and despite her obvious shock, she was able to give contact details for Michael King's next of kin.

When asked if she knew if Michael King had been a drug addict, she made the sign of the cross and said, "Oh, no. He was such a nice, clean boy."

CHAPTER TWENTY-NINE

BILLY PICKED UP A local newspaper on his way to the safe house. On the front cover, there was a picture of a battered old woman, who had been mugged on the Towers Estate. Billy studied the old lady's black eyes and read how the bastards had beaten her, even though she had handed over her handbag without putting up a struggle.

The headline above the shocking picture read, "Youths Attack Pensioner: Destitute Britain."

Billy couldn't agree more. The article made his blood boil. The muggers had been two school boys, still dressed in their school uniforms when they had set upon the poor woman.

Billy folded the newspaper and stuck it under his arm. This place had gone to the dogs. When he lived here as a boy, things were very different. The communal areas were well-maintained and kept clean. Signs, forbidding ball games, were adhered to. Now, the small communal gardens were full of rubbish and dog shit, and the kids stood around sneering at passers-by.

When Billy got to the safe house, the deputy and the runner were both there, sorting out their business for the day. The runner was dressed in his school uniform. With a grey, record bag over his shoulder, he looked like he was about to do a paper round. Billy shook his head. He knew for a fact the boy hadn't attended school for weeks, and he was about to go on a round of a very different kind.

Billy nodded to the deputy and set his paper on the kitchen table.

"All right, Billy? You want a cup of tea?" The deputy nodded to a saucepan of water simmering away on the cooker top. "The kettle is bust again."

Billy shook his head. "No, thanks."

"Keep an eye on it for me. I want to make a phone call."

The deputy walked out of the kitchen, and the boy swaggered over to the table and looked down at the front page of the paper. "Stupid old cow. She had it coming. She's always making complaints about the kids on the estate."

Billy turned around slowly. "Do you know who did it?"

The boy smirked. "'Course, I was there, wasn't I? Stupid old busy-body, always sticking her nose in."

Billy looked again at the picture of the old lady. "How could anyone do that?"

The boy made a tutting sound. "You wouldn't know, would you, Billy? You're too weak. You have to make them see you're in control."

"She's an old lady."

Billy watched the steam rise from the pan as the water bubbled away. He couldn't reason with him. Why was he even trying to have a conversation with the kid? Billy turned back to the boy.

Later, he wouldn't be able to say what made him snap, but

there was something in the boy's expression, the way he just looked so pleased with himself, that made Billy lose control.

He grabbed the boy's arm and clamped it to his chest, putting him in a headlock. Then he held the boy's other hand over the boiling water.

The boy's eyes widened and he let out a yell of sheer terror. "What are you doing, man?"

Billy didn't answer. He just pushed the boy's arm closer to the steam. The boy struggled, but Billy, pushing downwards, was too strong.

When the boy's hand broke the surface of the water, he screamed.

The deputy burst into the kitchen. "What the hell? What are you doing? Get off him."

Billy let the boy's hand come out of the water, but he didn't let the boy go. "Did he tell you what he did? Him and his friends. To that old lady?

"No, no. It wasn't me. I didn't do it. I made it up." The boy's eyes were streaming.

"Shit, Billy. Let him go," the deputy said. "He's just bigging himself up."

Billy relaxed his grip on the boy, but didn't let go. "He thinks that makes him sound big? That something like that will earn him respect?"

"I said, let him go," the deputy said.

Billy felt the cold metal of the deputy's gun against the base of his skull.

Billy released the boy, and then turned slowly to face the deputy. "All right."

The boy retreated to the corner of the kitchen, snivelling and rubbing his runny nose on the back of his school jumper. He cradled his scalded hand.

The deputy's dark eyes flashed with anger. But Billy liked that. It was better than the contempt he usually saw in the deputy's eyes.

* * *

That afternoon, Billy was summoned to see JT.

He wasn't worried, though. He knew that the deputy and the boy runner wouldn't tell tales, not when Billy knew about their little scam. They knew he could tell JT all about how they had been skimming the drugs and selling them for a tidy profit on the estate.

It was more likely that JT just wanted an opportunity to lord it over him again.

Billy walked into the bar at The Junction. It was quiet, as it usually was at this time of day. A skinny, young man stacked bottles of beer into the cooler behind the bar. Billy had seen him before, but couldn't remember his name, so he just nodded.

The bartender jerked his thumb. "He's in his office."

"Thanks."

Billy walked behind the bar and along the corridor towards JT's office. He could hear the clatter of plates from the kitchen. No doubt, Siobhan was still working away while JT had his feet up in his office.

He knocked on the office door and waited.

JT opened the door. "Oh, it's you."

"Deputy said you wanted to see me?"

JT nodded. "Yeah, yeah. Come in." He pointed at a chair.

Billy sat down and watched JT squeeze his bulk behind his huge, polished, wooden desk. Billy didn't know what wood the desk was made from, but it looked expensive. That was JT all over. Looks counted, despite the fact the bloody desk was so big, it hardly fitted in the room.

"So, Billy," JT laced his fingers together and put his hands behind his head. "How are you getting on in the organisation?"

Organisation? Billy wanted to laugh. "Pretty good, Justin. I wanted to say thanks again, for taking me on."

JT nodded.

Billy smiled, he couldn't hold it back. The man thought he was in the bloody Sopranos.

"I thought I'd better make sure you realise how important it is not to talk about any of my business dealings. I can't have you blabbering to anyone."

"Of course."

"Especially to Siobhan and Emily."

Billy nodded.

"They wouldn't... understand," JT said.

Billy nodded again. Of course, they wouldn't understand.

"This job was only temporary. A favour, because you are family." JT stared at Billy.

Billy felt a cold sweat break out on his forehead. "Yeah, I was on trial. But it went well." Billy licked his lips. "I've worked hard, made myself useful..."

JT paused for a moment. Billy knew he was enjoying his discomfort. "Deputy says you're doing okay at the safe house. So you can stay on, for now, but I am warning you, not a word to Siobhan."

Billy shook his head. "No, of course not."

JT turned his attention to his laptop and made a sweeping gesture with his hand. Billy was dismissed.

Billy left JT's office, closed the door behind him and walked a little further down the corridor to the kitchen.

Siobhan stood with her back to him, in front of the sink, arms up to her elbows in soapy water. Her back was bent over and made her look like she had the weight of the world on her shoulders. She hummed softly to herself.

"Hello, sis," Billy said.

"Bill!" she said, turning and grinning at the sight of him.

When she smiled, her dimples made her look twelve years old again. She wiped her hands on a dishcloth, crossed the kitchen and wrapped him in a hug. "Come and sit down. I'll put the kettle on."

Billy watched his older sister bustle around the kitchen, making the tea.

She put two cups of tea on the table and sat down opposite him. She cradled her own mug in red, chapped hands.

"You work too hard, Siobhan."

"Don't I know it."

"Can't Justin get someone else to help you out in the kitchen?"

"He could. But of course, he won't. Not when he can get me to do it for free." She softened her words with a smile, and the skin around her eyes crinkled.

She put a hand over Billy's. "Billy, don't worry about me. It's me that's supposed to worry about my little brother, not the other way around. Now, tell me how you are. How's the job going?"

Billy took a sip of his tea and then said, "Not too bad, he's got some real scum working for him, but you know, I'm just keeping my head down."

Siobhan nodded. "Does he still think I know nothing about his little empire?"

Billy just smiled.

Siobhan shook her head. "Honestly, that man must think

I'm deaf and blind." Her expression grew serious. "I just don't want Emily to find out. I couldn't bear it, Billy. But she's bound to one of these days, isn't she?"

Billy couldn't deny it. He covered Siobhan's hand with his own. "We'll cross that bridge when we come to it."

CHAPTER THIRTY

TERRY DOBBS WAS FEELING terrible. He sat in the armchair in front of his huge plasma screen TV and cradled his head in his hands.

"Can't you get her to shut up?" Terry shouted.

Michelle stood in the doorway with Chantal, their six-month-old baby, balanced on her hip. The kid never seemed to shut up these days. She was always bawling her lungs out, with her little fists clenched, and her face screwed up and bright red.

"I'm doing my best," Michelle said.

But Michelle wasn't really doing anything. She just stood still, holding the baby with one arm, while staring at the TV with blank eyes. She didn't even try to bond with the baby or distract her from her temper tantrum. Michelle was too busy keeping up-to-date with the Jeremy Kyle show.

Terry could really do without this. His mate was supposed to have come around with their fix, but he hadn't shown up yet. Stupidly, Terry had paid him up front. He wouldn't do that again in a hurry. He scratched at the marks on his arm.

Michelle laid the baby down on the sofa. "I need something soon, Tel. I'm feeling really bad."

Join the bloody club, Terry thought. "Yeah, all right. He'll be here soon."

Michelle shuffled out of the room.

"Where do you think you're going?" Terry yelled. "You can't leave a baby lying on the sofa like that. She's not a bloody doll."

Michelle glanced at the baby, then looked back at Terry. "You pick her up then. I can't do it anymore."

Terry stared at Michelle, noticing the change in her for the first time. She'd come off heroin when she fell pregnant, and Terry had done his best to cut down too. It hadn't gone to plan, but at least he had never taken it around her when she was pregnant. The pregnancy had gone well and Michelle was so excited about the baby and their future that Terry started to believe they really could make things work.

Within a week of having Chantal, Michelle had shot up. Terry had come home from work, to find her semi-conscious in the kitchen. She fed Chantal formula milk after that.

Now six months later, Michelle wore a grubby tracksuit and her greasy hair hung down around her face. She was a mess.

Terry wasn't feeling that great himself. He had a blinding headache. He put that down to withdrawal cravings.

They needed to take back control. They had managed it before and they could do it again. They'd start next week. He would get his mum to look after Chantal while he and Michelle went cold turkey.

"All right," Terry said. "I will look after Chantal. You go and have a nice hot bath or something, yeah?"

Michelle nodded. "Yeah, thanks."

Terry picked up Chantal, who was now grizzling, rather than screaming. Her nappy was soaked. No wonder she was so upset.

Terry pulled out the changing mat and the bag with the nappies and wipes. There were only two nappies left. Great. That meant he would have to go and get some more later, and nappies were so expensive.

With her nappy off, Chantal seemed much happier and waved her chubby legs in the air as she tried to clutch her toes with her little hands.

Terry entertained her for a minute, playing peekaboo. He smoothed on a bit of rash cream and put her in her new nappy and a new, pink romper suit. Then he handed her a soft toy, which she started chewing on.

Terry winced. This headache was getting worse. He could hear the water running for Michelle's bath and the sound hurt his ears.

He glanced at the clock. His mate was two hours late. He wasn't going to show. The bastard had taken Terry's money and cheated him. Terry shivered. If he didn't score soon, he was going to start feeling really ill.

Where the hell was he going to get more money from? It was hard enough trying to get the last lot together. He eyed the plasma TV. He could get a few quid for that.

He decided to give his mate another thirty minutes. By then, Michelle would be out of the bath, and Terry could go out.

He kneeled down on the floor beside Chantal, leaning over her. "You deserve a better dad, you know. I'm going to get straightened out. By the time you are old enough to remember, I will be clean. I promise."

There was a spot of blood on Chantal's pink romper suit. Shit! Where did that come from? Had she cut herself? Terry looked around the floor, but he couldn't see anything that could have hurt her.

He opened a couple of the poppers and peeled back the BabyGrow, revealing Chantal's soft skin. There wasn't a mark on her. So where was the blood coming from?

Another splash of blood.

Terry sat back on his heels. It was his blood. He raised a hand to his face. He had a nosebleed.

He grabbed some kitchen roll from the kitchen and held a wad of it to his nose. He felt dizzy, but the sight of his own blood had always affected Terry.

He sat back down on the floor beside Chantal, who looked up at him with interest.

"Do I look silly?" Terry said, smiling.

By the time Michelle finished her bath and came into the sitting room, Terry had used the entire roll to try to mop up the blood.

"Jesus. What has happened in here?" Michelle said.

"Nosebleed," Terry said. "It just won't stop."

Michelle tightened the belt on her dressing gown and ran a hand through her wet hair. "That's a lot of blood."

"Yeah." Terry stood up, with the kitchen roll held to his nose, his head spinning.

"I feel sick," he said and staggered out of the room.

The bathroom was still full of steam. Terry opened the window. He needed fresh air.

He took a couple of shallow breaths, hoping the sick feeling would go away. He had been like this since he was a kid. He hated the sight of blood. He had fainted at the doctors' surgery when he was eleven years old because one of the other kids in the waiting area had a cut lip.

Terry felt an odd, splitting sensation deep in his stomach, like something had burst open.

It was no good. He was going to throw up. He retched again and again.

Terry dropped to his knees. "Michelle, you better call an ambulance."

When Terry turned around, the lower half of his face was coated in blood, which dripped off his chin and dribbled down his shirt.

Michelle's screams were the last thing Terry heard before he passed out.

* * *

"Oh, God, no," said Roger Taylor.

"What is it, Roger?" Therese Daniels shouted so Roger would hear her over the ambulance siren.

"He's bleeding out. I'm losing him." Roger stared down at the man in the back of the ambulance. It seemed like he was bleeding from every orifice. Roger wore blue nitrile gloves, but his hands were slick with blood. The poor bastard was an addict, too, which meant he was a danger of infection, a high-risk patient.

"How much longer?" Roger shouted.

"Two minutes."

Roger bit down on his lip, trying to concentrate. Two minutes. He just had to hold this bloke together for the next two minutes. "C'mon, Terry, mate, hang in there," Roger said, swaying slightly as Therese steered the ambulance around a sharp bend.

"BP's falling," Roger said.

"I'll call ahead," Therese said, and Roger heard the static of the radio.

He needed to try and get the tube in. It was his only chance.

He could hear the man's breathing. It sounded more like gurgling. Roger positioned himself to insert the tube into Terry's throat. Just as he pried opened Terry's mouth, the man coughed and covered Roger's chest with droplets of blood.

"Shit!"

Roger did his best to ignore the blood and moved forward to try to clear the patient's airway, then the alarm sounded on the heart rate monitor.

"You need me to stop?" Therese shouted.

"No. Just get us to the hospital, like now." Roger quickly hooked up another IV line and squeezed the bag. The poor bastard was still breathing, at least, but if his blood pressure went any lower...

"We're here." Therese slammed on the brakes, and the back doors of the ambulance flew open.

The on-call registrar and three nurses stood by the ambulance bay, waiting for the patient. They all wore protective clothing.

"What have we got? He's a danger of infection one, isn't he?" the registrar asked.

Roger filled them in as they got Terry and the equipment out of the back of the ambulance and wheeled him through the double doors into the back of the Accident and Emergency department.

"I'll need six units of O-neg," the registrar said to one of the nurses. "Tell the on-call scientific officer, we'll need an emergency cross-match."

The registrar turned back to Roger. "Any idea what he has taken?"

"He's a heroin addict..." Before Roger could finish his sentence, one of the nurses screamed. Roger turned to see what she was screaming at.

The trolley and Terry were covered with bright red blood. The walls of the corridor were sprayed with it too.

The nurses and the registrar pushed the trolley as fast as they could. Their feet slipped on the floor, which was slick with blood. The doors smashed open as they flew towards the operating theatres.

Roger was left alone in the corridor. He turned in a slow circle, taking in the blood-drenched walls and the pools of blood on the floor. He'd never seen so much blood in his entire life.

CHAPTER THIRTY-ONE

CHARLIE PRICE, SARCASTICALLY KNOWN amongst hospital staff as "cheerful Charlie," wheeled his cleaning bucket down to the ambulance bay. His mouth always turned down at the corners, making him look perpetually depressed.

He wasn't. He told people at work that it was just the way his face was arranged, but that didn't stop them calling out, "Cheer up, Charlie," whenever they saw him.

Usually, Charlie was perfectly cheerful, thank you very much. But not today. Charlie definitely didn't feel very cheerful at the moment.

A hospital porter's day was never exactly glamorous. From taking the contaminated waste down to the incinerator, to cleaning up vomit and worse, porters always got the messy jobs, but this one took the biscuit.

Charlie sighed and looked around at the state of the corridor. There was blood everywhere. It would take him ages to clear all this up. It was even on the ceiling! Must have been an arterial spray, Charlie thought. He had seen that once before, in an operating theatre.

Sighing again, he picked up the bright yellow, plastic warning signs and set them down at either side of the corridor.

He pulled out the Presept and began to apply it to the floors and walls. The bright red blood turned a muddy-brown colour as soon as it was exposed to the bleach.

The chlorine tang of the Presept mixed with the metallic smell of blood. Charlie wrinkled his nose and stood back. He would leave it for a few minutes to kill any nasties, then start to mop it up.

Charlie was leaning on his mop handle, waiting, when Dr. Anna Sorensen walked down the corridor.

"Watch out, Doc," Charlie said. "You'd better watch your step. There is blood everywhere down here."

Dr. Sorensen stared at the mess. "What on earth happened?"

"Some poor bastard. He exploded in the corridor, apparently. Nurses told me there was blood squirting everywhere. And he was a danger of infection sample."

Dr. Sorensen paled. "Was he an addict?"

Charlie nodded. "It looked even worse when I first got here, believe me." Charlie gestured at the wall. "It looked like a slaughterhouse."

Dr. Sorensen put a hand against the wall to steady herself.

"Are you all right, Doc?" Charlie frowned. Okay, it wasn't a pretty sight, but surely a doctor should be used to the sight of blood.

Dr. Sorensen shivered. "Yes. It's just..."

"Yeah, it's not pretty," Charlie said. He understood why it was upsetting the doctor. He saw blood on a daily basis, too.

But this... This was something else.

CHAPTER THIRTY-TWO

DR. ANNA SORENSEN MADE her way to the pathology department, worrying about the man who had just been admitted. He was another addict. This was a coincidence too far. There had to be something in the heroin that was causing these people to bleed out.

When she entered the coagulation laboratory, she was pleased to see that Rita was the scientific officer on-call tonight.

"I'll be with you in a tick," Rita said. "I've just got to finish validating these results."

"Sure." Anna sat down on a stool by the lab bench.

In front of her was a collection of blood samples, which hadn't been processed yet. The blood samples were sent up to pathology in individual clear, plastic bags, together with a request form from the requesting doctor.

Different lab tests required different tubes. The colour of the lid on the glass sample tubes, indicated which test was required.

On the bench, there were three types of blood-filled tubes. For a full blood count, the lab needed a small sample tube with a pink lid. This tube contained EDTA as an anti-coagulant. If the anticoagulant was not present, the blood sample would simply clot in the tube. The platelets and cells would clump together, making analysis impossible.

A blood group test, or a request for a blood cross-match, needed a special tube with a red lid.

Blood samples used in coagulation tests were collected in glass tubes with purple lids. These tubes contained sodium citrate, another type of anti-coagulant, which was compatible with the coagulation tests. The sodium citrate bound the calcium ions in the blood, and without the calcium ions, the clotting factors in the blood could not work.

Rita turned to face Anna. "Right, I'm all done. What can I do for you?"

"A patient was brought in bleeding. I wanted to take a look at his blood work."

"Name? Hospital number?"

"Terrence Dobbs." Anna read out the hospital number from the file.

Rita typed the number into the computer, then scrolled down the screen. "Yes, got him. He was a danger of infection sample." Rita nodded at a sample on the machine next to them. It was covered in a bright yellow sticker. "Another addict?"

Anna nodded. All samples from known drug users were labelled with these yellow stickers. All samples were supposed to be treated as though they posed a health risk, but the yellow stickers were used if patients were drug users or known carriers of infectious diseases such as AIDS or hepatitis.

"I'm re-running the sample," Rita said. "To double check. He had an incredibly long clotting time."

Five minutes later, Rita pulled the results up on the screen.

Anna and Rita studied the results.

Rita frowned and turned to Anna. "The results are the same. This patient is in big trouble."

Anna picked up a pad of pathology request forms and pulled off a sheet. She carefully copied the patient's name and hospital number onto it, ticked four boxes, then signed the form and handed it to Rita.

"How soon could you run these tests for me?"

"Are they urgent?"

Anna paused, then said, "Yes they are, very urgent. It could tell us what is causing these patients to bleed."

Rita nodded. "I'll run them now."

CHAPTER THIRTY-THREE

MACKINNON GOT BACK TO Oxford in record time. There was no way he was going to let Katy down.

She opened the door as soon as he stepped out of the car. She had clearly been waiting for him.

"You've got five minutes," she said, looking at her watch. "Then we really have to go."

"No problem," Mackinnon said as he passed her in the doorway. "I'll just get changed."

He threw on a pair of jeans and a rugby shirt. He didn't fancy standing on the sidelines wearing a suit.

"Jack?" Katy called up the stairs.

"Just coming." Mackinnon descended the stairs two at a time. "It's all right; we've got plenty of time."

"It starts at seven, and I have to get changed there."

Mackinnon eyed her tracksuit bottoms and white airtex top. "Aren't you wearing that?"

Katy pulled him out the door, picking up her hockey stick

on the way. "I have to change into my skirt and put my shin pads on."

Mackinnon grabbed his coat and flicked off the light switch. "Okay, let's go."

The hockey match was being held at Katy's school. Wychwood was an independent school, on the Banbury road. It only took five minutes to get there in the car.

Mackinnon parked, then Katy jumped out of the car with her sports bag.

"I've got to go and change," she said. "You can wait on the pitch with the other parents. It's around the back." Katy pointed to a small path that disappeared along the side of the school, then dashed off.

Great. Now he had to find his way on his own. He would look like a strange man, prowling around an all-girls school. Thanks a bunch, Katy.

He locked the car and strolled over to the path, walking past a long, red-brick wall. He had only gone a few feet when he heard the sound of voices. As he rounded the corner, he spotted a bunch of adults huddled together at the sidelines.

One of the woman brayed with laughter. Mackinnon shuddered. The jolly, hockey stick brigade. He wasn't looking forward to this much.

Despite wanting to go and wait in the car, Mackinnon walked up to the group and smiled.

One of the women turned. "Oh, hellooo."

She looked him up and down so blatantly that if Mackinnon had been the type, he would have blushed. Instead, he just nodded back. "Hello."

The woman fingered her pearl necklace with the fingers of one hand, and held out the other for Mackinnon to shake. "I'm Daphne, Eleanor's mother. I haven't seen you before."

Mackinnon gave her hand a quick shake. "Jack. I brought Katy tonight as her mother couldn't make it."

As Mackinnon spoke, the Wychwood team ran onto the pitch. Katy turned and gave him an odd look, then ran up to take her position.

All the girls wore pleated hockey skirts with thick socks, bulky with their shin pads. They were playing a team from another Oxford girls' school as part of the Inter Oxford Schools' Hockey Tournament.

Mackinnon grinned at Katy and started to raise his hand to wave, but thought better of it and stuffed his hand back in his coat pocket. He didn't want to embarrass her.

The referee, a tall woman, with thighs bigger than Mackinnon's, blew her whistle to start the match. The girls flew at each other. Mackinnon winced and took a step back. This was brutal. They hacked at the ground and whacked each others' legs as many times as they hit the ball.

The referee blew her whistle as one player was forced to duck when her opponent's stick swung in the air, threatening to hit her at eye level.

Daphne, noticing Mackinnon's expression, said, "They play to win." She smiled at him, then shouted, "Come on, Eleanor, darling."

In the second half, Katy tore up the pitch with the ball. Mackinnon silently cheered. She was actually pretty good.

Then, out of nowhere, a girl from the other team flung her stick out at Katy's shins. There was absolutely no way the girl was aiming for the ball.

Katy went flying. She sat up, dazed, the front of her white shirt covered in mud. She got back to her feet, brushed herself off and picked up her hockey stick. Meanwhile, the other team had the ball and the referee hadn't even blown her whistle.

Was the referee blind?

"Hey," Mackinnon shouted. "She did that deliberately."

The referee shot him a nasty look, then made a zipping motion across her lips. Some referee, Mackinnon thought.

He turned to Daphne. "Did you see that?"

"Oh, yes. It happens quite a lot, I'm afraid."

Five minutes later, Katy had the ball back, and this time, there was no stopping her. She made a great shot at the goal. Mackinnon bit his lip as the goal keeper dived for it. It just slipped under the keeper's arm.

Mackinnon clapped, along with the other parents, and Katy excitedly hugged another girl from her team. Mackinnon pulled out his phone and typed a text to Chloe to let her know Katy had scored.

When the game ended, Mackinnon spoke to a couple of the parents while he waited for Katy to get showered and changed. After fifteen minutes, most of the other parents had left with their children, and there was still no sign of Katy, so he went looking for her.

He found her quickly enough. She was standing by the sports hall exit, chatting to a girl with long, brown hair. I should have guessed, Mackinnon thought. He opened his mouth to tell her to get a move on, but before he spoke, he heard the girl speak.

"My dad comes to every match. He never misses my games."

Katy shrugged. "Well, my dad's busy. He has an important job."

Mackinnon caught his breath. He had never given Katy's father much thought. When Chloe got pregnant, Katy's father didn't want to know and soon walked out on her. Chloe had never heard from him again, and as far as Mackinnon knew, Katy had never asked to meet her father.

Sarah's father was a different matter. A hot-shot business-man, who played a role in Sarah's life only when he felt like it. Sarah adored him, and in her eyes, he could do no wrong. Even after he moved to New Zealand, Sarah overlooked his desertion and found a way to blame her mother for it.

The brown-haired girl folded her arms. "Well my dad says nothing is more important to him than me."

Katy crouched down to pick up her sports bag. "I'd better go, my dad will be waiting."

Mackinnon felt like he had been hit by a ton of bricks. My dad?

The brown-haired girl nodded. "Was that your dad I saw tonight?"

"Yeah. I mean, he isn't my biological dad, but he's as good as."

Mackinnon retraced his steps back to the car, so they wouldn't know he had been eavesdropping.

When Katy arrived back at the car, he took her sports bag and loaded it into the boot. "Fantastic game, sweetheart. Well done. Shall we get pizza to celebrate?"

Katy grinned. "Yeah, okay. Has Mum's meeting finished yet?"

"I think she'll be another hour or so, so it will just be me and you. Is that okay with you?"

Katy nodded. "As long as we can get a Hawaiian."

Mackinnon pulled a face. "Really? I can't persuade you to go for pepperoni?"

Katy buckled her seat belt. "Nope."

"Okay, seeing as you did so well tonight, Hawaiian it is."

* * *

Mackinnon and Katy managed to polish off the extra-large pizza, and Mackinnon was just stacking their plates in the dishwasher when he got a text from Chloe. She asked if he could meet her in the Woodstock Arms in ten minutes.

Katy sat cross-legged on the floor in front of the TV, sipping a can of Coke.

"I'm going to the Woodstock Arms to meet your mum for a quick drink. We won't be long."

"Okay," Katy said, not bothering to turn away from the programme she was watching.

Mackinnon remembered what he had overheard earlier.

"Have you done all your homework?" Mackinnon asked. That sounded like a "dad" thing to say.

"Didn't have any."

"See you in a bit then."

"Okay."

CHAPTER THIRTY-FOUR

CHLOE WAS ALREADY IN the Woodstock Arms when Mackinnon got there. She had bought herself a glass of red wine and a pint of beer for Mackinnon.

"Hi," Mackinnon said, leaning over and kissing her on the cheek. "Why are we meeting here?"

Chloe smiled. "I just fancied a drink and a chat without being overheard."

Mackinnon took a sip of his pint. "Sounds serious."

"Not really. Just nice to spend a little time alone with you."

Mackinnon smiled. It was nice. It might even stay that way if they could avoid talking about Sarah for the evening.

"How was your meeting?" Mackinnon asked.

Chloe pulled a face. "Boring, very boring."

"Katy did well. She scored a goal."

Chloe smiled. "I got your text. She's quite the little sportswoman."

"I thought I might tag along to her next match, too."

"Oh?"

"It's next Saturday."

Mackinnon considered telling Chloe about what he overheard Katy saying earlier. But he wasn't sure now was the right time. She had been at work since eight and looked shattered, and he didn't want to add to her worries. She already had enough stress from Sarah.

Chloe took a sip of her wine and looked up at Mackinnon. She ran a hand through her hair, then bit her lip.

"I'm sure she's been taking something," she said miserably, looking down at her glass of red wine.

Well, Mackinnon thought, that didn't last long. They were back onto the subject of Sarah. Again.

"Have you asked her?"

"Well, she wouldn't tell me if she was." Chloe sipped her wine. "She won't talk to me. She dropped out of the sixth form at school to go to college, and now she won't go to college. She won't get a job. I'm at my wit's end. I just don't know what to do with her."

"Cut her off," Mackinnon said.

Chloe put her wine glass down on the table. "What?"

"She's almost eighteen. Tell her you won't give her any more money unless she goes back to college or gets a job."

"I can't do that."

"Why not?"

"Don't be ridiculous, Jack."

"She'll still have a roof over her head, but she won't be able to afford whatever it is you think she's taking." Unless she decides to steal to fund her habit, Mackinnon thought. He suspected Sarah may have already started down that slippery slope. Recently, he had found his wallet a little lighter than expected on a couple of occasions. A tenner here and there, not enough to be certain. He'd taken to locking his wallet in the bureau.

"For God's sake, Jack, that's something only someone without children would suggest."

Mackinnon sighed and picked up his pint glass. "I'm trying to help. What do you want me to say?"

"Nothing. I just wanted someone to listen."

Mackinnon's phone rang. He checked the caller ID. It was Dr. Anna Sorensen.

Dr. Sorensen told him another addict had been admitted, with the same uncontrolled bleeding.

As she filled him in, Mackinnon watched Chloe. Her shoulders slumped, and she stared at her wine without drinking it. She looked so forlorn.

Mackinnon interrupted Dr. Sorensen. "Just a moment, Anna. I'm finding it difficult to hear you in here. I'll call you back from outside.

After he hung up, Mackinnon put an arm around Chloe. "It'll be okay," he said. "I have to take this outside. Won't be long."

Mackinnon stood outside in the pub car park and called Dr. Sorensen back.

She answered on the first ring.

"DS Mackinnon, I have some interesting test results from the latest patient. Can you get to the hospital? I really think you should see these results."

"That won't be easy. I am in Oxford at the moment."

Dr. Sorensen was silent on the other end of the phone.

Mackinnon looked through the pub window, at Chloe sitting on her own. "Is it important?"

"You could say that," Dr. Sorensen said. "I have a theory."

CHAPTER THIRTY-FIVE

AS DR. SORENSEN DIDN'T want to elaborate on her theory over the phone, Mackinnon dropped Chloe off at home and promised to call her tomorrow.

He did feel a little bit guilty, but he was intrigued by what the doctor said on the phone. His guilt faded into the background as he headed for the hospital pathology department and mulled over what these test results might be able to tell them.

Dr. Anna Sorensen greeted him at reception. "DS Mackinnon, thanks for coming."

Mackinnon nodded. "Please call me Jack. So what are these results?"

"I think it would be easier to explain in the lab," Anna said.

She led him through the same corridors as before and through the labyrinth of labs. There were no scientists around, and the dimly lit laboratories had an eerie quality.

"Does no one get sick at night?" Mackinnon said.

Anna looked confused. "I'm sorry?"

"The place is deserted."

"Ah, I see what you mean. There is someone on duty. An on-call scientific officer for the haematology department. They will only process urgent samples. The routine samples won't get run until tomorrow."

"So where is the on-call scientist now?"

"Trying to get some sleep, I imagine."

"Sleep? Nice work if you can get it."

"Not really," Anna said. "The scientific officer on-call will have already worked a full day. So, including tonight, that is a twenty-four hour shift. If the scientist is cross-matching blood for me, I'd hope they would take any rest that they could."

"Ah, I see," Mackinnon said, suitably chastened.

Anna pushed open the doors to the coagulation lab and flicked on the lights. "Now this is what I wanted you to see."

Anna moved over to the computer, next to the large machine, which was humming gently. She tapped on the keyboard and brought up a screen of data.

"The patient's name is Terry Dobbs. He began bleeding at home, just a nosebleed at first, which got steadily worse. His girlfriend called for an ambulance and told the attending paramedics that Terry is a heroin addict. He was haemorrhaging badly when he arrived in the ambulance, bleeding from all his mucosal membranes. He was vomiting and excreting blood from every orifice. So far, he has had six units of blood. But his blood tests show-"

"This may be a silly question," Mackinnon said. "But if he has had so much blood pumped into him, how do you know the blood tests are reliable? I mean, it's not really his own blood anymore, is it?"

Anna straightened up. "It's not a silly question. Once a

patient is haemorrhaging like this and has had so much blood, it makes the problem worse. All the things the human body needs to form a blood clot, like clotting factors and platelets, are in effect, diluted by the new blood, so it's a vicious cycle.

"We did manage to get a pre-transfusion blood sample from him, though," Anna said. "And that has given us an interesting result. If you look here..." Anna pointed at the computer screen.

"We ran the sample on the automated coagulation machine. The machine adds calcium ions, which triggers the clotting process. The progress of the clotting reaction is measured optically by the machine and the time taken for the blood to clot is recorded. This measurement is then used to calculate something we call the INR. It stands for international normalised ratio."

Mackinnon was getting lost. Why didn't she just say the blood wasn't clotting fast enough, that he could understand. "Okay. I take it his INR was abnormal."

"I know this seems like quite a long-winded way to explain it to you, but the INR is important. Because the INR is high in warfarin patients."

"Warfarin?"

Anna nodded. "Yes. That is my theory. I think the heroin is contaminated with warfarin."

Mackinnon took a moment to think. "The stuff they use for rat poison?"

Anna nodded. "Well, yes. It is used as a rodenticide, but not so much these days as the rats are developing resistance. The elevated INR gave me the first inkling that it could be warfarin, or a similar coumadin, contaminating the heroin, but I wanted to be sure."

Mackinnon followed Anna as she walked back out of the

lab and along the corridor.

"I ran an HPLC assay on the serum of the blood samples. Both indicated the presence of warfarin in the patient's blood." Anna looked up at Mackinnon. "This is actually good news," Anna said. "It means we can treat the victims. Do you know much about warfarin?"

"Not much, other than it was used as a rat poison. Bleeding to death is a pretty nasty way to go, even for a rat."

Mackinnon tried to digest the information as Anna led him to the intensive care unit to see the two most recent victims of the contaminated heroin.

"Sorry about the science lesson, but I thought you needed to know why the test results suggest warfarin contamination. The clotting process is very complex, with many different factors coming together to form a cascade. Different drugs affect different parts of coagulation pathway."

"So the patient's abnormal INR is definitely caused by warfarin? You're absolutely sure?"

"The HPLC assay proves he had warfarin in his system," Dr. Sorensen said.

"We have given both patients a vitamin K injection, which should counter the effects of the warfarin. After the transfusions they were also given FFP-"

"FFP?"

"It stands for fresh frozen plasma, and it contains clotting factors, so that should help stop the bleeding," Anna said as they reached the doors to ICU.

Anna got them buzzed in and they walked across to the nursing station.

Anna whispered to the nurse.

The nurse frowned. "They are popular tonight. They already have a visitor."

Mackinnon turned to see a familiar figure leaning over a patient's bed.

CHAPTER THIRTY-SIX

MACKINNON LEFT DR. SORENSEN talking to the nurse and walked across to the ICU ward. DI Bruce Evans looked up as Mackinnon joined him at the bedside.

"What are you doing here?" Mackinnon whispered.

"I asked Dr. Sorensen to let me know if there were any more of these bleeding cases admitted."

Mackinnon looked around the ward. They weren't really supposed to be in here.

The lights were dim, and the only sound was the gentle beeps and humming noise from the machinery. There were six other beds in the units and two nurses were checking other patients. One of them gave Mackinnon the evil eye.

"I think we've out-stayed our welcome," Mackinnon said.

"I don't know Terry Dobbs, but I've seen this guy around," Bruce Evans said and nodded at the comatose figure. "I've seen him with Ronnie on a couple of occasions. He's got a record for shoplifting. He's only twenty-four. You wouldn't believe it to look at him, would you?"

Mackinnon had to agree. The boy's shrunken cheeks gave him a haggard appearance, and the pale, papery skin on his face looked like it belonged to an eighty-year-old man.

IV tubes were attached to his stick-thin arms, and he was wired up to a huge machine at the side of the bed. Two drips, containing clear fluid, stood beside him, entering his left arm. And a pouch of blood was attached to his right arm. Another tube entered his neck and was taped to his skin. Mackinnon supposed that was to prevent the tube from slipping.

Below the bed, there was a transparent bag, to collect the patient's urine. But the liquid in the bag was dark red, not yellow.

"Which one is Terry Dobbs?" Mackinnon asked.

Bruce pointed to the next bed. "That's him there. He's got a six-month-old little girl. His girlfriend was in here earlier. She told me they both shot up yesterday afternoon. Anna has admitted her for observation, but so far, she seems fine."

They stood there watching him in the dim light. Then they both jumped at a piercing beep from one of the machines.

Two of the nurses rushed over, with Anna close behind them.

"I'm sorry, gentlemen, but I'll have to ask you to leave now," one of the other nurses said. "We need to see to this patient."

"Of course." Mackinnon and Bruce Evans backed away.

Anna followed them to the exit, and pressed the green release button to open the door. Outside in the corridor, she turned to Mackinnon. "Have you told DI Evans my theory?"

"What theory is that?" Bruce Evans said.

"Anna thinks the heroin is contaminated with warfarin," Mackinnon said.

"Warfarin?" Bruce Evans raised an eyebrow. "Like the stuff in rat poison."

Anna nodded. "Shall we go and get a cup of coffee? Then I can explain. I'm nearing the end of my shift, and I feel like the living dead."

They went to the hospital staff canteen, got coffee from a vending machine and sat in the deserted seating area.

Mackinnon sat down beside Anna, and Bruce sat opposite them.

"You don't think this is deliberate, do you?" Bruce said.

"What do you mean?" Anna asked.

But Mackinnon knew. He'd already had the same ugly thought.

"This stuff is used to kill rats," Bruce said. "It's used to clear the streets of vermin."

"It's possible," Mackinnon said.

Bruce's intense expression relaxed into a smile. "No. Ignore me. I'm letting my imagination run riot."

Mackinnon took a sip of his coffee and thought about the wasted figure he'd just seen in ITU. He had a horrible feeling someone had contaminated this heroin deliberately.

CHAPTER THIRTY-SEVEN

MICHELLE HESITATED, HER FINGER hovered over the buzzer. She was supposed to be in her own ward, not up here in ICU. But she couldn't stay away, not when Terry needed her. Besides, if anything happened to her, if she started bleeding, the nurses here would help her.

She pressed the buzzer and the door was opened by a short Malaysian nurse, who gave Michelle a sympathetic smile. It was warm inside the ITU, but Michelle wrapped her arms around her midsection and shivered. She walked past the other patients, heading for Terry's bed.

There were six other beds in the unit. All the patients seemed to be asleep or unconscious. She had seen a few visitors come and go this afternoon, but there were no other visitors in here now.

Dr. Sorensen had admitted Michelle to hospital this afternoon. She said there was something bad in the heroin they'd been taking. Something that made Terry bleed. Dr. Sorensen didn't say as much, but Michelle knew the doctor thought she might turn out like Terry.

The nurse on the ward had hooked her up to a drip and given her some sort of vitamin, which was supposed to block the effects of the bad drugs. They had given it to Terry too. She hoped to God it worked.

She hadn't prayed in years, not since she was a little girl, but she did today. If only Terry would get better, they could have a fresh start. They could kick the stuff together and be happy again. Chantal deserved that much, at least.

Michelle's mother had collected the baby this afternoon. She arrived with her lips pursed and a deep frown on her face, like usual. She didn't approve of Michelle and Terry's lifestyle.

Michelle missed the feel of Chantal's little, warm body, tucked in close to her own. She missed the comfort it gave her. But she knew she couldn't keep Chantal here. The ICU was no place for a baby. Even worse, she could feel the withdrawal symptoms kicking in, the darkness closing in. She couldn't look after Chantal when she was like this.

Michelle felt a sharp pain in her stomach as it rumbled. She clutched a hand to her side. She had been suffering from terrible diarrhoea all day. It was another sign that her body was screaming for heroin.

She hardly recognised Terry when she looked down at him, surrounded by the life support equipment. He looked pale and thin, and there were so many tubes and wires attached to his body. She glanced at the computer monitor beside his bed, which contained data and images she couldn't understand.

She touched his pale, thin arm with her index finger.

"Terry," she whispered. "It's me."

Terry didn't react. What if he never opened his eyes again?

Michelle looked away. She focused on the drips and

machinery surrounding his bed, and concentrated on reading the labels, the names of drugs she had never heard of before.

"We'll be all right. We'll get ourselves sorted. Then maybe we can move away. We could get a place by the sea. Chantal would love growing up by the seaside, wouldn't she?" Michelle blinked away her tears.

CHAPTER THIRTY-EIGHT

DR. SORENSEN YAWNED. "SORRY. It's been a long day. Now, I can tell you a bit about warfarin, but I doubt it will help you track down the contaminated heroin."

"Background always helps," Mackinnon said.

"Well, warfarin has been around for a while. Way back in the twenties, in America, herds of cattle developed a mysterious illness. The cows were bleeding to death. At first, no one knew what was killing these herds, but eventually, it was linked to the cows' food. The affected herds were eating spoiled sweet clover hay." Anna smothered another yawn.

"It wasn't until the forties that scientists realised a compound found in the sweet clover, called coumarin, had been chemically altered by mould growing on the hay. And the chemically altered form, called dicoumarol, acted as an anti-coagulant." Anna took a sip of her coffee.

"So the dicoumarol was used to treat patients in the forties. Scientists then set about looking for other similar molecules. When warfarin was discovered, it was patented as a rat poison and considered too toxic for use in humans at first. But a few years later, clinicians started to use warfarin on humans, they found it was much more effective than the original anti-coagulant dicoumarol. And I think it was even used to treat Eisenhower, after he had a heart attack."

Mackinnon looked up from his coffee. "Can we be sure it is warfarin that is contaminating the heroin and not one of these related drugs?"

"Unless the drugs have been contaminated by some mouldy hay." Bruce grinned.

"The assay I ran confirmed that both patients' blood was contaminated with warfarin, and I think warfarin would be the easiest thing to get hold of. If someone wanted to deliberately contaminate the heroin."

"I really hope this is an accidental contamination." Evans drained his coffee. "The bloody heroin on its own causes us enough problems."

Anna shook her head. "I saw the public health notice in the papers this morning, but I'm not sure people are going to stop taking heroin. I think we should prepare ourselves for more casualties."

Mackinnon knew what she meant. How could they expect addicts to stay away from heroin? If it were that easy, they wouldn't be addicted in the first place.

CHAPTER THIRTY-NINE

THE NEXT DAY, MACKINNON rose early. He showered, dressed and left the flat before Derek woke. As he headed to work on the underground, his thoughts turned to the two patients he had seen in the hospital yesterday.

They looked so pale, so empty of life. Could Anna really be right? Would a quick injection of vitamin K really be enough to save them?

The lights on the train flickered as the train juddered to a halt inside the tunnel. There were murmurs of discontent from the other passengers. Mackinnon leaned back against the panel he was standing next to and glanced around at the other people on the train.

It was early so it was still pretty quiet.

There was a man dressed in a suit, his laptop bag resting on his knees. Next to him a young woman, with mascara-smudged eyes, wearing a short skirt, shifted uncomfortably in her seat. She had probably been out all night. On the opposite side of the carriage, an older woman sat, bundled up in an old winter coat; and next to her, a teenage boy with headphones sat back and scowled at everyone else on the train.

Any one of them might be addicted to heroin. You couldn't tell just by looking at them. One of them might be planning to meet their dealer, planning their next fix. None of them had probably heard about the contaminated drug on the street. None of them would know the dangers.

Press releases, warning signs on the walls of drug treatment clinics and charities, was that enough? The warning couldn't possibly get through to everybody.

Again, the image of Terry Dobbs in the ITU flashed through Mackinnon's mind. How many people would end up like him?

It had to be a mistake, an accidental contamination. Who would want to inflict that kind of death on another human being?

The train jerked into motion again, and Mackinnon gripped the handrail. They needed to get this dirty heroin off the streets. And they needed to do it fast, before it claimed any more victims.

CHAPTER FORTY

MACKINNON HUNG HIS JACKET up behind the door and walked over to his desk. It was covered with piles of paperwork, just as he'd left it. He switched on the computer, then went to get coffee while it booted up.

Collins was already at his desk. Mackinnon nodded and smiled. He didn't feel up to talking this early in the morning.

Back at his desk, Mackinnon started scrolling through the logs of incidents and crimes that had occurred over the past few days in the City area.

"Anything interesting?"

Mackinnon turned to see Charlotte cradling a steaming mug of coffee.

"A couple of vicious muggings." Mackinnon picked up his own coffee, then pointed at the screen. "There's a report here, an unusual death. An investment banker, Michael King, was found dead in his penthouse apartment. It says here that he hit his head and bled to death before anyone found him."

"He hit his head, or someone hit it for him?"

"The report suggests it was an accident. It caught my interest because it says drug paraphernalia was found at his apartment."

Charlotte blew across the top of her mug, then said. "You think he may have used some of this contaminated heroin?"

Mackinnon shrugged. "I'm going to find out."

He reached for the phone.

The officer he called wasn't very happy to be phoned at seven am. After a bit of moaning about how the officer was sure this could have waited another hour or two, he agreed to tell Mackinnon what he knew.

When Mackinnon hung up, Charlotte prompted him. "And?"

"Tox screen showed heroin in his system. They didn't test for warfarin, of course, but he did tell me something very interesting. He said that the head wound was superficial, yet the preliminary findings have shown that Michael King died from the amount of blood he lost."

Mackinnon would have to take this to Detective Superintendent Wright. Charlotte left him to plan his course of action. DS Baines emailed him a copy of the report and Mackinnon printed it off and headed to Wright's office, rehearsing what he would say once he got there.

Detective Superintendent Wright was obviously surprised to see Mackinnon when he knocked on the partially open door to his office. His assistant didn't start until eight.

"Mackinnon," the superintendent said and smiled. "Come in."

He had thought about what he was going to say while walking to his boss's office, and he had it all rehearsed in his mind. He needed the superintendent's help. They needed to get a sample of the heroin Michael King had taken and test it for warfarin.

"Sir, I need your help."

"Take a seat, Jack. What's the problem?"

Mackinnon sat down and looked into Wright's deeply hooded eyes. He started to lose his resolve. Wright was a good man and a great boss, but he had certain lines he wouldn't cross, and sticking his nose into another force's business was one of those lines.

Mackinnon forgot all his carefully planned, persuasive words and just blurted it out. "I think I have found another victim of the contaminated heroin."

Mackinnon pushed the printed report over the desk to the superintendent.

The superintendent's smile disappeared, and he frowned as he read the report.

"We need to get a sample of that heroin and have it tested for warfarin, sir."

The superintendent looked up. "It says here that Michael King lived in the Docklands." He tapped the printout. "That means it falls under the Met. I'll ring them and give them a heads-up. All the forces around the country have been alerted to this contaminated heroin, so I imagine, it won't come as a complete surprise."

"I'd still like to get hold of a sample, so we can test it here, sir."

"That isn't practical, Jack. The Met will have their own procedure to follow, and they will test the sample, using their own budget."

"But, sir. That could take ages."

For a moment, Mackinnon wasn't even sure if the superintendent had even heard him. His expression was blank. Did he regret giving this case to Mackinnon? Did he think Mackinnon would be satisfied with sending off a few press releases and sticking up a few warning posters?

No. If Wright had wanted someone to just go through the motions, he wouldn't have picked Mackinnon for this job. He would have picked someone like Tyler.

"In all probability, it will," the superintendent said. "But I am sure their lab will process it as quickly as possible."

"But sir, the turnaround time..."

"The turnaround time is not my problem, Jack. I don't make the rules. I just have to follow them. The samples have to be analysed by an approved lab, and unless we pay through the nose, they will take a couple of weeks to process."

"But by then..."

"I'll make this quick, Jack. I've got a lot to get through today. There is no way in hell I am going to use money from my budget to run lab tests for another force. Have you got that?"

CHAPTER FORTY-ONE

ITU NURSE, LILLY WATKINS, was in one hell of a bad mood. She had been on her feet for seven hours and was waiting for her break. Her cover hadn't shown up, and she couldn't leave the ITU. Her patient needed to have his vitals checked every fifteen minutes.

She loved her job, but she wasn't so keen on the salary or the lack of respect for her break times. She wasn't a machine, for God's sake.

She pushed herself up from the desk at the nurses' station and headed over to check on her patient. Man, her legs were killing her today. She'd give anything for a nice, long soak in a hot bath.

She looked down at the young man, propped up at a thirty degree angle. Scott. They still didn't have his last name. There had been a couple of police officers who came to visit him, but apart from that, nobody. It was incredibly sad. A young man, lying in a hospital bed, and nobody cared enough to visit.

Maybe he did have family, but they hadn't realised he was

missing? Lilly bit down on her lip. It made her glad she had such a close family. Between her mum and dad and five brothers and sisters, someone would notice if anything ever happened to Lilly.

Lilly slipped on a pair of protective gloves and set about checking Scott's vitals. She noticed that his gums were still bleeding, and his saliva was pooling at the corners of his mouth. She reached for the suction pipe to clean him up. But as her hand closed around it, the alarm sounded on one of the machines monitoring Scott's heart rate and blood pressure.

Aw, crap.

She reset the alarm and waited anxiously. It went off again. She slammed the heel of her hand on the emergency call alarm, and lowered Scott's bed, so he was lying flat.

"Stay with us, Scott," she whispered as the other ITU nurse arrived at her side, pulling the trolley containing the resuscitation equipment.

Within seconds, the room was filled with the rest of the team.

Scott started to tremble, then he began to shake. Lilly grabbed his arms, so he couldn't rip out the IV lines. "He is seizing!"

Dr. Patel moved forward. "Someone get the cart."

"It's here, Doctor," one of the nurses pushed the cart forward.

The senior nurse grabbed the syringe of epinephrine, Dr. Patel picked up the paddles, and Lilly squirted them with conductive jelly.

"Charge to one hundred," Dr. Patel said, rubbing the paddles together.

Everyone stood back from the bed.

"Clear," said the doctor, and applied the paddles to Scott's chest.

Scott jerked on the bed, then lay still.

Lilly watched the monitors. She shook her head. "He's still in v-fib."

"Charge to one fifty... Clear." The doctor put the paddles back onto Scott's chest, and again, the shock made his body rise off the bed, then fall back.

Lilly stared at the monitor, willing the display to change. Come on, Scott.

But nothing changed.

Dr. Patel pursed his lips together in a thin line, then said. "Charge to two hundred."

This time, Scott's body jerked even higher from the bed, but still no response. Lilly felt tears prick the corners of her eyes. She knew what was going to happen now.

Dr. Patel sighed and shook his head slowly. "He's gone."

As the doctor pronounced the time of death, Lilly look down at Scott's lifeless body and wondered if anyone would bother to claim him. Would anyone go to his funeral?

Lilly made eye contact with Dr. Patel. He put a hand on her shoulder. "So sad," he said. "Such a waste."

CHAPTER FORTY-TWO

RONNIE WAS WOKEN BY an alarm clock with the most annoying sound. He put an arm over his head, attempting to block out the noise.

Whose bloody alarm is that? And why didn't they switch it off?

Ronnie leaned forward and propped himself up on his elbows. Hang on a minute. Maybe that wasn't an alarm clock. It sounded more like a mobile phone. His mobile phone.

"Shit."

Ronnie peered around the room with bleary eyes. Where the hell was he anyway?

There was another guy in the room, crashed out on the sofa, with one hand trailing on the ground. But where was the phone? Ronnie lifted up his jacket, which he had been using as a pillow, and there was the phone, buzzing and flashing away.

Ronnie groaned, picked it up and tried to focus on the display. Oh no. His stomach twisted. It was DI Evans.

Ronnie raised the phone to his ear. "Hello?"

"Ronnie?" DI Evans said. "Where the hell have you been? I've been trying to get hold of you since yesterday."

"I... er... had a bit of business," Ronnie said, pulling at the scratchy, nylon carpet he was sitting on.

"Did you get the samples for me?" DI Evans asked.

Ronnie nodded. "Yeah, sure did. I have them with me now. Do you want to pick them up?"

DI Evans said he did, and told Ronnie to meet him in a couple of hours at their usual meeting spot.

Ronnie hung up and rolled over. Maybe he could get back to sleep for another hour or so. But the bloke who was sleeping on the sofa was snoring like a snorting pig.

Ronnie wondered why he hadn't thought to grab the sofa first. He had slept on the floor, and it was bloody uncomfortable. It was no good. He'd never get to sleep with this racket going on. He sat up, scratched his belly, and looked around.

He was in a friend's sitting room. Well, not really a friend, just someone he got high with now and again. The furniture was old and shabby, there were stains on the carpet and the place stunk of cigarettes, but it definitely wasn't the worst place he had slept in the past few weeks.

He'd lost his own flat. Last year, he was evicted by the council. Not that he could blame them. The place was disgusting by the time they chucked him out. It wasn't his fault, though. There were always low-lifes and hangers-on in Ronnie's life, who seemed nice and friendly when they needed a place to crash for the night; then they turned psycho and tried to wreck the place. Before he moved out, Ronnie had to get the council to replace his front door three times after some arseholes kept kicking it in.

Now, he didn't have to worry about that any more. Technically, he was homeless, and now he was the one crashing on people's floors.

Ronnie wriggled about a bit, trying to get the blood flow back into his legs. His hips ached from lying on the hard floor all night.

Ronnie and Scott used to look out for each other, watching each other's backs. He hadn't really known him that long, but he couldn't help wondering if Scott was okay. He looked terrible the last time Ronnie saw him.

He should have given the samples to DI Evans yesterday, before he got high. Now, he'd let Scott down.

Ronnie realised he was shaking. He could feel that horrible itching spreading through his veins. He needed more heroin.

And he had more.

Ronnie checked over his shoulder to make sure the snoring pig was still asleep. Satisfied, he pulled out his numbered samples of heroin. He picked one up, and his pulse quickened.

He could take one. Just one. He would give all the others to DI Evans. Surely, one less wouldn't make a difference.

He moved the sample labelled with a big, black "three" away from him. That one was from JT's runner, and Ronnie wouldn't touch it. That was the stuff Scott and Ronnie had taken before Scott got sick. No, he would not touch number three, but one of the others...

Ronnie grabbed the samples and shoved them back into his pocket. What was wrong with him? Was he so far gone that he couldn't take the time to help save people? To stop people like him from ending up like Scott?

Ronnie clenched his fists and drove his fingernails deep into the skin of his palms. No, he would give them to DI Evans as arranged. All of them.

Ronnie decided he would ring the hospital again today and

see if he had better luck finding out how Scott was doing. Last time he rang, the snooty nurse wouldn't tell Ronnie anything after Ronnie told her he wasn't family. This time when he called, he'd lie. He would say he was Scott's brother, or something.

Ronnie stood up and gathered his stuff together. He didn't have much, just his jacket and scarf.

The man on the sofa farted loudly and turned over.

Ronnie pulled a face. That was it. He was out of here. It might be the crack of dawn and freezing out there, but at least, he could get some fresh air and get away from the smell of stale cigarettes and body odour.

Ronnie left the flat and headed for the market. He knew a couple of the traders and sometimes they would give him a few quid if he helped them set up their stalls. When he got there though, most of them had already got their gear out ready.

Ronnie turned up his collar and shivered, watching them. There was one market trader, who hadn't got his stall set up yet. Ronnie didn't recognise him, but he headed over, smiling. "Need some help, mate?"

The stall-holder turned. He had a shaved head and small dark eyes. His cheeks were flushed from the cold. He shoved his hands in the pockets of his leather jacket and looked Ronnie up and down.

"All right. But don't go nicking anything. I've got my eye on you."

Ronnie put a hand to his chest. "You can trust me. I don't steal. You can ask around."

The man screwed up his face. "You can make a start by bringing those boxes over from the van."

Ronnie got to work. He unloaded four heavy boxes

containing white linens and dainty tea towels, and then helped the trader set them out on display.

Ronnie was careful not to get any dirt onto the bright, white tablecloths and linens.

When they were finished, Ronnie thought they had done a pretty good job. He beamed up at the trader.

The trader sneered at him. "What? You expecting something?"

"I thought..."

"What? You thought I'd pay you? A dirty little piece of scum like you?" The market trader put his face next to Ronnie's and laughed. "No chance. Clear off, you bloody tramp."

Ronnie took a step back and stumbled. That made the trader laugh harder. Ronnie looked around at the other stall-holders; none of them were laughing, but no one intervened either. No one stepped in to say it was unfair, not even the men Ronnie had helped out before.

Ronnie kicked one of the man's empty boxes on the floor.

The trader yelled, and lunged for Ronnie.

Ronnie took off.

When Ronnie finally stopped running, he was near Mile End station. He rested for a moment, breathing heavily. There was a phone box over the road. He could use it to find out about Scott.

Ronnie dug around in his pocket for change for the phone. There wasn't much. He had been relying on earning a bit at the market this morning, but he didn't have much luck with that, so he would just have to use the money he'd been saving for a cup of tea.

Ronnie had written down the phone number yesterday, which was just as well as the phone booth had been vandalised and there was no phone book.

This time, a man answered the phone, and Ronnie was very glad it wasn't the snooty nurse he spoke to last time.

"Could you tell me how Scott is please?" Ronnie said in his poshest voice. "I'm his brother," Ronnie added before the man on the phone could tell him he could only give details to relatives.

"Patient's last name please?"

"Oh, er, well..." Ronnie paused. Ronnie didn't know Scott's last name, but he couldn't very well say that after he'd just said he was Scott's brother. "It's er... Black," Ronnie said. "But I don't think you have his last name in your records."

"Just hold the line a moment, please," the man said.

"What? No! Don't put me on hold. I'll run out of money..."

But there was no answer. Ronnie stood in the vandalised phone booth, frantically searching for more change, a coin he'd missed before. But his pockets were empty. Ronnie waited until his money ran out, then slammed down the receiver.

As he hung up, the sleeve of his jacket rose to display the underside of his wrist. Ronnie blinked. What was that? He yanked up the sleeve of his jacket and studied his arm.

He had a rash.

Tiny little dots that looked like pin pricks of blood covered his arm.

CHAPTER FORTY-THREE

RONNIE STOOD IN THE reception area of St. Bart's, trembling. He knew he should probably go to A and E, but he wanted to speak to that nice doctor from last time. He waited in the queue. Any minute now, he might go the same way as Scott. He should have stayed at the hospital, like Dr. Anna told him to.

When the receptionist was finally free, Ronnie shuffled up to the counter.

"I'd like to speak to Dr. Anna, please."

The receptionist screwed up her nose. "Name, please."

"Um, Anna something... I think her last name begins with 's.'"

"I need your name, sir."

"Oh, I see. My name is Ronnie. Ronald Black."

Ronnie smiled, but the receptionist gave him a scowl in return. She busied herself filling in a form. When Ronnie was almost sure she had forgotten he was there, she turned to him. "Do you have an appointment?"

"An appointment? Not exactly. But I saw the doctor before, and she told me to come back."

The receptionist pursed her lips and wheeled her chair closer to the computer screen. She tapped something on the keyboard and studied the screen for a moment.

"Was it Dr. Sorensen?"

Ronnie beamed. "Yes, that's it. Dr. Anna Sorensen."

The receptionist nodded. "Take a seat."

Ronnie made his way to the edge of the room and sat on a grey, plastic chair. The other people in the room avoided making eye contact. That suited Ronnie. He waited until he was sure no one was looking, then rolled up his sleeve.

He felt a lump in his throat. It was still there. If anything, it was worse. He muttered a prayer, then blinked away tears. Stupid to be offering up prayers, promising God he'd never touch the stuff again, if only this time he was okay. But Ronnie knew himself too well. Those muttered promises meant nothing. Even now, with the threat of ending up like Scott a real possibility, he knew he wouldn't be able to stop taking the bloody stuff.

Ronnie had met DI Evans an hour earlier and handed over the samples. DI Evans had slapped him on the back and told him he was a good guy. But Ronnie didn't feel like a good guy now.

He sat with his head bowed, until he heard Dr. Anna's voice, "Ronnie, isn't it?"

Ronnie looked up at the doctor in her clean, white coat. He nodded. "I'm sorry I ran off last time. How's Scott?"

"I'm sorry, Ronnie. He lost a lot of blood, and had some bleeding in his brain, which caused a lot of damage. We did everything we could, but we weren't able to save him."

Ronnie stared at the ground.

Anna sat beside him. "And how are you feeling?"

Ronnie hesitated. All at once, he was overwhelmed by the need to run out of this room, to leave the hospital, to find his dealer and...

"Ronnie?"

Ronnie pulled back his sleeve. "I've got a rash."

* * *

Half an hour later, Anna stood beside Ronnie's bed in the Jenner ward.

"I'll run these tests, Ronnie. Now, you need to listen to me. You can't run off again. You need treatment, do you understand?"

Ronnie shivered and pulled the sheet up to his chin. "Is it the same thing that Scott...?" His voice trailed off.

"I need to run the tests first, so I can work out what is wrong, but try not to worry."

Ronnie stared at her. "Try not to worry?"

Anna smiled. "I know it is easier said than done, but you are in the best place you can be."

"It's just I keep thinking about him. Scott, I mean. About how awful it was and..."

"Look Ronnie, this may not be what you want to hear right now, but I could give you some numbers, perhaps we could get you onto an outpatient program..."

Ronnie shook his head.

"But it is more important than ever to give up with this stuff on the streets." Anna said. "Think of your little girl."

Ronnie winced, then rubbed the side of his nose with a finger. "Mind is willing, but the body is weak; isn't that what they say?"

Ronnie scrubbed his face with his hands. "Thing is, I tried. I tried so hard to do it for her, and I couldn't. And if I couldn't do it for her, then I can't do it at all..." Ronnie looked down at the floor.

Anna's bleeper sounded. "I'm sorry, Ronnie. I'm going to have to get this. But I'll be back to check on you soon, okay?"

He nodded and blinked back tears.

Anna gave his hand a quick squeeze, then left him to his memories and regrets.

CHAPTER FORTY-FOUR

AS SOON AS ANNA had seen to a patient in the Accident and Emergency department, who had broken three fingers by hitting his hand with a hammer, she shut herself in the on-call room and phoned Mackinnon.

She told him that Scott had died.

There was a pause before Mackinnon said, "Poor kid. I thought he was responding to treatment."

"So did I," Anna said, "But he had more internal bleeding, then went into shock."

Anna closed her eyes and leaned back against the wall. "I'm really hoping you are getting close to getting this stuff off the streets, Jack."

"We're working at it," Mackinnon said. "But I have some bad news. I think we may have had another of these bleeding cases, a man who bled to death in his bathroom from a head wound. I've asked Bruce to follow it up, and see if we can test for the presence of warfarin in his blood."

"Let me know what you find," Anna said. "By the way,

Scott's friend, the one who was with him when he was admitted, showed up today. He has a rash, so I have put him under observation and given him vitamin K."

"I don't understand," Mackinnon said. "Why are some of the patients who take this warfarin-contaminated heroin bleeding out, while others just get a rash?"

"I can't say for sure, but it is possible that Scott had a weakness in his gastrointestinal tract. He may have been bleeding already, but his body kept it in check. Blood coagulation is a complicated thing. It is a precarious balance of clotting and bleeding. Tip too far one way, and you end up with a blood clot; too far the other way, and like Scott, you bleed out.

"The simple answer is, some people get lucky, some don't."

CHAPTER FORTY-FIVE

JT SLAMMED HIS OFFICE door. That bloody woman. All he wanted was a bit of peace and quiet to get his head straight, and Siobhan was going on about needing more staff. If he employed someone to help out in the kitchen, what would Siobhan do all day? She would have too much free time, too much time to poke her nose into JT's business.

JT sighed, squeezed behind his desk and eased himself into his leather chair. He closed his eyes and leaned back, willing himself to calm down. He needed to relax so he could think things through. He couldn't make decisions when he was wound up, that would just make things worse.

Siobhan thought life began and ended with the bar. They had set it up fifteen years ago, when Emily was only tiny. They had a few good years together building it up. But it was hard graft, so JT looked for ways to supplement his income, and he found one. A great one. But it didn't come without stress.

The Bangladeshis on the Towers Estate were getting all wound up over his dealing. Someone had been making up lies, saying he was dealing on the estate. As if he'd be stupid enough to peddle his gear on the street. Why would he need to? He had everything he needed right here at The Junction, including a steady stream of customers looking for a little something extra to go with their drinks.

The Bangladeshis had definitely managed to get hold of the wrong end of the stick somehow, but JT would sort it out and smooth things over.

JT took a deep breath, stood up and walked over to the window. He looked out and watched a couple of city types rushing by. He leaned heavily on the windowsill and looked further along the road towards the churchyard.

In the distance, he could see the tops of the tower blocks that made up the Towers Estate. Depressing place. JT had been born there, but he would never go back. He had his bar now, in this swanky part of the city, and as long as he played the game, things could only get better.

JT smiled. The Bangladeshis were a problem, but JT didn't have to worry about them. Not when he had a secret weapon waiting in the wings.

CHAPTER FORTY-SIX

JT'S SECRET WEAPON STROLLED into the bar at lunchtime when JT was working behind the bar. JT looked up and grinned. He didn't have to worry about a thing. He had the best weapon a dealer could have to cover his back: a bent copper.

JT told Tom, one of his part-timers, to cover for him. Then he crooked a finger and beckoned DI Bruce Evans to follow him out the back.

Siobhan was still in the kitchen clanging pots together, her way of showing that she was still pissed off.

JT ignored the noise and led Bruce into his office, shut the door and turned to face him. "So what's the panic, Bruce?"

"What's the panic?" DI Bruce Evans' face flushed with anger. He pointed a finger at JT. "You should be panicking. I told you that your gear was contaminated. You need to get it off the streets. Now."

"Nah." JT waved him off and moved across to his desk. "I

told you the other day, must be some other dealer's stuff. I get mine clean. I pay top money for a clean supply."

"I'm serious. You need to pull that stuff," Bruce Evans said and started to pace around the tiny room.

"Have you any idea how much that will cost me? That's just not good business."

Bruce leaned on the desk, bringing his face close to JT's. "It's not exactly good business to kill your customers, either."

JT scowled. "Why do you care anyway? It's just a couple of addicts."

"It's more than a couple. How many does it have to be before you act? You going for a record? Aiming to beat Harold Shipman?"

"For Christ's sake, calm down." JT glanced at the door. "Keep your bloody voice down."

Bruce Evans lunged for JT and gripped his upper arms. "People have died. You need to take this stuff off the street now."

"No way." JT shoved Bruce away. "Now, get your hands off me and listen..."

There was a knock at the door. Siobhan looked in. "Justin, there's a soft drink delivery. I'm up to my eyes in the kitchen. Can you deal with it?"

Bruce turned away from the door so Siobhan wouldn't see his face.

JT nodded. "Yeah. I'll get to it in a minute."

After Siobhan closed the door, JT turned to Bruce and smiled. "Looks like we'll have to talk about this later."

CHAPTER FORTY-SEVEN

CHARLOTTE TURNED UP AT her nan's flat in East London at eight.

The block of flats smelled of fried onions and spices mingled with the chlorine tang of bleach. Nan had obviously cleaned the landing today.

She rang the bell and waited for Nan to open the door. There were just two flats per floor in this block, and the flats themselves were massive, easily three times the size of Charlotte's newer place, just five-minutes-walk away.

Nan had lived here for forty years. The council were always trying to get her to move to a smaller place, but Nan wouldn't hear of it.

Nan opened the door. "Hello, darling."

Charlotte leaned forward and kissed her on the cheek. She smelled of Olay moisturiser. "How are you?"

"Fine." Nan always said fine. Even if her arthritis was playing up and her knees were painful. Even when she broke her hip two years ago, and Charlotte visited her in the hospital and asked how she was feeling, Nan said she was "fine."

"What did you get up to today?" Charlotte asked.

"I went to the council. They wanted me to go in and see them. They are trying to get me to move."

"Again?"

Nan nodded. "I told them. Not bloody likely. I said, I am not moving into a poky, little place with plastic doors, just so they can fill my flat with a single mother, who's probably never worked a day in her life."

Nan had a thing about plastic doors. Charlotte didn't like them much either. It seemed like all the new blocks of flats had them.

"Well, they can't make you move if you don't want to."

"I'd like to see them try." Nan put her best "don't-mess-with-me" face on.

They ate dinner together and talked about various members of the family, including Charlotte's mum and dad. Nan found it very hard to understand why on earth they wanted to live in Spain.

"Better weather, I suppose?" Charlotte suggested.

Nan just shook her head.

After dinner, Charlotte insisted on doing the washing-up. She had just started running the hot tap, and squirted washing-up liquid in the bowl, when her mobile rang. She dried her hands and headed back to the front room.

Nan picked up the mobile and squinted at the front of it, just as Charlotte entered the room.

Nan handed her the phone. "Not sure who it is. Can't read those little screens."

Charlotte looked at the display. It said "caller ID withheld."

Charlotte felt a familiar feeling of dread building in her stomach.

"Hello?"

No answer.

"Hello? Anyone there? I can't hear you?"

For a moment, there was no sound at all. Then it started. The laughter. Mocking, cruel laughter.

Charlotte hit the red button.

"Who was that?" Nan asked. "Are you all right? You look pale as a ghost."

Charlotte put her mobile phone down on the coffee table and ran a hand through her hair. "No one. Think it was a wrong number."

"Another one?"

Charlotte shrugged and headed back to the kitchen to finish washing up.

She was up to her elbows in soapy water the next time the phone rang. She quickly dried her hands and rushed to the front room. But it was too late.

Nan had already answered the phone.

"Now, just you listen to me, you nasty piece of work..."

Charlotte took the phone from Nan and hung up. "Don't give him the satisfaction."

Nan stared at her. "How long has this been going on? Surely you can get something done about it?"

Charlotte took a deep breath and sat down on one of the armchairs. "It's just a nuisance caller. It's not worth the hassle. He'll get bored eventually." Charlotte smiled and tried to look convincing.

"He sounds like a bloody nutcase. Do you know who it is?"

Charlotte shook her head. "It's probably just some weirdo, who picked my number at random."

"Why don't you just stay here tonight?" Nan said.

Charlotte agreed to stay, telling herself she was doing it for Nan's sake, but the truth was, she didn't want to go back to her flat on her own tonight.

That was the last thing she wanted to do.

CHAPTER FORTY-EIGHT

DI BRUCE EVANS DIDN'T get home until after nine pm. The house was quiet. He thought perhaps they were all in bed. His wife, Fiona, had taken to turning in early these days.

He took his shoes off at the front door, then padded down the hallway to the kitchen.

Fiona, sat at the table, nursing a cup of tea. She looked up, but didn't speak.

"How was your day, love?" Bruce asked.

"Same as usual." She stood up, lifting her half-finished mug of tea. "You want one?"

Bruce shook his head. "I'll do it. You sit down."

Bruce watched his wife as he filled the kettle with water. "You look done in."

"I feel it." She massaged the back of her neck.

Bruce flicked the switch on the kettle. "I'm just going to say goodnight to the kids while this boils."

"They're asleep, Bruce. Don't wake them."

He looked back at her. "I'm not going to wake them, just look in on them."

He walked up the stairs, trying to shake off his irritation. She treated him like a kid at times. They were his children, too. It's not like he didn't take care of them all.

Bruce stopped at his daughter's room first. She'd kicked off the covers in her sleep, and her hand curled around Mr. Pink, her favourite teddy bear. She was mad about pink. The wall-paper, bedding, even the carpet, were all pink.

God knows where Fiona had managed to track down a pink carpet. They spoiled their daughter, no question, but they both worried about how she would react to her brother taking up so much of their attention.

Bruce gently lifted the duvet to cover his little girl and kissed her on the forehead.

Then he headed to her brother's room.

The KEEP OUT sign was still there from before. But neither Bruce nor Fiona had suggested getting rid of it. Most things they kept the same. Obviously, there had to be some changes. The bed for one. Luke had to have a special bed with raised sides. The doctors were worried he might have a fit in the night, and fall out of bed. So Bruce's seventeen-year-old son had to sleep in an oversized cot.

Bruce took a deep breath before he opened his son's door.

Luke lay on his back, his eyes open and staring at the ceiling.

"Hey, Luke. Buddy, are you still awake?"

"Aaargh"

Bruce stroked his son's dark, floppy hair. They'd have to get it cut again soon. That would be a palaver. Everything was these days.

"Did you have a good day, buddy?"

"Um arrgh."

Bruce reached over to the box of tissues by Luke's bedside, took one and wiped the spittle from the corner of Luke's mouth.

"That's better, isn't it, buddy?"

Luke's head flopped to the side, so he was facing away from Bruce.

Bruce knew he shouldn't take it personally. Luke wasn't trying to hurt him. But it felt like he was. It felt like he was punishing him for not looking out for him, not protecting him, like a father should.

Bruce felt his breath catch in his throat. He stood up. "I'll say goodnight then, son. Sleep tight."

As he exited the room, his mind flooded with images. Luke as a baby, taking his first steps. Luke riding his bike without stabilisers for the first time, taking him to his first football match. Then rushing to the hospital that night...

Bruce clenched his fists. It did no good to think like this, no good at all. He couldn't change the past.

He needed to focus on the things that mattered. The things he could change.

* * *

When Bruce got back downstairs, Fiona was still sitting at the table.

"There's another letter." She nodded to a brown A5 envelope on the counter next to the fruit bowl.

Bruce nodded. He recognised it straight away. "Right. I'll look at it later."

"It needs to be paid, Bruce. We're getting behind."

"I said, I'd see to it. Don't I always?"

"There's no need to snap at me."

There is every need, Bruce thought. He looked around at the poky kitchen. The walls seemed to close in on him.

"I need to go out." Bruce picked up the letter and stuffed it into his pocket. He didn't need to open it. He knew exactly what it was.

* * *

Bruce sat in his car, turned on the ignition and turned the heater up high. Then he pulled the letter out of his pocket and smoothed it against the steering wheel.

He stared at it for a moment, without opening it. Things were going too far and he was getting in too deep. But what else was he supposed to do?

He opened the letter. There in black and white was the final demand. The bills from St. Clare's rehabilitation centre had gone unpaid for two months. Two lousy months. They were supposed to be a care home. There wasn't much caring going on, as far as Bruce could see. It was all about money to them, just a business.

Bruce sighed, folded the letter and put it back in his pocket.

Fiona said the centre was really helping Luke. She said he was improving a tiny bit every time he went. Bruce didn't want her to get her hopes up, so he told her to be realistic, not to expect too much. That just made him the bad guy.

He would never be their old Luke again, but the staff at the centre said, with the right treatment, Luke might be able to sit up on his own. Surely, Luke deserved that, at least.

It wasn't just the costs for Luke attending the centre, although, they were pretty steep. The staff wanted him to buy special equipment Luke needed for his rehabilitation. Training bars, or something like that, and a new, fancy wheelchair. It all added up, and a police officer's salary didn't cover it. It didn't even come close.

Bruce sighed and the mist of his breath formed a white circle on the window. He wiped it away with his sleeve. He hadn't been to the centre yet. He knew he should, just to make sure they weren't pouring money down the drain for nothing.

To be truthful, the reason he hadn't gone along when Fiona took Luke to the centre was because he didn't think he could bear it if the centre wasn't all above board. How would he tell Fiona? How would they all cope if their last hope for Luke turned out to be a scam?

Bruce settled back in the driver's seat and put the car in gear.

He would find a way to pay for it. Of course, he would. It's not like he had a choice.

CHAPTER FORTY-NINE

JT THREW BACK THE duvet and rolled out of bed. A thin sliver of morning light entered the bedroom through a gap in the curtains. Siobhan was already up. He could smell the bacon cooking.

He felt like crap. He'd caught a cold and had been up coughing half the night.

He scratched his armpit, sniffed and stumbled over to their en-suite bathroom. They lived in the flat above The Junction. A year ago, JT paid top money to have it all done up. The builders installed en-suite bathrooms to both bedrooms and attached a dressing room to Emily's bedroom.

When he thought about his daughter, JT smiled. Emily would have already left for college. She worked so hard and was such a bright little thing. She'd be the first of his family to go to university, and JT almost burst with pride when he thought about that.

In the bathroom, JT blew his nose. God, his throat felt like sandpaper. JT peered at himself in the mirror over the sink.

He opened his mouth wide, and promptly clamped it shut again.

What the hell? He opened his mouth again, looking more closely. There was a disgusting, creamy coating lining the back of his throat.

JT retched and spat in the sink.

"Siobhan!"

Siobhan entered the bedroom, bringing the smell of fried food with her. JT retched again.

"No wonder my throat's sore," he said. "I've got a load of white stuff in my mouth."

Siobhan frowned and moved towards him, wiping her hands on her apron. "Let's have a look."

JT opened his mouth again and bent his knees, so Siobhan could see into his mouth.

"Looks like you might have a poison throat," Siobhan said. "An infection."

She put her fingers against the sides of his throat. "Hmm, seems like your glands are up."

She pressed a little harder and JT yelped in pain.

"Watch what you're doing, woman."

"I'll get you something for it."

As Siobhan left the room, JT inspected his throat again in the mirror. It really was foul. Tasted horrible, too. He needed to start taking better care of himself. It was no wonder he was run-down really. Those idiots working for him didn't help, and now his bent cop had started to get all self-righteous, discovering his long-forgotten moral code.

Siobhan came back into the bedroom, carrying a glass of orange-coloured liquid.

"What's that?" JT said, eyeing the glass.

"A health supplement. It's got vitamin C, echinacea and

zinc in it. Supposed to boost your immune system." Siobhan smiled and held out the glass.

JT took it and sipped the foul-looking mixture. It wasn't as bad as it looked, tasted a bit like orange squash. He swallowed some more.

"You better make me a doctor's appointment, too," JT said.

Siobhan nodded. "Do you want me to say it's urgent? They might be able to fit you in at the end of morning surgery."

"Of course, it's bloody urgent." JT snapped. "I've got white stuff in my mouth and I can barely swallow."

Two hours later, JT stood in the pharmacy at the back of Boots. He had been waiting in line for twenty minutes. Ahead of him, a little old lady leaned on her shopping trolley and cupped a hand to her ear.

"What's that? Can you speak up?"

The pharmacist, who had already been speaking loudly, ran a hand across his chest, to smooth his white coat, then he leaned forward and shouted, "One tablet, three times a day."

The old lady reared back, snatching the tablets from the pharmacist. "Well! There is no need to shout. I'm not deaf!"

She turned her shopping trolley around, bashing it against JT's legs, before wheeling it out of the shop.

Finally, JT thought. About bloody time.

JT slapped his prescription onto the counter. The pharmacist picked it up and squinted down at the form.

JT looked around the room. There was only one other customer nearby, and thankfully, no one waiting in the queue behind him. He hadn't felt this self-conscious in a chemist's since he'd bought his first pack of condoms.

JT cleared his throat.

Satisfied with the form, the pharmacist set it down on the counter and walked through a door at the back of the pharmacy.

JT hadn't even known you could get thrush in your throat. He'd heard of it before, of course, but he had always thought it was a woman's problem. The doctor told him it was basically a load of yeast cells growing in his throat. It wasn't common in someone JT's age, but the doctor said it could be because he was run-down.

The pharmacist returned and slid across a paper bag. "There you go, sir. Instructions are printed on the bottle."

JT flushed. Was the pharmacist looking at him strangely? He wanted to tell the pharmacist the medication was for his wife, but that wouldn't work because it was JT's name on the prescription. Instead, JT grabbed the bag, mumbled a quick thank you, and headed out of the chemist's as fast as he could.

CHAPTER FIFTY

DR. ANNA SORENSEN HAD been at work at the hospital since eight am. So far, her shift had been relatively uneventful, so she decided to go and grab a cup of coffee before she checked on Ronnie. That is, if he hadn't pulled another disappearing act.

She hoped he would stay put. There was something about Ronnie she liked. It was hard to put her finger on, but somehow, despite everything, there was a quiet nobility to him. If it hadn't been for the drugs...

She walked past a portrait of Elizabeth Blackwell, one of the earliest campaigners for medicine as a career for women. She was permitted to attend St. Bart's way back in 1850, but after she left, female students were excluded for another hundred years. Things had changed.

Anna sighed as she walked past another closed wing. Things were still changing. Most of the hospital departments were gradually being moved to the huge, new Royal London Hospital in Whitechapel. All the staff were a little on edge.

Anna just felt sad. St. Bart's was Britain's oldest hospital. It survived the Great Fire of London and the blitz in the second World War, and now parts of it were disappearing. She hoped it wouldn't vanish altogether.

Anna joined the queue in the canteen. It wasn't perfect, but she preferred the filter coffee they sold down here to the instant junk from the vending machine.

She smiled at Vera, the lady serving the coffee. "Thanks, Vera. White, no sugar, please."

Vera nodded. "I know how you like it by now, my love."

Vera handed her a steaming cup. "Did you hear about that poor bloke they brought in? The one whose blood squirted all over the corridor?"

Anna winced. She didn't really want to be reminded of that. She nodded.

"You don't often hear of cases like that, do you? I wonder what on earth was the matter with him?"

"I'm not sure," Anna said. "I suppose he must have had some kind of bleeding disorder."

Vera gave her a look as if to say, "that much is obvious," and moved on to serving the next customer.

Anna took her coffee to a table over by the window. An elderly man stood outside in the courtyard. He was hooked up to a drip, which he wheeled out with him, and in one shaky hand, he held a cigarette. He took a deep drag.

Anna wondered what was wrong with him. She was sure his doctor would have told him to stop smoking. But from Anna's experience, she knew it wasn't that easy. She once saw a man who was so desperate for a cigarette after he came round from heart surgery that he snuck out of the cardiac care unit, only to pass out in the corridor.

Addictions were funny things. Alcohol, cigarettes, drugs: once they got their claws into you, not many people escaped.

After Anna finished off her coffee, she headed upstairs to see Ronnie in Jenner ward. Walking up the stairs, she convinced herself he wouldn't be there, steeling herself for the disappointment.

But he was propped up in bed, the sheets pulled up to his chin. His floppy afro looked frizzier than before. She suspected one of the nurses had convinced him to have a shower and wash his hair.

"Ronnie, how are you feeling?"

"Dr. Anna." Ronnie brightened. "Not too bad." He held up an arm for her to see. "Rash is still there though."

Anna nodded and picked up Ronnie's medical notes at the end of his bed. "The rash might take a little while to fade."

She flicked through his lab results. "The lab tests look good."

Ronnie grinned.

"I'll be back in a minute, Ronnie. I just need to talk to the ward sister for a moment."

Anna spoke to the sister about Ronnie's progress and treatment so far, then scribbled out some more forms for lab tests. "I'll take the blood myself."

The ward sister, happy to be relieved of the work, collected the tubes and needles and gave them to Anna.

Ronnie grimaced when he saw Anna heading over to him with a disposable kidney dish containing the sample tubes. "Oh no, you're not taking more blood?"

"I'm afraid so, Ronnie."

Ronnie held out his arm. "At the rate you lot are going, I'll have none left."

Anna punctured his skin at the crease of his elbow. "Only two more samples, you'll barely notice."

When she finished, she pushed a ball of cotton wool against the puncture wound. "When I get these tests back, I'll see if you need anymore vitamin K injections, okay? So no running off."

"Yeah, all right," Ronnie grumbled, inspecting the mark on his arm left by the needle.

Anna put the used needles into the sharps bin, which would be incinerated, and swore under her breath as her beeper sounded. So much for a quiet shift.

She left Ronnie and made her way to the nurses' station to use the phone. She recognised the number on her pager. It was the haematology labs.

She punched the number into the phone, and Rita answered her call on the second ring.

"You better get down here," Rita said. "I think we've got another one."

Anna slammed through the double doors leading to the pathology department and grabbed the stethoscope around her neck to stop it falling to the floor as she rounded the corner.

In haematology, the scientific officers, busily bent over machines and microscopes, barely looked up as she shot past.

Rita sat in the coagulation laboratory, in front of the computer.

"Seems to be the same problem with clotting," she said, without preamble.

"Who is the patient?"

"Clarissa Meadows, nineteen. She was brought in by her parents. She is a known drug user."

"Heroin?"

Rita nodded. "Here's her coag profile. I've printed it off for you."

Anna took the sheet of paper and scanned the numbers on it. "Right."

"The odd thing is, her parents were insistent that she had kicked the habit," Rita said.

Anna frowned, then shrugged. "Sometimes, parents believe what they want to believe and ignore the facts, no matter how obvious."

Rita sighed, shook her head and slumped back in her chair.

Anna put a hand on Rita's shoulder. "Are you okay?"

Rita pushed her fringe out of her eyes and looked up at Anna. "Yeah. It's been a long shift. We've been cross-matching unit after unit. We had a twelve-year-old boy admitted who was hit by a train."

Anna put a hand to her mouth. "Christ. How?"

Rita shrugged. "Group of boys playing chicken at a level crossing, by the sounds of it. We have been cross-matching blood for hours, but as soon as they put it in, more blood came out."

"And now?" Anna asked.

Rita shook her head. "They pronounced him an hour ago."

Anna pulled a chair over and sat down next to Rita. "I'm sorry."

"Yeah, well, we've got Clarissa Meadows to worry about now. It never stops."

Anna turned her attention to the printout again. "Do you know if biochem has run their tests yet?"

Rita turned back to the computer and tapped on the

keyboard. "Here you go." Rita moved out of the way so Anna had an unobstructed view of the screen.

"Her liver function is shot," Anna said, pointing at one of the biochemistry test results. "We didn't see that with the others."

Rita frowned. "You're right. Do you think it's liver damage that is causing the bleeding?"

"Could be. I need to ask biochem for another test. I better speak to the requesting doctor first; who is that?"

Rita brought up a scan of the original pathology test request form. "It was Dr. Patel."

"Right. I'll page him, thanks."

After she had spoken with Dr. Patel, Anna went back to Rita. "He has already requested more tests. But he knows what it is. Apparently Clarissa regained consciousness long enough to tell the nurses she had taken an overdose of paracetamol."

"Oh, I just didn't think." Rita put her head in her hands. "I called you down here for nothing. I just thought..."

"Hey, it wasn't for nothing," Anna said. "It could easily have been another case, and it is important you're so vigilant. If we do have more cases, the faster we spot them, the faster we can treat them."

"Poor girl." Rita shook her head. "She probably regrets taking the tablets now. It was probably just a cry for help. Most of them are."

Anna nodded. Paracetamol overdoses could be horrific. If the victim is found in time and has his or her stomach pumped, the patient wakes up in hospital, and most of the time, things don't seem so bad when they come round. They usually change their minds, think they might give things another shot, but die anyway because they have damaged their livers beyond repair.

If the liver is damaged by paracetamol, it can lead to uncontrollable bleeding because the liver produces many of the clotting factors. So patients either die of liver failure or bleeding to death. Not a very nice end for anybody.

Rita stood up. "On that cheerful note. I better get home. I've been here more than twenty-four hours; my family are going to forget what I look like."

Anna smiled. "I'll walk upstairs with you."

Rita took off her white lab coat and collected her coat and bag, and they walked out of the pathology department together, talking about family, and avoiding the topic of work. They had just reached the main corridor, when Anna heard her name called.

A junior nurse, with flyaway hair, sidled up to them. "Dr. Sorensen? I'm sorry to interrupt, but a patient of yours has left the ward without checking himself out."

Anna sighed. "Which one?" She asked, although she knew very well which patient the nurse was referring to.

"Ronald Black."

CHAPTER FIFTY-ONE

CHARLOTTE HAD ONLY BEEN at home for twenty minutes when the front door bell rang.

She froze.

Who was that? No one said they were going to come around, and she didn't have many visitors these days, not since she had cut herself off from her old friends after the situation with Wayne.

She willed her tense muscles to move. It's probably nothing, she told herself, just a cold caller. The main entrance door hadn't buzzed, but then, people were always leaving the security door open, so that didn't really mean anything.

She slowly walked down the hallway towards the door, keeping her breathing deep and steady.

The doorbell rang again, and Charlotte jumped.

Oh, for God's sake, she thought, She was being pathetic. It was only someone at the door. Maybe someone needed to borrow a cup of sugar or something. It was hardly something to be scared of.

Charlotte pulled the deadbolt across, then turned the key at the top and the one at the bottom. She left the safety chain attached.

She opened the door as far as the safety chain would allow. "Hello?"

There was no one there.

That didn't make sense. She hadn't heard any retreating footsteps, and she hadn't heard the pinging sound the lift made when the doors opened. She removed the safety chain and opened the door, stepping out into the communal hall.

"Hello, Charlotte."

It was Wayne.

She stumbled back into her flat and tried to slam the door on him, but he blocked it with his foot. She stepped backward, hitting her head on the wall.

"Charlotte, what the hell is the matter with you?" He turned to the woman standing next to him, who Charlotte had only just noticed.

She was petite with long, dark hair. She looked at Charlotte as if she thought she were deranged.

"I told you what she was like," Wayne said.

The girl nodded.

"Just go away, Wayne," Charlotte said.

"Oh no, you're going to hear me out. Can we come in?"

"No!"

"All right. All right. I can say what I need to on the doorstep, if that will make you happy. This has got to stop. All the lies you've been spreading about me, getting your friends to threaten me. I've got a new girlfriend now. You've got to move on."

Charlotte stared at him. What was he talking about? Her friends threatening him?

She shook her head. "You've been making those calls, you bastard. Don't think I don't know it was you."

Wayne rolled his eyes and looked at his new girlfriend. "I told you this was a waste of time. I told you she was a psycho. Now do you believe me?"

The girl linked hands with Wayne. "Come on, let's go."

When Wayne removed his foot, Charlotte slammed the door, her fingers trembling as she tried to turn the locks. She sunk down to her knees, and listened out for the sound of the lift doors closing.

What sort of game was he playing?

CHAPTER FIFTY-TWO

THE FOLLOWING DAY, MACKINNON had the samples from Ronnie. After spending what felt like hours completing the paperwork and dealing with the officer in charge of physical evidence, the heroin samples were submitted to the forensics lab for testing.

He tried to get them run urgently, but Tyler said the super wouldn't go for it. Especially since the way they had been obtained meant they wouldn't be able to use the samples as evidence anyway.

After his previous conversation with the superintendent over budgetary constraints, Mackinnon was sure Tyler was right. But he still tried to persuade Tyler, telling him that the samples would lead them to the source of the dodgy heroin supply, and then Bruce's DCI could organise a raid.

Tyler screwed his nose up. "Well, get his DCI to pay for the lab tests then."

"Bruce said he won't stump up the money to run them urgently."

"Who is his DCI now?" Tyler asked. "I can't remember for the life of me."

"DCI Mark Rosser," Mackinnon said.

"DCI Rosser?" Tyler said. "Good luck with that one. You've got no chance. He plays things by the book and keeps a tight grip on the purse strings, too.

"Looks like you've wasted your time going after these samples, Jack." Tyler said. "There is no way the super will pay."

Mackinnon considered going over Tyler's head and asking the superintendent directly, but he didn't think that would work out well. He had to work with Tyler, after all.

"How's Bruce getting on?"

Mackinnon looked up, surprised. "Fine as far, as I know, why? You know him better than me."

Tyler shrugged. "We go back a long way, but since the accident, we're not close like we used to be."

Mackinnon paused. He sensed he was being played. Tyler expected him to bite, to ask about the accident. But Mackinnon couldn't resist. He had to ask.

"What accident?"

"Bruce's son, Luke. It's why he transferred, why he wanted to work at bringing down dealers."

Mackinnon nodded and waited for Tyler to go on.

"Luke went to a party one night, took Ecstasy, same as all his friends, but for some reason, things turned bad for Luke. He had a seizure. He got to hospital too late, ended up brain-damaged. It just about wiped Bruce out at the time."

"Yeah," Mackinnon said. "It must have."

"But then he seemed to get back into things. I think it helped to have a focus, tracking down dealers and stopping other kids turning out like his Luke."

Tyler stood up. "Anyway, it's good to know he's doing okay."

Mackinnon nodded.

"I'll leave you to your bowing and scraping then," Tyler said.

Mackinnon frowned. "What?"

"That's the only way you are going to get those samples run. You'll have to sweet talk the lab staff. That's your only option."

As far as Mackinnon could see, there was another option. There was one other person he knew with access to a lab and who would be willing to help.

He picked up the phone.

When Bruce answered, Mackinnon asked the question straight away. "Have you logged your samples with forensics yet?"

Bruce paused for a second, then said. "No, not yet. I've not filed the paperwork. Why?'

Mackinnon grinned with relief. "That's great news."

"Why?"

"Because I need them. You and I are going to run some experiments of our own."

When Mackinnon explained his plan, Bruce laughed, then said, "I thought you liked to play it safe."

Mackinnon ignored the comment.

"I have the lab report back for Michael King," Bruce said.

Mackinnon tightened his grip on the phone. "Yes?"

"High levels of warfarin were found in his blood. It looks like he got hold of some of this dirty gear."

"Thanks for letting me know." Mackinnon hung up and leaned back in his chair.

The tainted heroin had claimed another victim.

CHAPTER FIFTY-THREE

AFTER BRUCE HANDED OVER his duplicate samples, Mackinnon headed to Bart's. And for the first time, he managed to navigate the warren of corridors successfully and found Anna in the pathology department.

"Sorry about this. I guess this isn't usually the way you'd choose to spend your night off," Mackinnon said.

"No," Anna said. "But if it gets the stuff off the streets, then I'm all for it."

Mackinnon watched as Anna dissolved the samples of the drug into a clear liquid. She held up a small glass vial. "This is the control, pure warfarin."

She selected a small metal syringe from the lab bench, and used it to suck up some of the warfarin solution. "I'm going to inject this into this machine. It's called an HPLC. Basically, it separates molecules according to their properties."

She crouched down beside the machine and injected the solution into a central tube, near what looked like two pistons.

She looked up at Mackinnon.

"Now what?" he asked.

"Now we wait."

After a few minutes, a ream of paper started to scroll out of the back of the machine. "Results," Anna said, and looked down at the printout. "See this bump here?"

Mackinnon nodded.

"Well, that's warfarin," Anna said. "Now we are going to run the drug samples. If warfarin is present, we should see a bump in the same place."

"What's that other part of the machine for?"

Anna turned to face where Mackinnon pointed. "That's the mass spectrometer. It's a way to double-check the results. We think this bump in the chart is warfarin. The mass spectrometer will run a sample and confirm it."

Anna picked up the syringe again, and flushed it out with what looked like water. "Ready for the first sample? This could be a long night."

* * *

Four hours later, they had the results.

"So you're sure?"

"Absolutely." Anna stared down at the printout. "Only one of the heroin samples contains warfarin."

Mackinnon looked down at the printed sheet too. In the control, there had been one clean peak, but in the drug samples, there were peaks all over the place.

"Okay. That is good enough for me. I'll get in touch with Bruce."

"If you don't mind me asking..."

Mackinnon took his phone out of his pocket, then paused. "Go on."

"You said you had already submitted the drug samples as evidence."

"Yeah," Mackinnon said. "I did, but I knew there was no guarantee they would be sent out for testing."

"Why?"

"Bruce acquired the samples from one of his sources." Mackinnon said. "There are very strict rules about evidence, and unfortunately, Bruce's methods don't quite meet the guidelines."

"I see."

"I thought the samples could still give us answers. They might not be any good to the CPS, but they could help us narrow down which dealer this stuff is coming from."

"If you had already handed over the samples, then how did you get them back again to run these tests?" Anna asked.

"Bruce had a duplicate set of samples. He split them in half, and luckily, he hadn't submitted them yet."

A flicker of a frown passed over Anna's face. "That was lucky."

CHAPTER FIFTY-FOUR

THE FOLLOWING DAY, DI Bruce Evans drove over to Wood Street station to meet up with Mackinnon. They sat outside in Bruce's car, at his request.

"So Dr. Sorensen came through for us? She ran the samples?"

Mackinnon nodded. "Yes and they were all clean, except the third sample, which contained huge amounts of warfarin."

Bruce stared out the window. "The third sample?"

Mackinnon tried to see what Bruce was looking at, but failed to notice anything of interest. It had started to rain again and the windscreen was covered with droplets of water.

"Yes. Third sample. Which dealer was that from?"

Bruce seemed to rally himself. "Which dealer? Right, let me just double check..." he pulled a notepad out of his jacket pocket. "Uh huh. Thought as much. It was the Tower Boys' sample. Yeah, number three.

"Tell you what, Jack. I'll report this to my DCI. I had a word with him this morning, and he is prepared to authorise a raid. With any luck, this stuff will be off the streets by tonight." Bruce smiled.

"Good." Mackinnon reached for the door handle. "One more thing."

Bruce turned. "Sure, what is it?"

"There's no way Ronnie could have mixed up the samples, right? Because that could screw everything up."

"No. I'm positive. Ronnie's reliable, Jack."

"I thought it might be a good idea to get a second sample to confirm."

Bruce nodded. "That's a good idea. Consider it done. Thanks for all your help, Jack. I can handle it from here."

Mackinnon stepped out of the car. "You'll keep me updated?"

"Of course."

Mackinnon turned his coat collar up against the rain and watched Bruce drive away.

He had a funny feeling Bruce was hiding something, and Mackinnon intended to find out what it was.

CHAPTER FIFTY-FIVE

2001

TEN YEARS AGO...

Grace's father looked down at his beautiful, frail daughter.

She lay on the hospital bed, sleeping. She looked almost peaceful. She couldn't hear the beeps from the machine, monitoring her vital signs, or the sound of the respirator pumping air into her lungs, breathing for her. She didn't even know he was by her side, but he wouldn't leave her.

Every second was precious.

His daughter was a fighter, that's what he'd said when the doctor told him to prepare himself for the worst. Prepare himself? How was he supposed to prepare himself for life without his little Gracie? It wasn't possible.

He patted her hand. "It's all right, Grace, Dad's here, and I'll sit right here until you get better. You'd think the doctors would know you by now, wouldn't you? You've been in so many times. And every time, you get better."

Grace had fought so hard all her life, just to stay alive. All those operations she'd battled her way through, the infections she shook off, surely she couldn't die like this at the hands of those yobs. Not after she'd fought so bloody hard. Billy closed his eyes, took an unsteady breath, then said a silent prayer for his little girl.

CHAPTER FIFTY-SIX

2011

PRESENT DAY...

"I don't like the way he looks at her. I'm not having him coming here for dinner," JT said.

He sat at the kitchen table, eating a bacon sandwich that Siobhan had prepared.

"For God's sake, Justin. He's her uncle. What kind of dirty mind have you got?"

JT took a large bite of his sandwich, then spoke with his mouth full. "I don't care if he's her uncle or the queen of bloody Sheba. He ain't coming."

Siobhan turned back to the dishes. "You're a sick man, Justin. Don't tar the rest of us with the same brush. It's not normal."

"Stop going on about it, woman, and let me eat in peace, will you?"

Siobhan turned back to face him, with a wet plate in her hand.

"Have a heart, Justin," Siobhan said, softly. "He looks at Emily and he sees Grace. It reminds him of everything he's missing."

JT stood up, pushing his plate away and scraping his chair against the floor. His face was purple with rage as he approached Siobhan, but she didn't look away.

He slapped at the plate she was holding, so it slipped from her grasp and smashed on the floor.

She flinched.

"I said, he isn't coming." JT pushed his face right up to hers. "You got that, you stupid bitch?"

Siobhan glared back at him, defiant, but not quite brave enough to say anything else.

CHAPTER FIFTY-SEVEN

MACKINNON DIDN'T UNDERSTAND WHY he felt so uneasy. The results from Dr. Sorensen were conclusive, and now they knew which dealer was distributing the contaminated heroin. So why couldn't he relax and chalk it up as a result?

Handing it over to the drugs squad wasn't a problem. It was their remit after all. But Mackinnon kept wondering why Bruce was so keen to be a part of everything. Maybe he was one of those officers who didn't like people stumbling into his patch. Understandable, he supposed.

Mackinnon walked towards the tube station, his coat buttoned up against the biting wind. At least, the rain had stopped. He had just spoken to Dr. Sorensen, who told him the cases that had been treated with vitamin K were responding well. So that was yet more good news. He should be feeling good.

As he walked past the Old Bailey, Mackinnon had the sensation he was being watched.

He stopped at a small news stand, taking the chance to look behind him. But there was no one there. He scanned the line of people standing at the bus stop across the road, but no one was looking at him. A red double-decker pulled up and people clambered aboard, leaving Mackinnon staring at an empty bus stop.

He was imagining things.

He must be.

Mackinnon continued on his way, walking towards the underground station. But it was still there, that annoying, prickly feeling on the back of his neck.

He spun around quickly and felt like an idiot when he bumped into two schoolgirls, hurrying along behind him. They scowled at him.

"Sorry, sorry," he said, looking behind them.

Still no one. Just people going about their day-to-day lives.

He stopped next to the window of a mobile phone shop and pretended to study the latest BlackBerry on display. He watched the glass for reflections, but saw no one, apart from office workers scurrying along to the tube.

After another minute or two staring at the glass, he walked on. He had only walked for another minute at most when he felt it again. And this time, he was positive someone was following him. Mackinnon clenched his hand into a fist and turned into a narrow alleyway. Keeping his head down, he kept walking.

Soon he heard footsteps.

The alley ran along the back of a line of restaurants, bars and cafes. It was deserted, just scattered with bits of rubbish and smelly waste bins. Mackinnon held his breath as he continued past a bin that stunk of fish and rotting vegetables.

He heard the footsteps get closer and walked on, drawing

his pursuer further into the dark alley. He waited until he was halfway down the alley, then turned and saw who was following him.

The hooded figure spun around and started to run back down the alley.

"Oh, no you don't," Mackinnon shouted and ran after him.

He was fitter than the man he was chasing, and within a couple of seconds, Mackinnon grabbed him from behind and slammed him up against the wall.

The man's hood fell back, releasing the springy strands of his afro. It was Ronnie.

"Ronnie? What the hell are you following me for?"

"Can you let me go?" Ronnie asked. "Then we can talk."

Mackinnon loosened his grip a little, but he didn't let Ronnie go.

"So talk. I'm waiting."

Ronnie tried to smooth down the creases in his sweatshirt and pushed back his frizzy hair. "I was going to offer you a little information."

"And what information might that be?"

Ronnie frowned. He brushed off Mackinnon's hands, and Mackinnon let him.

"All right, Ronnie," Mackinnon said. "Let's hear it."

Ronnie looked back towards the entrance to the alley, as though he expected someone to be there. Mackinnon looked too, but the alley was still deserted.

"Out with it," Mackinnon said. "Why didn't you just come up to me earlier? Why all the cloak and dagger stalking stuff?"

"I wanted to make sure you were alone."

This set off alarm bells for Mackinnon. "You mean you didn't want DI Bruce Evans to hear this."

Ronnie nodded.

"Okay, Ronnie," Mackinnon said. "Tell me what you don't want DI Evans to know."

Ronnie pulled away from Mackinnon and tried to get a little dignity back, tried to hold himself a little higher.

"I thought I had better let you know that your colleague might not be as snowy white as you think."

"Go on."

Ronnie shrugged, looking slightly less sure of himself now. "I only know what I heard."

"And what did you hear?"

"Just that DI Evans keeps a foot in each camp."

Mackinnon swallowed, looked away, then back into Ronnie's eyes.

"You're saying he's bent?" Mackinnon asked in a voice barely above a whisper.

Ronnie nodded.

"How? Is he taking bribes? Involved with the drugs?"

"Hey, hey..." Ronnie held up his grimy hands. "I don't know all the details. I just thought you should know, that's all."

Mackinnon paused for a moment, then said, "How do you know I am not crooked too?"

Ronnie looked up, eyebrows raised, as if he hadn't considered that possibility. Then he smiled, showing a few craggy and blackened teeth.

"No way, man. I'm a good judge of people, and you're straight as they come. I could tell that the first time I saw you."

CHAPTER FIFTY-EIGHT

MACKINNON AND RONNIE WALKED out of the alley together. Ronnie kept a safe distance from Mackinnon, walking on his toes, like he was a sprinter about to make a dash for it.

Mackinnon said he'd buy Ronnie a cup of tea at the cafe around the corner. From the way Ronnie's jeans appeared to be slipping off his hips, Mackinnon thought he had better splash out on a meal for him too.

They slipped into a booth in Greg's cafe. Mackinnon ordered a cup of tea, and Ronnie picked the biggest thing on the menu: the extra large, all-day breakfast.

Mackinnon's stomach turned as Ronnie started to gobble it down.

"What else can you tell me?" Mackinnon asked.

Ronnie paused with his fork halfway to his mouth. "Just that DI Evans is pretty tight with JT."

"JT?"

Ronnie frowned as he finished chewing a large chunk of bread and butter. Then he said, "Yeah. JT, the guy who is dealing the dirty heroin."

"Hang on..."

Ronnie's jaw dropped open and he closed his eyes. "I'm not supposed to know that, am I?"

Mackinnon leaned forward. "Why did you say that, Ronnie? Have you spoken to DI Evans?"

Ronnie shook his head. "No." He took a deep breath, then said. "I knew it was JT's stuff that was bad all along."

Mackinnon felt the tension between his shoulder blades ease a little. "I see. You're just guessing."

"I wish I was. The fact is, I saw one of my friends almost bleed to death after taking stuff from one of JT's guys."

"You sure he didn't get it from anyone else?"

Ronnie cocked his head to one side and bit his lip. "It was definitely from JT's guys. I know because..."

"How do you know?"

Ronnie looked down at the table. "I know because it was me that bought it for him. We both shared it," he said in a trembling voice. "It's my fault."

"Ronnie, if that was the case, you would have been ill, too. I don't think you can blame yourself for your friend. He must have taken the dirty heroin on another occasion."

Ronnie looked up, his eyes flashing with anger. He yanked up his shirtsleeve. "I was ill. See, I still have the rash, but I didn't get as bad as Scott because Dr. Anna treated me."

Mackinnon pushed his chair back from the table. He needed to take all this in. Was Ronnie telling the truth? He couldn't be. They knew from Anna's tests that sample three contained the warfarin but... they only had Bruce's word for it that sample three was from the Tower Boys. Why would Bruce lie about that?

"Look, Ronnie, are you sure Scott didn't buy any heroin from the Tower Boys?"

Ronnie gave a little smile then it faded. "Did DI Evans tell you the bad gear was coming from the Tower Boys?"

Mackinnon nodded.

Ronnie put his knife and fork down and pushed his plate back. "I gotta go."

"Why? Sit down and finish your breakfast."

Ronnie shook his head and swallowed hard. "No. I gotta go."

Mackinnon put a hand on Ronnie's arm. "Ronnie, sit down and finish your meal first. Tell me what has got you so spooked."

Ronnie sat down.

But he couldn't finish his meal, he just pushed the food around his plate until it got cold. When Ronnie started stabbing the congealed egg with his fork, Mackinnon decided enough was enough. He moved Ronnie's plate to the edge of the table.

"Tell me."

"Nothing to tell."

"Either you're worried about something I just said, Ronnie, or you've got a split personality. You were on cloud nine a minute ago, now you can't wait to get out of here."

Mackinnon studied him, watching the way his eyes flitted around the room.

"I didn't mean any harm. It's not like I was hurting anyone." Ronnie said. "Didn't mean for this to happen. I was trying to help."

"All right," Mackinnon said. "I'm sure you didn't mean any harm. What happened, Ronnie?"

"I just reckoned DI Evans didn't want a sample from JT's because he thought he was a small time player."

Mackinnon nodded. He was pretty sure he knew where this conversation was going.

"But I knew Scott had used JT's stuff before he got sick, so I wanted to help. I wanted to make sure you got a sample of the bad stuff."

Their conversation paused as the waitress came over to clear their table. "Can I get you any more tea or coffee?"

Mackinnon declined and Ronnie just stared down at the table, looking miserable.

Once the waitress had moved away from their table, Mackinnon said, "That's okay, Ronnie. I understand what you are saying, but maybe your friend, Scott, took some of the Tower Boys' heroin the day before."

"But DI Evans told you the dirty heroin is from the Tower Boys, but it can't be!"

"You could be mistaken, Ronnie. Or perhaps, both the Tower Boys and JT could be supplying the contaminated heroin. It doesn't mean that DI Evans is lying."

Ronnie's leg was shaking, banging against the table leg. He was really getting agitated now. "No! He is lying. I never got any samples from the Tower Boys' runner. So the thing is, it couldn't be the Tower Boys' drugs, could it?"

Christ.

Mackinnon reached inside his pocket and pulled out a pen and one of his cards.

"Ronnie, this is really important. You got the samples and labelled them yourself, right?"

"Uh huh." Ronnie nodded. "I wrote the numbers on the bags."

"Then I need you to write the numbers down for me, and next to the numbers I want you to write who you got the sample from, okay? Can you remember?"

Ronnie looked up towards the ceiling, then smiled. "Yeah. I can remember."

He took the pen and bent his head over the card, carefully writing the list in his scratchy scrawl that Mackinnon recognised from the sample bags.

Ronnie thrust the list over to Mackinnon when he finished.

Mackinnon scanned the list, then looked up at Ronnie. "You're sure about this?"

Ronnie nodded.

"And this is the same list you gave DI Evans?"

"Yes."

Mackinnon's hand tightened around the list, crumpling it at the edges. One of them was lying. Ronnie or DI Bruce Evans, and Mackinnon was pretty sure he knew which one.

On the list, next to sample three, Ronnie had written "The Junction."

"Ronnie, tell me about The Junction."

"It's run by a man called JT, mostly from his bar up at Cemetery Junction, but sometimes they deal on the side in the estates."

"What is JT's real name?"

Ronnie shrugged. "No idea."

Mackinnon sat back and stared at Ronnie, until Ronnie broke eye contact and looked down at the table.

The drug addict in front of him was making serious allegations against a fellow officer. Why should he believe Ronnie over Bruce? Didn't he owe Bruce some loyalty? But then again, why would Ronnie lie? What was in it for him?

"You don't believe me, do you?" Ronnie asked.

Mackinnon looked up. "These are serious allegations. Maybe you should come back to the station with me."

Ronnie's eyes widened. "No way. I told you as a favour. You take me in, and I'll deny I said anything."

CHAPTER FIFTY-NINE

THE TAXI DOOR OPENED, and a long-legged young woman, wearing a sorbet-coloured, chiffon dress, stepped out.

The doorman stared as the young woman approached the hotel entrance, tossing her fair hair as she walked. The gold bracelets on her arm, diamond studs in her ears, and a leather handbag, worth over a thousand pounds that hung on her shoulder, all spoke of class.

She raised her sunglasses and smiled at the doorman. He stumbled forward to open the door for her and held out his hands to take her overnight bag.

She waved him off. "I can carry it myself, thank you."

She could feel his eyes on her as she walked through the lobby, her high heels clicking on the white marble floor.

She paused at the reception desk. Two members of the hotel staff came towards her, a young, dark-haired woman, her eyes narrowed with suspicion; and a young man, with a cute smile, his eyes widened in appreciation.

The man stepped in front of his colleague. "Can I help you, madam?"

"Natasha Green. I have a room reserved for one night." Natasha pushed her passport over the polished wood of the reception desk.

The man started the check-in process, making little jokes and looking up at Natasha like a lovesick puppy.

"Have you stayed with us before, Miss Green?"

"Once," Natasha said. She didn't elaborate. In her profession, it wasn't a good idea to stay at the same hotel frequently. She tried that at the beginning, using one hotel as a base and paying a senior member of staff to look the other way, but there were always other people sticking their noses in.

It wasn't a hardship. There were plenty of hotels in London. This one, Threadneedles, on Threadneedle Street, was a particularly fine Victorian boutique hotel. Natasha looked up at the glass-domed ceiling, stained with vivid colours.

"Could I have your credit card, madam?"

Natasha handed over her gold card and glanced at her Cartier watch. She had thirty minutes before her appointment. That was good, very good. She didn't like to be late; that was unprofessional.

The hotel receptionist handed Natasha back her passport and her credit card. "Would you like some help with your bags?"

"I can manage, thank you." Natasha picked up her tan, leather, overnight bag and headed toward the lifts.

Inside the hotel suite, Natasha placed her bag on the luggage rack and looked around. Everything was fine. She ran a hand over the Egyptian cotton sheets. She took her mobile out of her handbag and sent a text to her client, telling him the room number.

Then she rummaged in her bag for her toiletries and took them through to the marble bathroom. There was even a plasma TV in the bathroom. Not that she would have much use for that.

She stared at herself in the mirror. She was looking a little pale. She inspected the bruise on her inner thigh.

Damn.

It looked even worse now. She tried to cover it with Mac's Face and Body foundation. She found the foundation in her toiletry bag and dabbed on some more. It looked a little better.

Natasha didn't even know how the bruise had happened. She couldn't remember knocking her leg or anything.

Natasha shrugged. It would heal soon enough. She wasn't worried, but she needed to look her best, and bruises weren't attractive.

She picked up her toothbrush and began cleaning her teeth. As she spat the toothpaste in the sink, she noticed it was pink. Natasha rinsed her mouth with water, then examined her mouth in the mirror. Around each tooth was a small amount of blood. She had obviously flossed too hard last night.

She rinsed her mouth again, and tidied away her things in the bathroom, before sitting down to wait for her client.

He arrived dead on time. Frank Rivers, forty-five years old, reasonably attractive, with a wife and two kids. Natasha got the business side out of the way first, and took payment. Then she linked her hands behind him and pulled him across to the bed.

Afterwards, he lay breathing heavily by her side. "Do you fancy coming out with me tonight? I've got to go to a function at the Guildhall."

Natasha smiled, and said, "I'm sorry. I can't. I have plans for this evening."

Frank reached across and stroked her arm. "I can pay you."

Those four magic words.

Natasha leaned into him and rested her head on his chest. "I suppose I could cancel my plans."

Frank left the hotel suite twenty minutes later, after arranging to meet Natasha that evening in a small wine bar, near the Guildhall.

Natasha was glad he was gone. She was feeling a little off colour and had sharp pains in her stomach. She rolled over and hoped a nap would help.

But of course, it wouldn't.

What she really needed was her next fix.

CHAPTER SIXTY

MACKINNON LEFT RONNIE WITH enough money to get a cheap bed for the night and headed back to Derek's on the underground. He called Chloe on the way, to ask her how her day had been. It was amazing how much better they got on now that they only saw each other on weekends. It seemed absence really did make the heart grow fonder.

He stopped at the Chor Bazaar and picked up a takeaway curry, getting an extra rice and naan bread in case Derek was home. Mackinnon was actually glad he wasn't seeing Chloe tonight. It gave him a chance to think over this problem with DI Evans.

Derek was home and gratefully tucked into half the curry. They ate on their laps in front of the television.

Derek's dog, Molly, came to sit next to Mackinnon's feet.

"Why does she always sit next to me when we eat?"

Derek gestured with his fork. "Because she's been with me long enough to know she won't get anything off me."

The Border Collie, tilted her head and looked up at Mackinnon with soft brown eyes.

"Women always think I'm a soft touch."

"Because you are," Derek said. "You've always been soft."

"Whereas you've always been highly successful with women?"

"You said it."

"I seem to remember you writing poetry to some girl in our second year at university," Mackinnon said. "That's a bit soft."

"Low blow," Derek said, throwing a cushion at Mackinnon that narrowly missed his lamb rogan josh.

After polishing off the curry, they channel-surfed for a while.

"Nothing on," Derek said in disgust and chucked the remote at Mackinnon. "I'm off to bed."

"Have you gotten rid of those irons yet?" Mackinnon called as Derek left the room.

"Tomorrow."

"If I believe that, I'll believe anything," Mackinnon muttered and switched the channel to Sky news.

He couldn't concentrate on anything else. Mackinnon tried to process what Ronnie had told him today.

He tried to fit the pieces of the puzzle together, but none of it made sense. He should have gone straight to the superintendent with it, and told him his suspicions about Bruce, but something held him back.

If he told Superintendent Wright about this, he would have to explain from the beginning. He would have to tell him about the little experiments they set up on the side. Mackinnon didn't want to screw up his career, but if even a small portion of what Ronnie suggested was true, Mackinnon would have to do something about it. Even if it messed up his own career.

He tried to think of a logical explanation, a way to reconcile what Ronnie had told him, with the facts Bruce had given him. Ronnie insisted that he hadn't managed to get a sample of the Tower Boys' supply, so why did Bruce Evans tell Mackinnon the contaminated heroin was from the Tower Boys?

Was it a simple mistake, or something more sinister?

CHAPTER SIXTY-ONE

NATASHA WAS FEELING WORSE. She gripped the bed sheets as another spasm of pain shot through her stomach. She felt weak and sweaty. She threw off the bed sheets and headed to the bathroom.

She would have to go out and score.

Natasha wrapped herself in a fluffy, white, hotel dressing gown and sat on the lid of the toilet and put her head in her hands. This wasn't good. She kept needing more and more of the bloody stuff.

She looked down at her feet. She tried to inject in a place where it wouldn't be seen too easily. She needed to stop, otherwise she would have to kiss goodbye to all this. She'd be selling herself on the street if she wasn't careful.

Natasha stood up and nausea flooded over her. She staggered over to the sink. The nausea passed as she took big gulps of air. She shivered.

Just as she thought she might be okay, that she might head back to bed, her lungs felt like they had filled with water. She tried to clear her throat. It was horrible. She couldn't breathe properly.

The tickle at the back of her throat developed into a chesty cough. She bent double. It felt like she was coughing up her insides. When the coughing fit was over, out of breath, Natasha looked down at her hand and saw that it was covered with blood.

"Oh Jesus Christ!" What was wrong with her?

She felt faint at the sight of her own blood. She wobbled as she walked towards the door. She needed help. She needed to get to hospital.

Natasha stepped out into the communal hallway and the door clicked shut behind her. Too late, she realised she should have phoned for help. She hadn't picked up the hotel key card, and now she was locked out of her suite.

She staggered down the hallway, banging on doors.

"Somebody help me, please," she screamed between bouts of coughing.

The front of the white dressing gown was now covered with her blood.

Oh God. Why didn't anybody answer?

She looked down and saw blood dripping down her legs. She whimpered in horror.

Maybe she should just lie down here, on the carpet. Maybe the blood would stop if she did that. She felt so faint.

God, she was going to die, here in the hotel corridor. Why didn't someone help her?

She sank to her knees in front of the last room in the corridor. She hammered on it with her fists. She couldn't die here, not now. She was only twenty-two years old.

Why did she leave the room? She could have called for help by now. The hotel would have gotten an ambulance.

She slumped against the door, black spots appearing in front of her eyes.

When the door she had been leaning on opened, Natasha fell into the room.

A woman's voice said, "Oh my God!"

"Help me," Natasha said.

Natasha felt the woman's hand gripping her arm. "Stay with me. I'm calling 999. Just hang on. Help will be here soon."

"Thank you," Natasha said, then she closed her eyes and didn't feel anymore pain.

CHAPTER SIXTY-TWO

WHEN NATASHA CAME AROUND, she was on a stretcher, surrounded by people. She stared up at the ceiling. Bright lights flickered past. They were moving.

Fast.

She realised the people surrounding her were doctors and nurses. She had made it to hospital.

Natasha grabbed a women's arm. "Help me. I just started bleeding. I don't know what's wrong. You have to help me." Natasha struggled to sit up.

"Lie back down for me. I'm Dr. Sorensen. We are going to help you."

Natasha fell back on the stretcher as they came to a stop. The stretcher was rotated, then the people around her counted to three and lifted her onto the bed.

Natasha looked around the room for Dr. Sorensen. People were rushing around everywhere and it was difficult to see. The black spots in front of her eyes re-appeared.

"I don't feel so good," Natasha said.

A nurse by her bedside, who was attaching things to a drip, said, "You've lost a lot of blood. We are going to give you a transfusion to replace it. That should make you feel better."

Another face appeared by Natasha's bedside. It was Dr. Sorensen again. She held a clipboard in front of her. "The staff at the hotel said your name is Natasha Green, is that correct?"

"Yes."

"Okay, Natasha. I need to ask you a few questions, to help us figure out how to treat you."

Natasha nodded, but she couldn't focus on the doctor anymore, the lights were getting dim.

* * *

When Natasha next came around, she was in a ward with other patients, and she was dressed in a blue patterned hospital gown. All her jewellery was missing.

"Hey! Hey you! What has happened to my jewellery?"

A plump nurse made her way over to Natasha's bedside. "We removed them during treatment. I'll see that they are returned to you."

"Make sure you do."

The nurse rolled her eyes. "I'll tell the doctor you are up to answering her questions now, shall I?"

Natasha ignored the nurse's question and shifted uncomfortably. She was still attached to a drip and what looked like a bag of blood. She shuddered.

* * *

Dr. Anna Sorensen took the call from Jenner ward and gathered up her notes. She needed to ask Natasha Green some questions.

Natasha looked one hundred times better than the last time Anna had seen her, two hours ago. The blood had been cleaned from her face and hair, and her cheeks had a little more colour. Her ash blonde hair was pushed back from her face.

"Hello, Natasha. I'm Dr. Sorensen. Do you remember me?"

Natasha nodded. "What's wrong with me?"

"That's what I'm trying to find out. You had a bleeding episode and lost a lot of blood. Your haemoglobin levels are still very low."

Anna went through her questions, completing the medical history form. "Have you taken any medication or any non-prescribed drugs in the past few months?"

"No," Natasha shook her head.

Anna paused. She had been certain they were looking at another poisoned heroin case when Natasha was admitted, but Anna had been perplexed by the absence of track marks. Anna had been about to order bleeding disorder screens and specialised coagulation panel tests when Dr. Patel pointed out the marks between Natasha's toes.

What did the girl think Anna was going to do? Run off and report her to the police? Tell her mother? Natasha was prepared to lie and put her life in danger. It defied belief.

Anna's silence was making Natasha nervous. She picked at the bed sheets. "Do I look like a drug addict?" She tossed her long, fair hair.

"If you tell me what a drug addict looks like, I'll tell you."

Natasha scowled.

"Do you really think I couldn't run a tox screen to find

out?" Anna shook her head. "This is very important. I need to know if you have taken heroin in the last couple of weeks."

Natasha's face crumpled and tears rolled down her cheeks. "I last injected yesterday afternoon. I'm sorry. You can still treat me, can't you?"

Anna wanted to be hard on her, to tell her by lying she could have delayed the treatment that could save her life, but she didn't. She patted the girl's hand. "Yes, we can still treat you."

CHAPTER SIXTY-THREE

AFTER A SLEEPLESS NIGHT, Mackinnon got to the station just after six. It was so much easier to get to work from Derek's. He didn't miss the commute from Oxford at all. He did miss Chloe, though, in a nice way.

He grabbed a coffee from the ancient machine in the corridor, as the canteen wasn't open yet. He'd just managed to extract the cup, without spilling any, as he normally did, when he heard footsteps behind him.

"Hey, Jack. You're in early."

Mackinnon looked up as Charlotte walked over. "Yeah. Thought I'd better catch up on the paperwork. I've been avoiding it."

"Don't blame you. I've got my own pile to catch up on before Brookbank's briefing starts at seven. I meant to ask, how is that drug case of yours coming along?"

Mackinnon took a sip of coffee while Charlotte punched the numbers for hers into the vending machine.

"Actually, it is getting complicated. I could do with a chat, if you have the time?" Mackinnon said.

Charlotte looked up. Despite the fact she looked shattered, she grinned. "For you, Mac, I'll make time."

They took their drinks into the empty canteen and sat at a table near the bar area, facing each other. Mackinnon struggled to come up with the right words. "I don't really know how to put this, it's... sensitive..."

Charlotte shrugged. "Whatever it is, you can tell me. It won't go any further."

Mackinnon knew he could trust Charlotte, but he still found it hard to tell her what he was thinking. Once he put his suspicions into words, it would be out in the open and he'd have to act on it.

"It's about another officer, the one in the drugs squad, who I've been liaising with on the contaminated heroin case." Mackinnon paused.

"You think he's bent?" Charlotte asked.

Mackinnon raised his eyebrows.

Charlotte shrugged. "Well, it is a bit of a cliché isn't it? A drugs squad cop taking bribes to clear the way for some scummy drug lord."

"It's not quite like that."

Charlotte blew over the top of her steaming coffee, took a sip, then asked, "Are you sure he is bent, Jack?"

Mackinnon took a sip of coffee. "No. I'm not sure, but my instinct tells me..."

"You can't rely on your instinct. You need proof. If you're wrong, you could screw up his career... and your own."

Mackinnon stared down at the table. She was right. If he was wrong and made an allegation like this... No one would ever trust him again.

"One of his sources, an addict from the Towers Estate, told me he is working with a dealer called JT."

"That's all you have? The word of a drug addict? This source might have a grudge? He probably isn't reliable?"

Mackinnon nodded. "It's not great evidence, I know."

Charlotte looked around the canteen, checking they were alone, then leaned forward. "I take it we're talking about Bruce Evans, DI Tyler's mate."

Mackinnon paused for a moment, then nodded.

Charlotte exhaled a long breath and folded her arms. "I don't think you should say anything. Not yet, at least. There is no way you can trust the word of a drug addict over a detective inspector."

"It's not just that. What I'm really worried about is the samples we have for this case. DI Evans arranged for one of his sources to collect five samples of heroin from different dealers over the City and Tower Hamlets area. When the samples were analysed by the lab, they found that the third sample was heavily laced with warfarin, which is the stuff making the unlucky addicts bleed to death."

Charlotte screwed up her face. "Nasty."

"Bruce Evans told me the contaminated sample came from a certain dealer, and his team are planning a raid. But when I spoke to his source directly, the addict that actually went out and got hold of these samples, he told me he didn't even get a sample from that dealer. He told me sample three was from a different dealer entirely."

"Hang on," Charlotte said, frowning. "Are you telling me Bruce Evans lied about where the contaminated heroin is coming from?"

Mackinnon nodded. "I think he did, and I need to find out why."

CHAPTER SIXTY-FOUR

2001

TEN YEARS AGO...

Billy was losing her, losing his Grace.

He knew that now.

He sat beside her bed, watching her chest move up and down as the respirator pumped air into her lungs.

He barely noticed the bustling nurses who came to check her vitals, ignoring their looks of pity.

He concentrated on holding Grace's hand, willing her to squeeze his hand, willing her to respond.

But she didn't.

An hour later, he was still holding Grace's hand when she slipped away.

Away from him forever.

CHAPTER SIXTY-FIVE

2011

PRESENT DAY...

SARAH turned over on the sofa bed and yawned. She snuggled back down into the duvet. She had been having such a great dream, if she could fall asleep again, she might get the dream back.

No chance. She could hear Jessica's mum calling them from downstairs.

Sarah flung back the duvet and sat up, rubbing her eyes with her fists. God, she was so tired. She glanced over at Jessica, who was still buried under her duvet.

Sarah stretched and yawned again. They'd had a really good night last night. Jessica hadn't been feeling very well, so they stayed in and watched DVDs, munching their way through a mountain of popcorn, just like they used to do when they were younger.

These days, it was all about going to parties in skanky places, or finding a new way for Jessica to get high. Her mother would freak if she knew what Jessica got up to. Sarah was a saint in comparison.

"Girls, time to get up. I'm cooking pancakes," Mrs. Mahon called from downstairs.

Sarah's stomach rumbled loudly. Pancakes. Just what she needed.

"Jess. Jess, wake up. Your mum's cooking us breakfast."

Nothing. Not even an imaginative swear word, which was how Jessica normally responded when she was woken up.

Jessica had always been a heavy sleeper. Sarah gave her a firm prod.

"Hey, Jess, wake up!"

Still nothing.

"Fine. I'll just go and eat your share of the pancakes too."

Sarah reached over the bed to shake Jessica's shoulder. Grasping it, she rolled her over. "Will you... Oh my God....!"

Blood saturated Jessica's pillow and was smeared all over her nose and mouth.

Sarah screamed.

CHAPTER SIXTY-SIX

DR. ANNA SORENSEN GOT the call from Rita on her mobile.

"I'm sorry to disturb you at home. But we have another bleeding case, an addict. Her profile matches the others. Dr. Patel has administered the vitamin K, but he thinks it might be too late to save her."

"I'll be right there."

Anna only lived a twenty-minute bus ride from the hospital, but this morning, it seemed to take forever. The traffic was backed up and the bus crawled along. Anna rang the bell and got off one stop too early. She was sure she could walk faster. She walked briskly and took a footpath that led to the back of the hospital.

Rita had given her the details on the phone, so she went straight to ICU and met Dr. Patel as he was coming out.

"How is she?"

"Not good."

"But you have given the patient vitamin K?"

Dr. Patel nodded. "I have, but I believe we were too late.

She had a massive intracerebral haemorrhage before she was admitted."

"Brain damage?"

"Irreversible, I'm afraid. We'll have to switch the machine off. Such a pretty, young thing, such a waste."

Dr. Patel rubbed a hand over his face and sighed. "Now, I shall have to tell her family."

Before she had a chance to really think it through, Anna said, "I'll do it. I'll tell her family."

Dr. Patel raised his eyebrows. "Really?"

"I feel like I should. I've been working with these cases and..."

Dr. Patel nodded furiously; he wasn't about to look a gift horse in the mouth. "Well, if you're sure... I do have my rounds to be getting on with."

Anna left Dr. Patel to get on with his rounds and entered the ICU ward. One of the nurses on duty directed her to the patient, Jessica Mahon, nineteen years old.

Anna stared down at the pretty, doll-like girl. She felt overcome with sadness as she looked at her young face. She was fair-skinned and had long, delicate, pale eyelashes. The blood had been washed from her hair and her blonde curls were still slightly damp.

Her nails had been recently manicured. Everything about this girl spoke of money and privilege. She didn't fit the image people usually conjured up when they thought of a heroin addict.

She looked so much younger than nineteen. Anna felt tears prick the corner of her eyes.

Anna had been too confident. She thought that now they knew what was causing the addicts to bleed to death, she could save them. She thought there wouldn't be any more deaths. How wrong she was. How naive.

First Scott, and now this poor, young girl. Despite treating them both, it hadn't been enough.

The nurse appeared at Anna's side and made her jump. She quickly wiped away her tears.

"Sorry. Silly of me. You would think I'd be used to it by now."

The nurse smiled. "Not at all. I don't think it is possible to get used to it, and I don't think I would ever want to."

CHAPTER SIXTY-SEVEN

CHLOE WALKED AS FAST as she could without running. Her mouth was dry, and her heart was pounding. She was terrified. She drove down from Oxford as soon as she received Sarah's tearful phone call.

Sarah had been staying in London, at Jessica's mother's house. Chloe assumed she'd be safe there.

She burst through a set of double doors, almost knocking down a porter trying to come through the doors at the same time. "Sorry," Chloe called out as she hurried on her way.

She arrived in the corridor outside the Intensive Therapy Unit and saw Sarah and Dawn Mahon, Jessica's mother, sitting next to each other on plastic chairs set back against the wall.

"Mum!" Sarah looked up with eyes red and bloodshot from crying. She stood up and flung herself into Chloe's arms.

"I got here as fast as I could, darling," Chloe said. "Are you all right?"

Sarah hiccoughed and wiped her tear-stained cheeks. "It's Jessica, she was bleeding, it was all over her pillow, and I didn't know what to do..." Sarah buried her face in Chloe's shoulder and sobbed.

With one arm hugging Sarah, she reached out with her other hand to Dawn Mahon. "Any news, Dawn?"

Dawn looked up in a daze. "No. No news. Nothing yet."

"We are waiting for the doctor," Sarah said between sobs. "The nurse said he would come to speak to us."

"And where is Mike?" Chloe asked, thinking about Jessica's father. He still lived in the old family home in Oxford. Chloe cursed herself for not thinking earlier, she could have picked him up on her way.

Dawn shook her head. "I tried to ring him, but he hasn't answered my calls yet."

"Right. Well, you can leave that to me. I'll try him again."

Dawn nodded but didn't look up.

Chloe let go of Sarah's hand and went outside so she could make the call. Her hand shook as she dialled the number. She wanted to help Dawn, wanted to make it easier for her. God, what that poor woman must be going through.

As she listened to the ringing tone, Chloe broke out in a cold sweat. How the hell did you tell someone their daughter was lying in the ICU? There wasn't an easy way to do it. She would just have to tell him straight. There was no way to make it sound less scary. It was the phone call every parent dreaded.

But he didn't answer. Chloe tried once more, then decided to send a text message. She agonised over what to type, but in the end settled for: URGENT. Jessica is in hospital. St. Bart's.

It seemed so cold and such a horrible way to break the news, but it was important to make sure he got there as quickly as possible.

When Chloe got back inside, she saw a woman talking to

Dawn and Sarah. She walked up to Dawn, who was shaking her head vigorously.

"Are you okay, Dawn?" Chloe put a hand on Dawn's shoulder and looked up at the newcomer, a tall, willowy woman, wearing a soft pink shirt.

The woman said, "My name is Dr. Anna Sorensen. Are you family?"

Chloe looked down at Dawn. She could feel Dawn's shoulders trembling. "I am a friend of the family. What's happened? Do you have any news about Jessica?"

Chloe felt awkward, asking questions when it wasn't really her place to, but Dawn was staring vacantly at the wall. She looked like she was in shock.

Dr. Sorensen nodded. "We did all we could, but I'm afraid we couldn't save Jessica."

Chloe stared at her. "Jessica's dead?" She turned to face Dawn, who was still staring at the wall, shaking her head.

After a moment, Dr. Sorensen continued awkwardly, "I'm very sorry for your loss."

"But what happened?" Chloe asked.

Dr. Sorensen looked down at Dawn. "I've explained the circumstances to Mrs. Mahon, but I think it's a bit much to take in. Jessica had a bleed in her brain, by the time she got to the hospital, it was too late..."

Dawn stood, suddenly. "I know that you did all you could. Thank you, Doctor. Jessica carried a donor card she always wanted..."

Anna nodded. "I see... Unfortunately, that won't be possible in this case."

Dawn Mahon clutched the doctor's sleeve. "No, you don't understand. It's what Jessica wanted."

"Perhaps," Dr. Sorensen said, "we could discuss it later."

Chloe put an arm around Dawn Mahon's shoulders. "She's right. Why don't we go somewhere and get a cup of tea?"

"No!" Dawn yanked again on the doctor's arm. "You have to. She wanted to be a donor."

Dr. Sorensen ushered the three women into the nearby family room, with Dawn still clutching her arm.

"It was very important to her," Dawn said. "Don't you see that?"

"Yes, but I'm afraid that, as Jessica was an intravenous drug user, she isn't a suitable donor."

Dawn snatched her hand away as if she'd been burned.

They were cruel words to say to a woman who had just lost her child. It was the ultimate rejection, a kick in the teeth when she was already down.

Chloe's mouth opened in shock. The doctor must have this wrong. There was no way Jessica was an intravenous drug user. No way.

"I'm sorry, Doctor, but I think there has been some kind of mistake..." Chloe said.

Dawn gave a strangled sob, then said, "That's what I thought, too, but then your daughter told the doctors that Jessica had been using heroin."

Chloe whirled around to face Sarah. That couldn't be true. Jessica who loved making cupcakes when she stayed at Chloe's for a sleepover. Jessica who cried over her braces. Jessica who had been Sarah's best friend since infant school.

Then Chloe looked at her daughter and knew that it was all true.

Terror constricted her chest as she realised Sarah might have taken heroin too. "Did you?"

Sarah shook her head. "I haven't taken any."

Relief and an almost primal desire to grab Sarah and get

the hell out of there swept through Chloe. She wanted to go somewhere where Sarah would be safe, where she couldn't be hurt.

Thoughts flooded her mind. She remembered standing by Sarah's cot when she was a baby, scared that she might stop breathing. She remembered her fear when Sarah set off on her first bike ride without stabilisers, her fear on Sarah's first day at school because she might be bullied.

She remembered wanting to cocoon Sarah away from the pain of her father moving to half way around the world.

But she couldn't take Sarah and run because Jessica's mother needed them.

Dawn gave an anguished cry, and her legs buckled.

Chloe tried to support her, but Dawn leaned back against the wall and slid down it, sobbing. Chloe got down on the floor beside her and hugged her. Sarah just stood there with silent tears rolling down her cheeks.

CHAPTER SIXTY-EIGHT

CHARLOTTE SAT IN THE main meeting room at Wood Street station, listening to Brookbank's briefing. They were closing in on the gang that was planning a huge robbery. It should have been exciting, but Charlotte's mind was elsewhere. She was worried about Mackinnon.

She didn't want him throwing his career away based on the word of a drug addict. Jack Mackinnon wasn't exactly the reckless type, but he did have flaws. They all did. They were all just trying to do the best job they could.

Mackinnon's major problem was the fact he always wanted to do the right thing. Obviously, that wasn't a bad attribute to have, but he did have a tendency to see things in black and white, and seemed blinkered to the grey. This meant, on occasions, he would bulldoze his way into situations that probably required a more delicate touch.

If Charlotte suspected one of her colleagues was involved in something dodgy, she would keep quiet, while she collected proof of her suspicions. Mackinnon was more likely to confront DI Evans straight away, which could have nasty consequences.

Charlotte stifled a yawn. This briefing was taking a long time. At least, she had managed to get a good night's sleep last night, though. It was the first time in ages that she had slept right through. In fact, Charlotte was feeling pretty good today. She hadn't had any more calls, and when she left home this morning, she only had to check the locks once. Her good spirits were only slightly marred by worrying about Wayne's new girlfriend. The poor girl had no idea what she was getting into.

Charlotte tried to push that thought to the back of her mind and concentrate on what Brookbank was saying. But it was no good, within a couple of minutes, her thoughts returned to Mackinnon.

If Bruce Evans was innocent, he could easily make a complaint to a senior officer and that would leave a nasty mark on Mackinnon's record. If DI Evans were guilty, then confronting him would just give him time to cover his tracks.

And if DI Evans was seriously corrupt, then the question was, how deeply was he involved? Was he taking bribes to look the other way? Or involved even deeper? Was he taking a cut in the profit and involved in the supply chain?

Charlotte chewed on the end of her biro. She didn't like this, at all. She would talk to Mackinnon again after this briefing and tell him not to confront DI Evans alone.

He needed to be careful.

DI Evans might be a rat, but a cornered rat could be dangerous.

CHAPTER SIXTY-NINE

"JESUS, SIOBHAN!" JT SCREAMED out. "Oh God! No!"

JT stood in their bedroom dressed in just his boxer shorts, staring at himself in the full-length mirror.

Siobhan entered the room, slightly out of breath from running up the stairs. "What on earth's the matter?"

JT studied his reflection, turning around and tilting his head to one side.

"Well, what is it, Justin?" Siobhan folded her arms.

"Look at this." JT held out his arm. "My skin's peeling off."

Siobhan took hold of JT's wrist and looked closely at the loose skin on JT's forearm. "Maybe it is some kind of allergic reaction."

She turned his arm slightly and moved him into the light so she could see better. "Have you used any new skin products lately?" Siobhan asked.

"Any new what? No. Don't be ridiculous." JT pulled his arm away, inspecting it himself. "Jesus. I knew I was ill. Make me an appointment with Dr. Stacey."

Siobhan nodded. "I'll try to book an emergency appointment for afternoon surgery."

"You do that," JT said. "Tell them my bloody skin is falling off."

CHAPTER SEVENTY

JT STOOD IN DR. Stacey's examination room and pulled his tee shirt over his head.

"See, Doctor. It's everywhere. Great big patches of my skin are falling off."

Dr. Stacey snapped on a pair of gloves and approached JT. He motioned for JT to turn around, which JT did.

Dr. Stacey poked and prodded for a little while until JT lost his patience.

"Okay, Doctor. Give it to me straight. What have I got? I've been feeling like crap for weeks. Now this. I'm falling apart."

Dr. Stacey took off his glasses and rubbed the bridge of his nose. "To be honest with you, Mr. Theroux, I'm not sure what this is. It looks like it might be an allergic reaction to something. New washing powder, perhaps?"

JT pulled his tee shirt back on.

* * *

JT was silent all the way home in the car and he ignored Siobhan's questions. He just stared out of the window when she asked him what the doctor had said.

He waited until they were back inside their flat, above The Junction, before he let Siobhan know how pissed off he was.

Siobhan switched the kettle on. "How about I make us a nice cup of tea? Then you can tell me what the doctor said."

JT pulled out a chair and sat down at the kitchen table.

Siobhan moved over to him. "You know, if it is bad, I'm here for you. Always."

JT grunted. Then he stood up, walked over to the sink and opened the cupboard beneath it.

"What are you looking for? I'll get it." Siobhan's voice sounded high-pitched and nervous.

JT bent down and picked up a box of washing powder. He held it up and shook it. "New washing powder! You stupid cow. You made me look like a right tit. I went to the doctor's because I reacted to some bloody washing powder."

JT leaned forward and delivered a vicious back hander to Siobhan's jaw. He watched with satisfaction as she dropped to the floor like a sack of spuds.

Pathetic woman. He turned and stalked out of the room.

CHAPTER SEVENTY-ONE

2001

TEN YEARS AGO...

Grace's father sat in the court and waited for justice for his daughter.

All the nights he had lain awake, the days spent staring at her grave, they all came down to this one moment. Retribution. Punishment. Vengeance. This is what he had waited for.

The judge, a short, wiry man, sat at the front of the courts. Billy was disappointed by his appearance. He wanted someone larger than life, someone powerful to deliver the verdict.

The judge scratched the side of his nose and looked around at the court.

Billy turned to look at the first defendant in the dock. With his hair smoothed down, wearing a navy blue suit, he was playing the young professional.

But Billy knew he wasn't.

Billy knew this was the man who had smashed a lamp into the back of Grace's head, not just once, but repeatedly cracking it against her skull.

The judge and jury wouldn't fall for his act. They had to see through his pathetic attempts to pretend he was an honourable member of society. Billy raised his eyes to the ceiling and prayed.

* * *

Just a few short weeks later, Billy stood on the steps outside the court, stunned.

He couldn't believe it. Those two yobs, the thieving, drugged-up scum, who had murdered his Grace, had got off.

And it was because of the drugs.

He had listened to the judge's closing statement and looked around at the other people in the courtroom. This had to be a mistake. Surely, someone would say something, tell the judge he was spouting a load of left-wing rubbish.

But no one said anything.

He watched as the families of those two pieces of scum came forward, smiling, clapping each other on the back, celebrating...

Billy had always believed in the system; he trusted that the law would deliver justice. He served in the Army for this country, and was prepared to sacrifice his life for it. He believed they would be punished. He might have preferred capital punishment, but he knew that couldn't happen. But at the very least, he expected them to serve life in prison.

A life for a life. Wasn't that fair?

Bile burned its way along Billy's throat and he gagged. He

sat down on the stone steps outside the court and rested his head on his knees.

The judge said because the defendants were on drugs during the time of the attack, they could not be held accountable for their actions – "diminished capacity."

Billy couldn't take it in. Drugs were illegal, but they weren't being punished for using them. Instead, they were treated leniently because they were on drugs.

What sort of world was this?

His Grace was gone, and those scumbags didn't get sent to prison, not even for one day.

CHAPTER SEVENTY-TWO

2011

PRESENT DAY...

JT arrived at the Accident and Emergency department of St. Bart's with Siobhan. He sat on one of the orange plastic chairs next to an old man with what looked like half his dinner down the front of his jacket. JT's chest wheezed every time he took a breath. Siobhan stood in line at reception, waiting to fill in his registration form.

"Asthma, is it?" The man next to him said.

JT didn't want to waste his energy on chatting. He shook his head.

"Thought so," the man said, ignoring JT's response. "My eldest had that. He had some terrible attacks."

JT concentrated on his breathing. In and out. He just couldn't get enough air in. He knew he mustn't panic. He had woken up, in the middle of his afternoon nap, covered in sweat, gasping for air.

Although he did manage to calm his breathing, he still

couldn't take in enough air. It felt like an elephant was sitting on his chest. He could only take short, pathetic gulps of air.

Siobhan kept insisting it was a panic attack and would pass when he calmed down.

Panic attack, his arse. He demanded she drive him straight to Accident and Emergency. He knew something wasn't right.

JT glanced over at the digital display. Approximate waiting time was two hours. He wasn't sure he could wait that long. Surely, they could give him something in the meantime. An oxygen mask perhaps. He'd seen those on TV.

He tried to gesture to Siobhan, but she had her back to him. Stupid woman. He'd have to sort it out himself, as usual.

JT got to his feet and had taken two steps when he felt a tight band encircling his chest. He'd never felt anything like it. When he tried to take a breath, a soaring pain shot across his chest.

He couldn't breathe. He was going to die.

He took one more stumbling step, before falling to the floor.

When he came to, JT was lying in a hospital bed, in a cubicle, surrounded by blue curtains. He had a clear mask strapped over his nose and mouth. So they had finally got around to giving him some oxygen. About bloody time. It was probably a new NHS policy: Wait until the patient collapses before giving them any treatment.

Siobhan was on his right, and a doctor stood at the foot of his bed.

"Ah. Mr. Theroux." The doctor leaned forward and peered at him. "I see you're back with us."

"My chest hurts," JT said. In truth, the pain had subsided, but his chest still felt heavy, like it was clogged up.

The doctor pulled up the file attached to the end of JT's bed. "I'm not surprised. You have a very nasty infection."

JT shot a look at Siobhan, to say, "See? I told you I was really ill."

The doctor clipped an X-ray image onto a small, white light box. "This is a picture of your lungs, Mr. Theroux. This white stuff you see here." The doctor pointed to a fuzzy white area on the X-ray. "That's fungus, growing inside your lungs."

"Fungus?" JT felt his heart beat a little faster. "What's that? Is it like bronchitis or something?"

"No. It's actually very unusual."

"What? Why is it unusual?"

"It is normally only seen in patients with severely compromised immune systems."

"What... the hell... does that mean...? Speak English..." JT gasped for breath.

The doctor looked at Siobhan, then back at JT. "It means, Mr. Theroux, your immune system is not working properly. And we need to find out why."

CHAPTER SEVENTY-THREE

"OH, GOD, JACK," CHLOE said, as Mackinnon walked through the double doors.

Sarah sat on the plastic seat, next to her mother, looking shell-shocked.

Chloe stood up.

"I came as soon as I got your message," Mackinnon said. "Is Sarah all right?"

"Sarah?" Mackinnon touched her arm, and she nodded.

Chloe bit down on her lip. "It was awful. Poor Jessica... and Dawn's beside herself."

Mackinnon wrapped his arms around Chloe and hugged her tightly.

Sarah looked up at them. "Jessica's dad's not even here yet."

Chloe ran a hand through her hair. "He is on his way now."

"What happened?" Mackinnon asked.

"She was taking drugs. The doctor told us she had obviously taken some bad stuff, and when Sarah tried to wake her this morning..."

Mackinnon's stomach twisted. Surely not? This couldn't be happening.

Sarah started to cry. "She was bleeding... there was blood everywhere."

Mackinnon felt his stomach knot again. "Sarah, you haven't taken anything, have you?"

Sarah shook her head, and Chloe said, "She hasn't. We've talked about it, and she knows how important it is to tell the truth. I told her I wouldn't be angry."

"I haven't taken it," Sarah said. "I promise."

Mackinnon exhaled the breath he hadn't even realised he was holding.

Dr. Anna Sorensen exited the ICU ward, with her head down, reading patient notes, so she didn't see Mackinnon until they were almost level.

She did a double take. "DS Mackinnon? Did we have a meeting?"

Mackinnon shook his head. "This is my family," he said, squeezing Chloe's hand.

Anna's eyes widened. "Oh, I am so sorry."

Mackinnon stood up. "I won't be a minute," he said to Chloe.

He and Anna walked through the double doors into the main corridor.

"You knew Jessica Mahon?" Anna asked.

"Yeah, what are the chances of that? Here I am worrying about getting the word out, putting in notices in rehab centres, and then... so close to home..."

"God. I'm so sorry. We did everything. Dr. Patel gave her

the vitamin K, but by the time she got here, it was too late," she looked up at Mackinnon.

"I know you would have done everything you could. It's just so bloody tragic, such a waste."

Anna nodded. "I'll let you get back to your family. If there is anything I can do, let me know."

Mackinnon started to walk away, then turned back. "I suppose the body won't be released for a while."

"I'm sure they'll process her as soon as possible, but in a case like this..." Anna shrugged.

Mackinnon nodded and walked away. The words "process her" stuck in his head.

Mackinnon sat down next to Chloe and held her hand.

"Thanks for coming, Jack, but you don't have to stay. I know you have to get back to work."

"Not yet I don't," Mackinnon said. "I'm staying here with you."

CHAPTER SEVENTY-FOUR

MACKINNON ENDED UP SPENDING half the day at St. Bart's with Chloe and Sarah. They waited for Jessica's father to arrive, and sat with him while the poor man tried to process the fact he would never see his daughter again. Jessica's mother was unresponsive; no doubt, she was still in shock.

All in all, it had been an absolutely horrendous morning.

From what Sarah told them, it sounded like Jessica was using heroin for at least a couple of months. Mackinnon was amazed she had managed to keep it so well hidden from her parents.

Chloe offered to drive everyone home, but Mackinnon ordered them a taxi. He said he would drive Chloe's car back to Oxford tonight.

Now more than ever, Mackinnon needed to get the truth from Bruce Evans. He decided there was no point in delaying the confrontation.

Mackinnon would tell Bruce what Ronnie had told him and see how he reacted.

The police station where Bruce Evans worked had been recently refurbished. The walls were all painted cream, and everything else seemed to be made of metal and glass – the reception desk, the chairs, even the small coffee table scattered with leaflets. He could still smell the new paint.

Mackinnon gave his details to the duty officer and requested to see DI Evans. He then settled back into a chair in the waiting area. Bruce wasn't expecting him, so Mackinnon knew he might be in for a long wait.

Mackinnon pulled out his mobile and scrolled through his messages. He had missed a call from Charlotte. He considered calling her back, but then decided against it. He knew she would try to talk him out of confronting Bruce.

He typed out a quick text message to Chloe, saying he hoped she got home safely, and he would see her tonight.

The internal door buzzed, then opened and DI Bruce Evans walked out into reception.

"Jack. Good to see you."

Bruce held out his hand for Mackinnon to shake, and gave him a slap on the back, like they were old pals. "Did we have an appointment? I must have forgotten."

"Thought I'd drop in for a chat," Mackinnon said. "I hope it isn't an inconvenient time."

"Not at all. Come on up. We'll go and grab a couple of coffees. Actually, I'm glad you came by. I can update you on the progress from our end."

Bruce opened the door wide, and gestured for Mackinnon to go first. "It's up the stairs, second floor."

Mackinnon headed for the metallic staircase. It was one of those fancy ones, which had a gap between each step that allowed you to look down to the floor. Mackinnon kept his eyes fixed straight ahead.

They walked up the stairs in silence, Mackinnon mentally puzzling over how to broach the subject with Bruce. He usually went for the direct approach, didn't see the point in wasting time, but this time, he wasn't sure. Mackinnon glanced over his shoulder at Bruce, who smiled back at him.

Bruce had such an open, expressive face and always had a ready smile. Was he really as straightforward as he seemed, or was he hiding dark secrets behind that friendly smile?

Bruce led the way into a small office, with one internal window that looked out into a larger, open-plan space.

"It's not much," Bruce said. "But at least, I don't have to share."

The walls of Bruce's office were lined with bookcases and two filing cabinets, which made it appear even smaller. With the desk and two chairs shoe-horned in as well, it was cramped.

Bruce nodded to a chair, and Mackinnon sat down. Bruce reached over to the filing cabinet behind him and pulled two mugs out of a drawer. A small coffee machine was perched on the other filing cabinet.

"Could you do the honours?" Bruce said and handed Mackinnon the two mugs. "I'm afraid I don't have any milk."

"Black is fine." Mackinnon took the jug from the coffee machine, poured the hot liquid into the two mugs and handed one to Bruce.

"Cheers. It's not the best, but it's better than the stuff they serve at the canteen." Bruce smiled again.

Mackinnon sat down with his own mug of coffee. Lying awake last night, he convinced himself Bruce was involved in something dodgy, but now sitting opposite him, with Bruce tearing open a packet of bourbon biscuits, the whole thing just seemed too far-fetched, like something out of an American cop show. Surely, Bruce wasn't the type to get mixed up in something like this.

Mackinnon leaned forward and accepted a biscuit. "I spoke to Ronnie. He tracked me down."

Bruce looked up, but his face remained impassive. "Oh, really… What for?"

"He told me something that didn't tally with what you told me about the samples of heroin." Mackinnon paused, waiting for Bruce to tell him that Ronnie couldn't be trusted, or Ronnie had a grudge against him and was prone to making things up.

But Bruce just took a large bite of his biscuit, then sipped his coffee.

"He told me that sample three, the one contaminated with warfarin, was actually from a dealer called JT," Mackinnon said, watching Bruce closely for his reaction. "He told me the sample was not from the Tower Boys' crew."

Bruce put down his mug. "You're kidding?"

Mackinnon shook his head.

Bruce exhaled loudly. "Jesus. We are planning a raid on the wrong place." He rubbed a hand over his face. "I don't believe this. Christ, I was stupid to let him label the samples himself. What was I thinking?"

Mackinnon didn't answer.

"You warned me about that, didn't you? I'm sorry, Jack. I should have listened."

Bruce reached for the telephone on his desk. "I'd better call DCI Rosser. He'll have my balls for this one." Bruce shook his head. "Thank God, you let me know in time to stop the raid. Seriously, Jack, thank you."

"That's okay," Mackinnon said.

Mackinnon watched Bruce as he made the call to his DCI. From the faces Bruce was pulling and the fact that he couldn't seem to get a word in edgeways, Mackinnon could tell the news wasn't going down well with Bruce's DCI.

When he got off the phone, Bruce said, "I don't think I am going to live this one down in a hurry. Look, I'm sorry to rush off, but I have to go to the DCI's office and try to explain how this screw-up happened. You understand, don't you? I'll give you a ring this afternoon."

Mackinnon stood up, but Bruce put his hand on Mackinnon's shoulder. "No stay, finish your coffee at least. You can finish off the bourbons, too. It's the least you deserve after just saving my neck."

As Bruce grabbed his suit jacket and dashed out of the office, Mackinnon reached for his mug of coffee. Through the whole meeting, Mackinnon had been studying Bruce for signs of deception. A slight sheen of sweat along his browline was the only sign he was lying, but having his DCI scream down the phone at him may have been the cause of that.

CHAPTER SEVENTY-FIVE

AS BRUCE RAN UP the stairs to DCI Mark Rosser's office, he felt his heart pounding. His mouth was dry, and he wished he had finished off his coffee before coming up. He was sure as hell the DCI wasn't going to offer him any. His stomach churned. The bourbon biscuits had probably been a bad idea.

DCI Mark Rosser was a great boss, just so long as you didn't mess up. He had no time for screw-ups. He worked hard and conscientiously, and he expected his team to do the same.

Bruce reached the DCI's door and hesitated. The fact that he liked and respected his boss just made Bruce feel worse. He knew he had let him down badly, and he deserved the grilling he was about to get, and a whole lot worse.

He didn't have a clue whether Jack Mackinnon had fallen for his act. He was too perceptive, nothing like DI Tyler. But Bruce had bigger things to worry about now. He had to bluff his way out of this situation with his DCI.

He had to give the performance of his life. He had no choice.

He knocked on the DCI's door, and DCI Rosser yanked it open. "Come in, Bruce."

Bruce entered the office and shut the door behind him. The DCI was going to shout, and Bruce didn't want the whole building to hear.

DCI Rosser walked behind his desk. There was no trace of his usual smile. The DCI put his hands on the desk and leaned on it heavily. His face radiated exasperation. "What the hell happened?"

"Well, sir..."

DCI Rosser hit the desk with his palm. "How could you have got it so wrong?"

"The thing is..."

The DCI held up one hand. "I haven't finished. We have everything set up for tonight. I had to move heaven and earth to get this raid brought forward. The superintendent was very reluctant to waste months of work, just to raid a safe house and bring in a couple of small time runners. He wants the ringleaders. We only brought the raid forward because we need to get this dirty gear off the streets before anyone else dies. And now you are telling me the contaminated heroin isn't even there! Now what am I supposed to do? I'll have to cancel."

This time, Bruce didn't answer. He thought he should let the DCI have his rant first, and let him get it out of his system.

After a few choice expletives and some pacing about the room, DCI Rosser finally seemed to calm down. He flopped down in his chair. "I don't know what to say to you, Bruce. I'm incredibly disappointed."

"It is an unfortunate result, sir."

"Unfortunate? It is a damn sight worse than that. It is a catastrophe, that's what it is."

Bruce licked his lips and took a deep breath. "I think we can still get a good result with this one, sir."

The DCI narrowed his eyes. "Oh? How?"

Bruce took another deep breath. His legs felt like jelly. If JT found out he was double-crossing him, he'd be dead, but the way Bruce saw it, he didn't have another option.

"We've had a tip-off. I know one of the runners from this dealer's crew. I can bring him in. We'll find out where they are storing their stash. I can get you a result, sir. I promise."

CHAPTER SEVENTY-SIX

JT WOKE, GASPING FOR breath. The sheets were wrapped around him, ensnaring his arms. He peeled off the covers, detaching them from his sweat-covered body. He tried to take a deep breath, but his wheezing chest couldn't take it in. He spluttered, then coughed, in deep, hacking bursts that racked his body with pain.

He tried to focus on the feeling of the cool air against his damp skin, and to relax his clenched muscles, forcing himself to release his grip on the sheets. It was so much worse when he panicked.

The doctors had allowed him to come home. They gave him some horrible medication, which had made him vomit on the journey home, and instructed him to return for an outpatient appointment in two days time.

The pain just under his ribs had been so bad, he didn't think he would be able to sleep, but he nodded off eventually. The painkillers probably helped. They were the old-fashioned sort that made you sleepy, thank God. He didn't want any of that new, non-drowsy stuff. He wanted to fall asleep and only wake up when he felt better.

He had fallen asleep long enough to have a terrifying dream. He could feel tendrils of the fungus spreading through his lungs, burying themselves like the roots of trees in his tender flesh, slowly suffocating him.

JT reached out a hand, trying to reach the painkillers on his bedside table. When had he last taken one? Surely it was time to take another? And where was Siobhan? She was supposed to be looking after him.

The painkillers were just slightly out of his reach. He started to sit up, but a shooting pain sliced through his chest, and he collapsed back onto the pillows. The pain made his eyes water. He blinked. Would he ever feel normal again?

"Siobhan... Siobhan." JT tried to shout, but her name came out like a whisper.

Once more, he reached across for the tablets. This time, his fingertips touched the edge of the bottle. Frustrated, his fumbling only made the bottle of tablets slide further away. He grunted with the effort to edge a little closer. He nearly had them. He stretched, grasping for the bottle, but again, it slipped by his fingers. This time, it teetered on the edge of the table.

Annoyed, JT made a last desperate grab for the tablets, which sent the bottle crashing to the floor.

JT groaned in frustration.

The sound brought Siobhan running into the bedroom. "What happened?" she said, putting her hand to her chest. "You gave me such a fright."

JT tried to tell her, tried to explain it was her fault. He was just trying to get his tablets. She shouldn't have left them out of his reach. Even to JT's own ears, the hoarse, wheezing words coming out of his mouth were inaudible.

Siobhan bent down to pick up the tablets. Then she turned the bottle over in her hands.

JT grunted.

"Were you trying to take these?" Siobhan asked, then pursed her lips. She glanced at her watch. "You're not due to take these for another hour. I think I had better put these over here."

She walked across to the far side of the bedroom and put the tablets on the dressing table.

JT slammed his fist down against the mattress, and Siobhan jumped.

"I'm only thinking of you, Justin. If you take too many, you might overdose." She moved closer to the bed and put her hand on his. "I'll make you a nice cup of tea, okay?"

JT turned his head the other way, determined to ignore her. If he didn't know better, he'd think she was enjoying this, the bitch.

Siobhan soon returned, carrying a cup of tea.

JT shook his head.

"Please, Justin," Siobhan said. "You have to drink something. If you don't keep your fluids up, the doctor said you'll have to go back to hospital and have a drip."

JT stared at her for a moment, then tried to push himself into a sitting position. Siobhan moved to support him. At first, he slapped her hands away, but in the end, he had to accept her help. He couldn't do it alone.

Once he was sitting up, Siobhan fussed around him, plumping up his pillow and straightening the sheets.

"Let me... drink... in peace," JT said.

Siobhan sighed and stepped back. She handed him the cup, but she didn't leave the room. She was obviously going to wait to make sure JT finished his drink like a good little boy.

JT scowled. If this was how life would be from now on, he would make sure he bloody overdosed on those painkillers.

CHAPTER SEVENTY-SEVEN

BILLY WAS WALKING TO the safe house. It had been raining all day. He strode through puddles, ignoring the water seeping into his shoes. His mind was focused on more important things.

He passed the newsagents, where he usually picked up his newspaper and had a quick chat, without stopping.

A boy on a bike sped past, purposefully riding through a puddle so water sprayed up and soaked Billy's legs. As the boy rode off laughing, Billy didn't even glance back.

On another day, he might have noticed something was wrong earlier. He might have noticed the twitching curtains or how quiet the street was. But he was so preoccupied that he had turned the corner and was just about to reach the entrance to the flats before he saw it.

He stopped dead.

A police van was parked outside, and he saw police officers, dressed in black, carrying a large cylindrical object.

A battering ram.

Billy blinked.

The rain started to fall more heavily. He pushed his wet hair back from his forehead. He couldn't quite take it in. After all this time, all this planning, it was over.

Billy turned on the spot and began walking away. He zipped up his coat all the way to the chin, shutting out the wind.

It's over.

He did as much as he could in the time he had.

CHAPTER SEVENTY-EIGHT

JT HAD STARTED TO feel a little better. He still felt like he'd been kicked in the ribs by a dozen bucking broncos, but it was a start.

JT reckoned the medication must have kicked in and started killing all that disgusting white stuff growing in his lungs. About time, too. He had never felt so ill in his life.

Siobhan had helped him into the sitting room. He was just glad they lived in a flat; he wasn't sure he could make it downstairs to the bar on his own yet.

JT glanced across at Siobhan, who was sitting in an armchair with her eyes glued to some stupid reality show on TV.

"Turn it down," JT wheezed.

Siobhan turned. For a minute, he thought she might snap at him and remind him that he was the one who turned it on in the first place. But she didn't. She got up, walked across and picked up the remote from the table next to JT's armchair.

JT smirked.

Siobhan pressed the button to lower the volume, and the god awful singing stopped. She took the remote with her and sat back in her armchair.

She'd only just sat down when the phone rang.

With a sigh, she got to her feet and answered the phone.

"Hello... I'm sorry, who?... Are you sure you have the correct number?... I'm afraid he isn't very well..."

"Who is that?" JT asked. A horrible sensation tingled in the pit of his stomach.

Siobhan covered the mouthpiece with her hand. "Someone who wants to speak to you. He said he is your deputy, or the deputy?"

"Give it here," JT said, gesturing wildly.

Siobhan carefully unhooked the lead, so the phone would reach where JT was sitting.

"Hurry up, woman!"

Siobhan handed JT the phone, just as Emily walked into the room.

"Good day at college, love?" Siobhan asked.

Emily flopped down on the sofa. "It was alright." She pointed at the TV. "Can we turn it up?"

Siobhan nodded at JT. "Your dad's on the phone."

JT hissed into the phone. "I thought I told you never to call me at home... My mobile?...Well, I've been in hospital..."

JT was silent, for a moment, clutching the phone to his ear.

"Shit. All right. Don't say anything. I'll get you a brief, a good one, but you had better keep your mouth shut... Just don't tell them anything, or you'll regret it. I promise."

JT put the phone down. He could feel his blood draining away.

"What's wrong, Justin? Who was that?" Siobhan asked.

Emily had rolled over on the sofa and was now looking at JT with interest.

"Go... to your room, Emily," JT said.

"But, Dad..."

"Go!"

As Emily stormed out, Siobhan crossed the room and sat on the arm of JT's chair. She stroked his hair. "What's wrong, love?"

JT put his head in his hands. "It's over Siobhan. I'm finished."

CHAPTER SEVENTY-NINE

MACKINNON WAS TALKING THINGS over with Charlotte, in an empty meeting room at Wood Street station, when he got the call from DI Bruce Evans.

"It's him." Mackinnon said, holding up the phone so Charlotte could see the screen. "I'll put it on speaker."

He put the phone down on his desk and answered the call. "Mackinnon."

"Jack, it's Bruce. I just wanted to keep you in the loop."

"Appreciate it," Mackinnon said.

"The raid went down late this afternoon. Went like clockwork. We recovered a large amount of heroin, not sure of the exact amount yet."

"That's great news."

"Yes. We've got a couple of suspects in custody, people we think were involved in Theroux's operation. One of them is barely more than a kid. He can't be older than fifteen, but he keeps shooting his mouth off. We need to get someone in so he can be interviewed officially, but in the meantime, he has given us loads of information."

Mackinnon frowned and looked up at Charlotte. "Because he's scared?"

"No. It's like he is showing off. Scary really. It's almost like he is proud of it."

"Who is the other suspect?"

"His name is Nathaniel Fletcher. The boy has been referring to him as the deputy. We think he is probably pretty high up in Theroux's command. So far, he's not saying a word."

"And Justin Theroux himself?"

"He is in hospital."

"Oh. Playing the "too-ill-to-be-interviewed" card?"

"Well, he won't get out of it that easily," Bruce said. "I'm heading over there now."

There was a pause, then Bruce said, "Do you want to tag along?"

Mackinnon looked up at Charlotte, who shrugged.

"Sure," Mackinnon said.

"Right. I'll be with you in ten minutes."

They heard the beep as Bruce disconnected the call.

Mackinnon picked up his phone and put it in his pocket. "Well what do you think?" he asked Charlotte.

"I don't know, Jack. He didn't say anything to make me think... I mean, if he was dealing with JT on the side, would he really want you to go with him now?"

Mackinnon didn't have the answer to that.

Bruce was either innocent, or playing a very clever game.

CHAPTER EIGHTY

SIOBHAN SCRAMBLED TO HER feet as the doctor entered JT's hospital room. She had just been dozing off. She hadn't slept at all last night and she was shattered.

"Is he going to be okay?" she asked. "I had to call an ambulance. I was so scared when he collapsed at home."

The doctor, a short man with glasses, piggy eyes and drooping jowls, stepped over to JT's bedside, bent over JT and adjusted his oxygen mask, then glanced over at Siobhan. "He's still sleeping. Has he been sleeping since you brought him in?"

Siobhan nodded. "I thought the medication was working, Doctor. He seemed to be getting better. Then he got a phone call and collapsed right in front of me."

The doctor patted her hand. "It must have been quite terrifying."

"It was horrible. I didn't know how to help him."

The doctor nodded at the seat Siobhan had just vacated. "Please, sit down, and we'll have a chat."

"Okay." Siobhan perched on the edge of the chair.

The doctor didn't speak straight away, and the only sound in the room was JT's rasping breathing. Siobhan shifted in her chair.

"I'll be back in just a moment," the doctor said and pulled the curtain to one side and disappeared through it.

Siobhan frowned. For goodness sake, why couldn't the doctor tell her what was wrong with JT? She stared at JT's prostrate form and tried to block out the horrible sound of his breathing. She couldn't stand this. If that doctor didn't come back soon, she was going to have to go outside.

The doctor reappeared a few seconds later. He carried a chair. "Now, we can both sit down, and I can answer your questions."

Siobhan frowned. He kept her waiting so he could get a chair? How ridiculous.

She clutched her handbag to her stomach. "I would appreciate it if you could tell me what is wrong with my husband."

The doctor bowed his head and said, "Of course. Mr. Theroux has a condition termed 'invasive aspergillosis'."

Siobhan looked at him blankly.

"You've probably never heard of it."

No, thought Siobhan, I haven't. And neither, I suspect, have ninety-nine percent of the population. She folded her arms. What she really wanted to do was reach out and give the doctor a good shake.

The doctor took off his glasses and began to polish them on the sleeve of his white coat.

Siobhan gritted her teeth. God, she wanted to throttle him.

"It's caused by a type of fungus," the doctor said. "In your husband's case, he doesn't seem to be fighting it off. We've looked for reasons why. Typically, this is seen in people who are immuno-compromised somehow. For example, they have some type of cancer, or AIDS, and this weakens their immune system."

Siobhan raised a hand to her mouth, but the doctor was quick to reassure her.

"We have found no evidence of those conditions in your husband, yet your husband does not seem to be fighting off the infection."

The doctor frowned. "I'm afraid his immune system is very weak."

JT coughed and then groaned as he shifted in his sleep.

Siobhan looked down at her hands, then looked the doctor directly in the eye.

"Will he recover?"

The doctor took a deep breath. "In patients with weak immune systems like your husband, there is a chance the fungus could migrate from the lungs."

Siobhan bit her lower lip, then said, "Please, doctor, I want the truth."

The doctor looked at JT, then shifted his gaze back to Siobhan. "If the fungus does migrate from the lungs, into the bloodstream, it could reach the brain," he said. "In which case, it could be fatal."

CHAPTER EIGHTY-ONE

MACKINNON AND DI BRUCE Evans had to wait an hour before they were permitted to question Justin Theroux, and even then, the doctors only very reluctantly gave them access.

Bruce entered the cubicle first, and Mackinnon paused behind the curtain.

"You have to help me," a croaky voice said. "You need to..."

Mackinnon pushed back the curtain, and the man in the bed stopped talking and raised the oxygen mask to his face.

Justin Theroux looked ill. If he was faking, he could have earned an Oscar. His face was pale, the skin around his eyes looked bruised and swollen, and with every breath he took, he made a crackling sound.

Sitting at Theroux's bedside was a middle-aged, red-headed woman Mackinnon guessed to be his wife. She glared at Mackinnon and DI Evans with open hostility.

"What do you want? Can't you see he is ill?" she snapped.

Bruce stepped forward to take charge. "I'm Detective Inspector Bruce Evans and this is my colleague, Detective Sergeant Jack Mackinnon."

Justin Theroux regarded Mackinnon with wary eyes.

"Can this not wait?" the redhead asked.

Bruce turned his attention to her. "And you would be? Siobhan Theroux? Justin's wife?"

Siobhan nodded.

"I'm afraid it can't wait, Mrs. Theroux," Bruce said. "We are investigating the poison your husband has been selling."

Siobhan looked at JT, who lowered his oxygen mask. "I don't know anything about it."

Bruce nodded at Mackinnon, who took his cue. "Putting the drug-dealing aside for a moment, what we really want to focus on are the murders."

Justin Theroux's eyes darted to Bruce, then back to Mackinnon. "Murders? I'm not involved in any murders."

"We're pretty sure the drugs you were dealing were spiked with a lethal substance," Mackinnon said. "Deliberately."

"Spiked?"

Bruce smiled. "Come on, Justin. They're your drugs. Are you trying to tell us you knew nothing about it?"

"Spiked?" JT repeated again and blinked rapidly. "No, listen to me, that's nothing to do with me. If the drugs were bad, then that's down to whoever supplied them."

"I'm afraid not, Justin," Mackinnon said.

"Of course it is. Why would I do that?" He shook his head. "I mean, just say, hypothetically, I was a dealer. Why would I ruin my own stuff? It would be bad for business." He looked up at Mackinnon. "Wouldn't it?"

Mackinnon shook his head slowly. "The drugs you supply

are from the same batch of heroin as at least four other dealers in the City area and none of their drugs are spiked, Justin. None of them. Only yours."

JT coughed then sucked in a breath. "No... that can't be right." He looked at Siobhan, who placed her hand on his arm.

"Unless..." JT turned slowly away from her. "Unless it was that crazy brother-in-law of mine...Yeah, it sounds like something he would do." JT broke off, panting. "That's who you want to speak to, Billy Donnelly, that stupid bastard..."

Siobhan stood up and replaced the oxygen mask over JT's mouth, muffling his words. "Don't be ridiculous, Justin," she said, swatting away his hands as he tried to remove the mask again.

She turned to Mackinnon and Bruce. "You're upsetting him. Can't you see he is having trouble breathing?" She tightened the straps on the oxygen mask to keep it in place. "He has to wear this mask so he gets enough oxygen. It's not a fashion accessory."

After they finished talking to Justin Theroux, Mackinnon and Bruce Evans stood in a brightly lit hospital corridor and talked things through. Bruce was confident they could track down Theroux's brother-in-law, Billy Donnelly.

"Shouldn't be too hard. I'll get the team on straight away," Bruce said.

"Right."

"It's a good result, Jack. We've got that dirty brown off the streets," Bruce said, misinterpreting Mackinnon's stony response. "I know you're disappointed that we haven't found out who was spiking the stuff. But remember, it may have been accidental."

"You said yourself, the other samples were clean."

"Yeah, and from the lab analysis it looked like most of the samples we collected came from the same batch originally," Bruce said. "I know it was only Theroux's sample that was contaminated with warfarin, but it could have been accidental. Maybe this Billy Donnelly messed up. Maybe he was surprised more than anybody when it turned out that the bulking agent he used did a lot more than just bulk out the drug."

"Maybe."

Mackinnon was so close to asking Bruce what was going on, asking him straight out if he was in Justin Theroux's pocket.

But he didn't do it. He kept thinking about what Charlotte said, that he should wait until he had proof. A feeling wasn't enough.

After Bruce headed back to his East London station, Mackinnon went in search of Dr. Anna Sorensen. He felt she deserved an update.

Mackinnon took the lift down to the basement, his mind running over and over everything Bruce had said. He shifted to the side, as a group of people entered the lift on the second floor. One of the women was crying, and had a soggy tissue screwed up in one hand. She made him think of Jessica's parents and what they must be going through.

Anna met him by the vending machines in the corner of the waiting room near the ICU.

"How are your wife and daughter doing?"

Mackinnon didn't bother to correct her. "They are still a bit shaken up. How are Terry Dobbs and Natasha Green?"

"Hanging in there," Anna said, moving across to the vending machine and feeding it a pound coin. "He is still in ICU, but his blood work is looking good. We had a few worrying hours when he needed surgery for a burst ulcer, but I think he is past the worst of it now. She is out of ICU and in Jenner ward. She is still under observation, but I think she is going to be okay."

"And Michelle, Terry's girlfriend?"

"Fine," Anna said. "She hasn't shown any symptoms at all, even though she and Terry both used the same source of heroin."

Anna punched numbers into the digital pad of the vending machine, and a muesli bar dropped down the chute. "It's the nature of the coagulation pathway," she said. "It is such a delicate balance, usually correcting itself, but if it is tipped too far one way..." Anna shrugged. "Everyone is different. Some people are more susceptible to bleeding, some have a greater tendency to get blood clots."

Anna gestured at the vending machine. "Can I get you anything?"

"No," Mackinnon said. "I'm fine. I actually wanted to give you some good news."

"Oh?"

"DI Evans' team has discovered the stash of contaminated heroin during a raid on a flat in the Towers Estate. The investigation is still ongoing, but I hope there won't be any more of these bleeding cases."

Anna smiled. "I hope you are right. Do you think you've got all of it?"

"We think we have the main stash, but there might still be a small amount knocking about with the runners. But runners won't carry much on them."

Anna unwrapped her muesli bar and took a bite. "Do you know how the warfarin ended up in the heroin? Was it accidental?"

That was the question Mackinnon wanted the answer to. "We are still looking into it," he said.

CHAPTER EIGHTY-TWO

MACKINNON KEPT REPLAYING THE scene over and over in his mind. Why had Justin Theroux stopped talking to Bruce so abruptly when he saw Mackinnon?

Then there were the looks Theroux kept directing at Bruce, like he was trying to communicate something.

When Mackinnon tried to explain it to Charlotte, he just ended up sounding like he was paranoid. But there was something going on, Mackinnon knew it. He wasn't crazy. Bruce was hiding something.

Mackinnon tapped some details into the computer, and came up with nothing. He stared down at the printout in front of him.

Bruce's team had dug up information on Justin Theroux's brother-in-law easily enough. Billy Donnelly, fifty-two years old, had served five years in the Royal Engineers, then went through a series of unskilled jobs, until he had disappeared from the system entirely ten years ago.

Of course, Siobhan insisted she had no idea where her brother was. A likely story.

Mackinnon entered a different combination of words into the system. No record. It was like he had just vanished.

Mackinnon clicked the mouse and brought up a web browser. When in doubt, he thought, Google it.

He didn't want to narrow the search down too much. He might miss something. So he typed in "Billy + Donnelly + 2001," the year Billy had vanished.

Over a million results. Great.

He needed coffee.

The canteen was closed, so he had to settle for the vending machine stuff. He had just taken his first sip and was walking back through the incident room, when DI Tyler walked in from the other end.

"I hear you've been having an interesting time with Bruce, Mackinnon."

Mackinnon nodded. "Yeah, hopefully the contaminated stuff is off the streets for good now. We just..."

"Oh, I know," Tyler said. "Bruce told me. I've just been filling the superintendent in on our progress. He's very pleased."

Our progress?

"Oh, don't look like that, Jack. I told the super what a good job you've been doing. Watch out. You're spilling it." Tyler pointed at Mackinnon's plastic cup of coffee.

Mackinnon relaxed his grip. "You're heading off home, then? Goodnight," Mackinnon said. "Don't let me keep you."

Tyler chuckled. "There's no point staying late to impress Superintendent Wright. He's already gone home."

Mackinnon turned back to his computer and started to scroll through the results.

"Suit yourself," Tyler said. "See you tomorrow."

Mackinnon looked at his first page of results: an optician in Kansas, a few dozen Linked-in pages and a few Facebook pages. Not much to go on. He hoped Bruce and his team were having better luck.

Two hours later, when he was almost ready to throw in the towel and head home, he saw it. A newspaper article from 2001. He clicked on the link, then swore.

On the screen was a message: *The page you are trying to reach requires a paid subscription. Please log in to access this page.*

Mackinnon reached into his pocket and pulled out his wallet. If it got him answers, he'd pay.

He typed in his credit card details, and opened the article.

He leaned close to the screen, skimmed the text, then smiled.

This was the Billy Donnelly they were after. Mackinnon was sure of it.

CHAPTER EIGHTY-THREE

MACKINNON CALLED BRUCE AS soon as he finished reading the article, and Bruce invited Mackinnon to his house to discuss it.

Mackinnon pulled out the printed article as he walked up the steps to Bruce's front door. He lived in a three-storey Victorian townhouse in Twickenham, which must have cost a packet. The lights were on in the rooms downstairs, and he could hear a child laughing.

A woman answered the door. "Jack?"

"Yes. Hello, is Bruce about?"

The woman opened the door wider. "Come in. I'm Fiona, Bruce's wife."

Mackinnon stepped into the hallway.

Fiona bent down to pick up a soft toy from the floor. "Welcome to the madhouse," she said and rolled her eyes. "Bruce has just popped out to take one of our daughter's friends home. It's only five minutes away, so he won't be long."

Fiona started to walk down the hallway. "You're welcome

to wait for him in the living room, or you can keep me company in the kitchen while I make the kids' dinner."

"I'll keep you company," Mackinnon said and followed Fiona down the hall to the kitchen. The kitchen was large. It looked like two rooms had been knocked into one. A breakfast bar stood in the centre of the room and a dining table sat against the wall.

A boy in a wheelchair sat next to the breakfast bar.

Fiona walked up to the boy and put her hand on his shoulder. "This is Luke, our eldest."

"Hi Luke," Mackinnon said.

Luke rolled his head back against the headrest and flung out one of his arms.

Fiona smiled. "Can I get you tea? Or would you like something stronger?"

"Tea would be lovely, thanks."

Luke seemed to have inherited his looks from his mother, dark hair, low hairline, plump lips, but his eyes looked liked Bruce's. Wide, blue, expressive eyes.

Mackinnon turned as he heard the front door close.

Bruce walked into the kitchen, apologising. "I thought I would be back before you got here. Sorry."

"I'll take Jack in the front room, honey. We've just got a bit of work stuff to talk about. It won't take long."

"Okay. Would you like to stay to dinner, Jack?" Fiona asked, handing Mackinnon a cup of tea.

Bruce answered for him. "Oh no, we'll be done in five minutes." Bruce led Mackinnon out of the kitchen. "So what have you got?"

Mackinnon handed Bruce the printout of the article, and waited for him to read it.

While Bruce read, Mackinnon was thinking about Luke,

about how much it would cost to buy a new wheelchair, or a specially adapted car. He tried to bury the thoughts. It didn't mean anything. They probably got financial support from the health authority for things like that.

Bruce looked up from the article. "So now we know why he did it."

Mackinnon nodded. "His daughter was killed during a robbery and the perpetrators went unpunished, so Billy decides to deal out justice on his own."

Bruce sighed. "It looks like Billy Donnelly is our man. But how the hell do we find him?"

CHAPTER EIGHTY-FOUR

BRUCE AND MACKINNON MULLED things over for a while, but they didn't come up with any answers. Bruce said he'd get the team on it first thing in the morning, so Mackinnon decided to call it a night. On his way back to the car, he called Chloe. When she answered, her voice was thick with sleep.

"Sorry," Mackinnon said. "Did I wake you?"

"I fell asleep on the sofa. What time is it?"

"Eight thirty. How are you?"

"Okay, I guess. It's just been a hell of a day."

"How's Sarah doing now?"

"A little better. She's been a bit clingy this afternoon, but she's sleeping now. It's horrible that it takes something like this to realise..." Chloe sighed. "It's just such a bloody waste."

"I'm leaving London now. I'll be there..."

"No don't, Jack. Stay at Derek's tonight. It's silly you coming all the way back here, when you'll have to be up at the crack of dawn to go back to work tomorrow."

"Are you sure? I didn't want you to be on your own tonight."

"I'm not on my own, the girls are here, and to be honest, I'm done in. I'm going to head up to bed now anyway."

"Are you really okay? You're not just saying that?"

"I'm really okay, Jack. I'll see you tomorrow night."

* * *

Mackinnon got to Derek's flat just after nine. A delicious scent of beef stew hit Mackinnon as he entered the flat.

Derek, wearing a Hawaiian shirt and old faded jeans, stood in front of the cooker, stirring the contents of a saucepan.

"That smells amazing," Mackinnon said, his mouth watering. "When did you learn to cook? I thought you were strictly a beans on toast and takeaway man?"

"Don't get any ideas," Derek said. "It's for the dog."

"You're cooking that for Molly?"

Derek turned back to his saucepan to give it another stir. "She's got a delicate digestion. She likes her meat cooked well."

Mackinnon's disappointment must have been clearly stamped on his face. Derek took pity on him. "If you're hungry, there is a ready-meal lasagne in the freezer."

"Cheers." Mackinnon shuffled items around in the freezer, found the frozen lasagne and started to unwrap it.

"Bad day?" Derek asked, and switched the oven on.

"Not the best."

"Grab a beer from the fridge, I'm a good listener."

Mackinnon got two bottles of beer from the fridge and put one on the counter for Derek. "It's just work stuff. I feel like I'm going around in circles."

Derek crossed the kitchen, opened a low cupboard and pulled out an amber bottle. "We'll crack this open tonight. Things always seem better after a dram."

They ate the lasagne on their laps and watched TV. Molly stuck to Mackinnon's side like glue again.

"After I slaved away over a hot stove, she just wants some of your lasagne," Derek said. "I don't believe it."

Mackinnon grinned. "It's nothing to do with your cooking." He held up a tumbler of scotch. "She just prefers to sit next to me."

The rest of the night passed in a bit of a blur, with Derek putting the world to rights. He informed Mackinnon that all estate agents were evil, and men like Nicolas Sarkozy, wearing stacked shoes was just wrong; they were heels, no matter which way you looked at it.

They spent a while debating which was the better album: Queen's "News of The World," or Bowie's "The Rise and Fall of Ziggy Stardust and the Spiders from Mars." Mackinnon backed Queen, and ignored Derek's argument that Bowie was the "most awesomest thing" ever.

They put on an old Dr. Hook album and laughed like school kids over the lyrics of "Everybody's Making It Big, But Me."

They finally stumbled to their respective bedrooms at two am, with Mackinnon swearing loudly when he stubbed his toe on one of the boxes of irons.

"I'll get rid of them tomorrow," Derek mumbled. "Tomorrow."

CHAPTER EIGHTY-FIVE

THE FOLLOWING MORNING, MACKINNON was woken by his mobile. He looked at his watch: seven thirty. Damn, why did he let Derek talk him into the whisky last night? He had wanted to get to work early this morning.

He pressed the green button on his mobile. "Mackinnon."

"Jack, it's Bruce. We've got the results back from the lab. I thought you would want to know as soon as possible."

"Yeah, thanks." Mackinnon rubbed the sleep from his eyes and tried to focus.

"The drug seized from Theroux's safe house contained extremely high levels of warfarin," Bruce said. "It has been confirmed by the reference lab."

Mackinnon flung back the bed covers. "Could the warfarin have been added higher up the supply chain? Could there be more of this dirty stuff out there?"

"I think we have it all. I can't be one hundred percent positive, but according to the samples we received from various sources in the area, no other dealer appears to have a supply contaminated with warfarin."

"So you still believe that the contamination occurred after the heroin got into JT's safe house?"

"Yes. The composition of the heroin is similar to that from a couple of other dealers, but their heroin contains no trace of warfarin."

"Right," Mackinnon said. "So Billy Donnelly is still our guy. We need to find him."

"Yes. I've got my team working on it," Bruce said. "Don't worry, we'll track him down."

Mackinnon disconnected the call, and left Derek's spare room in search of coffee.

"Oh lovely! Exactly what I don't want to see when I've got a hangover," Derek said, grimacing.

"What?" Mackinnon said, yawning.

"You, walking around in your boxers. Can't you put a dressing gown on?"

"Don't have one." Mackinnon said and nodded at the coffee pot. "I'll have what you're having."

Derek shuffled over and grabbed a mug from the cupboard above the sink. "I feel bloody awful. Whose idea was the whisky?"

"It was your idea." Mackinnon squinted. "I never noticed how bright it was in here. This place is a sun trap in the morning."

Derek grunted, poured Mackinnon's coffee, then handed it to him. "You want some headache tablets with that?"

"Please."

Mackinnon gratefully accepted the paracetamol, and ten minutes later, after a shower, he began to feel human again. Ten minutes after that, he was on his way to the station.

He rang Chloe as he walked to the underground station. She told him Sarah was doing okay, considering everything that had happened. Mackinnon promised to be home by seven so they could all have dinner together.

He disconnected the call, thinking about Jessica's family and how devastated they must be. She was their only child. What would they do now? How would they get past it? They would be starting to think about the funeral. He hoped Jessica's body would be released quickly for burial, so her parents could say their goodbyes. He'd mention it to DI Bruce Evans.

He stopped walking.

Jessica's parents would want to say goodbye. Of course, why hadn't he thought of that before? Billy Donnelly would want to say goodbye to his daughter, too.

CHAPTER EIGHTY-SIX

MACKINNON GOT OFF THE underground at Bank, but instead of heading for Wood Street station, he turned right, walking toward the bar Justin Theroux owned, The Junction.

He could have searched for the information he needed at the station, but he wanted an answer quickly, and he was pretty sure that Siobhan could provide it.

When he arrived, the bar was still closed. It was only just after eight am, after all.

The shutters were down, so Mackinnon couldn't look through the windows. He rang the doorbell and waited.

No answer.

He stepped back from the doorway, into the street, and looked up at the windows. He couldn't see any lights on. Siobhan might have stayed at the hospital with her husband. He decided to try once more and hammered on the door.

A light came on upstairs, and thirty seconds later, the door opened a crack. The safety chain was still on. A pair of brown eyes appeared, the rest of the face was in shadow.

"What do you want?"

Mackinnon moved closer and saw a teenage girl with dark hair, gripping the door. She looked on edge, ready to bolt at any minute.

"I'm DS Mackinnon, City of London Police." He held up his ID, and she looked at it, then shrugged.

"I'd like to speak to Siobhan Theroux."

The girl stepped back from the door but didn't release the safety chain. "Mum," she shouted. "There's a police officer down here. He wants to speak to you." She wandered off, leaving the door open just a crack.

Siobhan took her time, but eventually, she appeared, wearing jeans and a huge, cream jumper that was several sizes too big for her. Mackinnon wondered if it was her husband's and if she was wearing it for comfort. She pushed back her frizzy red hair from her face.

"What is it?" she asked. "Has something happened to Justin?"

She undid the safety chain and opened the door.

"It's not about Justin. I wanted to ask you where your niece was buried."

Siobhan's eyes widened, then filled with tears. "Oh."

She blinked rapidly, then reached for her coat, which was hanging on a stand next to the door. "I'll take you there. It's not far. A ten-minute walk."

At first, they walked in silence. The back streets were still quiet, but they could hear the rumble of traffic from the main road.

"How is Mr. Theroux?" Mackinnon asked. "Is he feeling

any better today?"

Siobhan kept her head down, looking at the pavement. "No, I don't think he is."

They reached the cemetery gates, and Siobhan stopped. "I know why you wanted to come here. You think he'll come here, don't you?"

Mackinnon nodded. "I think he might."

Siobhan sighed. "You might get lucky. But it's still early."

They walked through the cemetery gates and along a paved walkway. Mist and fine rain hung in the air. The sun was trying to break through and shimmered on the wet ground. The noise of the traffic seemed to die away, and a blackbird darted across the path in front of them.

"She was buried over here," Siobhan said, pointing to the left. "It's an old family plot."

As they got closer, Mackinnon could see a figure standing by one of the graves. Was it him? He squinted through the misty rain. It looked like a man.

Mackinnon turned to Siobhan to gauge her reaction. Her jaw was tightly set, like she was clenching her teeth.

A middle-aged man, with reddish blond hair, wearing a leather jacket and dark blue jeans, stood beside a line of small marble headstones. On the ground in front of him, were delicate yellow flowers.

Siobhan walked right up to him, before he noticed her. She put a hand on his shoulder. "Billy, love, it's time."

The man looked up and smiled at his sister, then turned to face Mackinnon. "Police, are you?"

Mackinnon showed Billy Donnelly his ID.

Billy nodded. "Well, that's it then. I've done as much as I could."

Billy Donnelly looked like a broken man. His hand shook

as he ran it through his hair. His jeans were soaked. He had been here a while. Mackinnon wondered if he had been here all night.

He looked like he couldn't hurt a fly.

Mackinnon began to read Billy his rights.

"Is that really necessary?" Siobhan snapped.

Billy touched his sister's cheek. "It's all right, Siobhan."

Siobhan gave a muffled sob and turned away. She bent down and ran a hand over her niece's smooth, white headstone.

As they were about to leave, Billy turned and nodded at the yellow flowers on the ground. "Can you finish off for me?"

Siobhan began to pick up the flowers and put them into the tiny vase beside the headstone. "Of course, I will." She wiped away her tears. "Don't you worry."

CHAPTER EIGHTY-SEVEN

MACKINNON BROUGHT BILLY TO Wood Street station. It would probably piss off DI Bruce Evans and his DCI, but Mackinnon couldn't care less. He would let Detective Superintendent Bob Wright deal with the politics. Mackinnon just wanted answers.

While Billy Donnelly was being processed, Mackinnon headed upstairs to update the superintendent and let him know he might have to deal with an irate DCI from the Met soon.

Mackinnon supposed he should tell DI Tyler too, although he would have preferred to keep him out of it as much as possible.

Unfortunately, Tyler was the first person he ran into as he passed through the incident room on his way to the superintendent's office.

"All right, Mackinnon?" Tyler said, then gave a large yawn.

"I've just brought in Billy Donnelly." Mackinnon carried on walking.

Tyler seemed to wake up suddenly. "The suspect in the contaminated heroin case?"

"Yes, I'm going to see the super now."

Tyler scurried after him. "I'm coming too."

Mackinnon knew Tyler just wanted to share the glory, but Mackinnon didn't care. He wanted answers before Bruce heard about this. He still wasn't sure where he stood with DI Bruce Evans.

* * *

But the news travelled fast.

DI Tyler was still planning the interview strategy when Bruce Evans arrived at Wood Street station. Smiling, he shook everyone's hand in turn, coming to Mackinnon last.

"I hope I'm not late, Jack. I got here as fast as I could."

Before Mackinnon could answer, DI Tyler called Bruce over. "Bruce come and have a look at these interview questions. Tell us what you think."

Mackinnon was left fuming while Tyler, Superintendent Wright and Bruce decided on the appropriate questions and the direction Billy Donnelly's interview should take.

He expected Tyler to fall for Bruce's act, but he thought Superintendent Wright would see through it. Bob Wright was an intelligent man, surely he'd notice something wasn't quite right with Bruce?

Mackinnon should have gone to the superintendent with his suspicions about Bruce straight away. He'd left it too long.

* * *

DI Tyler and DI Bruce Evans interviewed Billy Donnelly.

Mackinnon had to settle for watching the action from the viewing room.

He stared through the mirrored glass at Billy.

Could this middle-aged man really be responsible for murder?

Billy licked his lips and reached for his plastic cup of water. He wasn't talking.

Tyler and Bruce rephrased their questions time and time again, but Billy didn't bite. He stared up at the clock.

Bruce leaned forward. "Stop wasting our time. We know exactly what you did, and why you did it. You're finished, Billy. It's over. So you may as well start talking."

Billy blinked. Then gave a little smile and nodded. "You're right, officer. I'm finished. But it's not over, not by a long way."

Billy's words hit Mackinnon like a bolt of electricity.

Mackinnon found Charlotte at her desk, swearing at her computer. "Bloody thing. It keeps saying it needs to shut down every time I try to save a document. It hates me."

"Can you come with me now?" Mackinnon asked.

Charlotte looked up. "Why? Where are we going?"

"I hope I'm wrong about this, but Billy just said something in his interview that has me worried. I'll explain on the way."

Charlotte grabbed her coat and followed Mackinnon out into the corridor. "So where are we going?"

"To The Junction," Mackinnon said. "We can call the super from the car and tell him that Billy said it isn't over, and I think they're planning their next victim."

"Whose they?"

"Billy and Siobhan."

CHAPTER EIGHTY-EIGHT

SIOBHAN HELPED JT OUT of the taxi. She struggled under his bulk. Although he had lost weight since falling ill, he was still a big man. She felt his hands trembling as he gripped her arm.

"Let's get you inside, Justin. You can have a nice rest, and I'll fix you some dinner."

JT nodded listlessly.

They took tiny steps towards the door of The Junction. "Do you think you can make the stairs? I could make up a bed for you in your office downstairs."

JT shook his head. "I can do the stairs."

It took them more than five minutes, with JT stopping on every other step to catch his breath, but they made it up the stairs. Siobhan settled JT in his armchair, wrapped a blanket around his knees and switched on the television.

She put the TV remote on the arm of the chair. "I'll just go and make you something to eat, all right love?"

JT stared straight ahead at the TV.

Siobhan went to the kitchen and took a casserole out of the fridge. Her friend, Margie, had brought it round this morning. She knew how bad things were with Justin. Siobhan spooned some of the casserole into a bowl and put it in the microwave to heat through.

As the dinner heated, Siobhan opened the cupboard under the sink.

It was the perfect hiding place.

No one else ever washed up, so no one else would find them.

She pulled out the bright yellow rubber gloves and put her hand inside one, feeling around. Her fingers closed around a capsule, and she pulled it out. There weren't many left now, but that didn't matter. She wouldn't need many more.

The microwave pinged, and Siobhan took out the bowl of casserole. She reached for the capsule and carefully pulled the two halves apart. She sprinkled the white powder all over JT's dinner.

She gave the casserole a quick stir, then put the bowl on a tray and carried it through to Justin.

"Justin, dinner's ready."

CHAPTER EIGHTY-NINE

FIVE MINUTES LATER, MACKINNON and Charlotte arrived at The Junction. Siobhan let them in.

"Where is he?"

"You mean Justin? He's upstairs."

"Can we see him?"

Siobhan stepped back and gestured for them to enter. "Be my guest."

Siobhan led the way through the bar, which smelt of stale beer. The floor was sticky underfoot. Siobhan stopped at the foot of the stairs. She looked like she might be about to say something, but then appeared to change her mind and started to climb the steps.

She opened the door to a living area. JT sat in a black leather armchair. He looked like an old man. He had a tartan-patterned blanket tucked around his legs, and he hunched over a tray of food on his lap.

"Don't eat that," Mackinnon said.

"What?" Justin Theroux looked at his fork, mystified.

"What the hell are you lot doing here? I'm too ill for your questions."

But Siobhan knew what Mackinnon meant.

She clapped her hands. "Very good, detective, but you're too late."

"Too late for what?" Justin looked at Siobhan and coughed. "What the hell are you talking about?"

Siobhan ignored her husband and focused on Mackinnon. "He's been taking it for months. How can I put this? He's past the point of no return," she said, cheeks flushed, eyes shining.

Justin dropped his fork, and it clattered down to the tray. "What? What have you done?"

Siobhan faced her husband, and smiled.

"You bitch," JT screamed. "It's you! You have been making me ill."

Justin flipped the tray out of his lap and lunged to grab his wife's arm. But he was weak and unsteady on his feet. Siobhan just stepped out of his reach, and Justin stumbled, falling head first onto the floor.

Siobhan looked delighted and jabbed him in the ribs with her foot.

Charlotte ushered Siobhan out of the room, and Mackinnon tried to lift Justin Theroux back into his armchair.

"Hold on to my arm, Mr. Theroux, that's right," Mackinnon said, putting his hands under Justin's armpits, ready to lift him.

Justin flung his head back. "Did you hear that? I want the bitch arrested. She tried to kill me."

Being so close to Justin, Mackinnon could see the scabs on his face, and what looked like green fuzz growing along his jaw line. It was hideous. Mackinnon suppressed a shudder.

Mackinnon left Justin wheezing in his chair and went to find Siobhan and Charlotte.

He saw them in the kitchen. Siobhan had calmed down enough for Mackinnon to take a moment to call the superintendent. Mackinnon filled him in, telling him they needed a team sent down to search the house for the drugs Siobhan had used on her husband.

In the kitchen, Siobhan and Charlotte sat at the table. Siobhan was talking. They both looked up as Mackinnon entered, but Mackinnon didn't say a word. He wanted Siobhan to keep talking. He took a seat on the opposite side of the table.

"It all seemed so right," Siobhan said. "Like poetic justice."

"What was poetic justice, Siobhan?" Charlotte asked.

"I think your colleague has guessed by now," Siobhan said, nodding at Mackinnon.

Siobhan started chewing her nails, then looked up again. "I didn't think it would work, but it did, much better than I'd hoped."

Siobhan locked eyes with Mackinnon and she leaned towards him. "Justin's drugs killed her, and now her drugs have killed him."

Charlotte raised her eyebrows and looked at Mackinnon for help. "Her drugs?"

"Grace Donnelly," Mackinnon said quietly. "Billy Donnelly's daughter and Siobhan's niece. Grace had cystic fibrosis, and she had a heart and lung transplant, which meant she had to take immuno-suppressants." He turned back to Siobhan. "Have you been giving your husband Grace's old tablets?"

"Oh, no," Siobhan said, shaking her head.

"No?" Mackinnon frowned. He had been so sure.

"No. There weren't enough of Grace's tablets left, and we needed a very high dose to have the effect we wanted."

"So where did you get the drugs?"

"Ordered them over the internet," Siobhan said, as if it was the most obvious thing in the world.

"I suppose that is where you and Billy got hold of the warfarin, as well?"

Siobhan nodded. "Rat poison."

Was there anything you couldn't buy on the internet? Mackinnon and Charlotte were both speechless for a moment.

Mackinnon looked around the kitchen, then remembering the teenage girl who opened the door to him earlier, he asked, "Where is your daughter?"

Siobhan pushed back the arms of her shirt. "She's staying at a friend's."

"What's that?" Charlotte said, reaching for Siobhan's arm.

Mackinnon just caught sight of a large, yellowing bruise before Siobhan yanked her sleeve down to cover it.

"Does your husband hit you?" Charlotte asked.

Siobhan laughed, a bitter humourless laugh. "Do you think I should say it was self-defence?" She gritted her teeth, put her face right up to Charlotte's and said, "Yes, the bastard hit me, but in the end, I won."

CHAPTER NINETY

LATER THAT AFTERNOON, MACKINNON sat at his desk and tried to call Dr. Anna Sorensen. Justin Theroux's poisoning had been reported through official channels, but he felt he owed it to Anna to tell her the details personally. She didn't answer, so he left a message on her voice mail and hung up.

He sat back in his chair and looked down at the paperwork in front of him. He didn't even know who had to file the different reports, the City or the Met. In all probability, both forces would end up filing their own.

He circled his neck, trying to release the tension. It had been a hell of a day, but a good result in the end.

The phone on his desk rang. It was Anna. He told her that a suspect had been arrested.

Her relief was obvious from the tone of her voice.

"Oh, thank God," Anna said. "I can't see what would drive anyone to do something like that, to want to poison so many people."

She told Mackinnon that rumours were circulating around the hospital staff, people were saying that the drug dealer responsible was a man they were treating for multiple infections after his wife had poisoned him with immuno-suppressants.

"News travels fast," Mackinnon said.

Mackinnon told her that Justin Theroux's wife had been arrested for attempted murder.

"He's been admitted to the isolation ward," Anna said. "But it doesn't look good."

"But if you know which drugs his wife was poisoning him with, won't you be able to treat him?" Mackinnon was looking forward to seeing Justin Theroux in handcuffs and sent to prison for a very long time.

"I'm not so sure," Anna said. "The immune system is a tricky thing. He might recover, but..."

"He might die?"

"It's a possibility."

* * *

Mackinnon had just started on the first of the reports when he felt a hand on his shoulder. He spun around on his chair. It was Bruce.

"Got a minute?"

Mackinnon put the lid back on his pen and stood up. "Sure. Do you want to get a coffee?"

Bruce nodded. He looked less slick than usual, his toothy smile didn't make an appearance.

"So," Mackinnon said as they started to walk down the corridor to the canteen. "We got a good result in the end."

Bruce cocked his head to the side, then nodded. "We did. In the end."

They walked in silence until they reached the canteen. Mackinnon opened the door, letting Bruce enter first.

"Drugging her own husband," Bruce said. "I didn't see that one coming."

"No," Mackinnon said, heading over to the serving area.

"But you did, though."

"Sorry?"

"You did see it coming, Jack. And you chose to keep me in the dark."

Mackinnon turned to face Bruce, whose face was flushed with anger. "First: going solo to bring in Billy Donnelly; then to The Junction to confront Siobhan. What's the matter with you?"

There were only four other people in the canteen, but they all turned as Bruce raised his voice. "It was my case. I kept..." Bruce prodded his finger into Mackinnon's chest, "...you in the loop. And you didn't have the decency to extend me the same courtesy."

Mackinnon took a breath, pausing to keep his temper in check. Bruce had a point. Mackinnon hadn't wanted to keep him involved because he didn't trust him.

"Okay, you're right. I should have kept you informed."

"So why didn't you?" Bruce said, opening his arms wide. "Why the hell didn't you?"

"Because I didn't think you could be trusted."

Bruce paled. Mackinnon had done it now. He couldn't take it back. He had to explain.

"All that stuff, getting the samples mixed up. Theroux asking you for help, before he saw me behind you at the hospital."

Bruce's eyes narrowed and he stepped forward, crowding Mackinnon. "What are you saying, Jack?"

Mackinnon stared back at him. "Are you taking bribes?"

Bruce moved so quickly, Mackinnon didn't have much chance to respond. He managed to take half a step back, before Bruce took a swing at him. Bruce's fist grazed Mackinnon's jaw, knocking his head to one side.

Mackinnon turned back to face Bruce, furious. Bruce was coming back for more, but there was no way Mackinnon was going to let him have another shot.

"Jack!" DC Collins shouted from the other side of the canteen.

It was enough to bring Mackinnon to his senses. He moved away from Bruce, and with great effort turned and walked out of the canteen.

It took every last drop of his will power to walk away.

CHAPTER NINETY-ONE

IT TOOK ALL OF twenty minutes for Charlotte to appear at Mackinnon's desk.

"I take it you've heard then?" Mackinnon said.

"Of course, I've heard. Everyone's talking about it. You know what this place is like. What happened?"

Mackinnon held his hands up. "I know. You told me not to."

"You told Bruce you thought he was bent?" Charlotte crossed her arms. "Great. How to win friends and influence people, eh?"

"I had to do it. I had to get it off my chest," Mackinnon said. "Besides it was better this way, better than sneaking off and reporting my suspicions behind his back."

"Was it?"

"Look, Charlotte. I don't have the energy for this. I'm going home. I'm going to spend a nice evening with Chloe and the girls and try to forget all about this stuff with Bruce Evans."

Charlotte nodded. "All right. I'll shelve the lecture. I'm just worried that–"

"Yeah, I know, but don't worry. It's done now. I can't take back what I said. I'll see you on Monday, okay?"

Mackinnon could feel Charlotte's eyes on his back as he left the incident room.

* * *

Luckily, the evening improved. When he arrived at Chloe's house, he could smell dinner. After spending most of the week eating takeaways, the garlic bread and pasta smelled divine. After a few glasses of red wine and dinner with Chloe and the girls, he felt himself begin to relax.

Sarah was subdued, but stayed at the table to eat dinner with them, and even helped Katy with her English homework. After dinner, the girls went to their rooms, and apart from the thumping base from Sarah's music, it was peaceful.

Mackinnon put his arm around Chloe as they watched some rom-com DVD that Katy had borrowed from one of her friends. Mackinnon didn't think much of it, and apparently neither did Chloe as within five minutes of the start, she was fast asleep, leaning on Mackinnon's shoulder.

When the clock chimed eleven pm, Mackinnon decided to wake Chloe.

"Time for bed, sleepy."

Chloe sat up and looked at the blank TV screen. "Oh. Has it finished?"

Mackinnon smiled, nodded and held out his hand.

Chloe stood up and linked her arms around his neck. "I missed you, Jack."

He kissed her forehead and said, "I missed you, too. It's good to be home."

* * *

Mackinnon had only been asleep for a few minutes when he was woken by the sound of his mobile phone. He fumbled for it in the dark, anxious to mute the ringing before it woke Chloe.

He pressed the green button, put the phone to his ear, then pushed back the duvet.

Chloe sighed and rolled over, burying her face in the pillow.

"Mackinnon, it's Bruce."

Great. That was all he needed.

Mackinnon got out of bed. "What do you want?"

"To talk."

"It's midnight. I'm at home in bed. I'll talk to you on Monday."

Mackinnon was just about to hang up when Bruce said, "I know."

"What do you mean, 'you know'?"

"I'm outside."

"Outside?" Mackinnon crossed to the window and pulled the curtains back. What the hell was Bruce playing at? He scanned the street below, looking at the parked cars. He couldn't see anything out of the ordinary. The bastard was winding him up.

Mackinnon reached for the curtain, to pull it shut, when he saw a flash of light. The interior light went on in one of the cars across the street."

"What are you doing outside my house at midnight? Do you want me to report you for harassment?"

"No, Jack. I just want to talk to you." Bruce paused for a beat, then said, "I'm sorry about earlier."

Mackinnon rubbed his jaw. "So you should be."

"Can you come outside? We can talk in my car."

Mackinnon looked at Chloe, fast asleep, curled up in a tight ball. "Yeah, all right. Give me a minute."

Mackinnon pulled on a pair of jeans and a jumper, then headed downstairs, slowly and quietly so he didn't wake the girls. He pulled on the shoes he'd left at the door.

He thought about taking some kind of weapon with him, then dismissed his paranoia. Even so, he decided to write a note. If anything did happen, at least people would know he'd gone to meet Bruce. He left the note on the kitchen table.

Mackinnon climbed into the passenger seat of Bruce's car, then said, "What's all this cloak and dagger stuff then?"

Bruce's face looked pale and sallow under the car's yellow interior light.

"Sorry," Bruce said. "But I knew I had to talk to you tonight. I need to get this off my chest."

This was it. Bruce was going to confess.

"Why did you do it?" Mackinnon asked.

"Why does anyone do it? The money." Bruce turned to Mackinnon, his slick veneer had disappeared, leaving a desperate man behind. "After Luke's accident. There were so many things we needed. Treatments he had to have, equipment the centre told us he couldn't do without. I got out of my depth. I was tempted and I was weak, but you have to believe me, I have regretted it every day."

Mackinnon pushed away the image of Luke that came into his head and tried to ignore the pity he felt. "That isn't an excuse."

"No, but it is the reason."

Mackinnon stared out of the windscreen.

Bruce said, "So what are you going to do?"

"You mean, am I going to report you, officially?"

Bruce nodded.

"Who else are you involved with?"

"No one, it was only Justin Theroux. I didn't want to keep doing it, but as soon as I had taken the money once, he had a hold over me."

"Why did he target you?"

"They have their ways, Theroux and his kind of people. They find out who is struggling, who would be an easy target." Bruce turned to Mackinnon. "I guess they just pick the ones who can't say no."

"I think you should come clean."

"I can't do that. I'd lose everything. Luke... Fiona..."

Mackinnon put his head back and closed his eyes. "You're asking me to lie for you. I can't do that."

CHAPTER NINETY-TWO

FOR THE REST OF the weekend, Bruce played on Mackin-non's mind constantly. He picked up the phone a couple of times, but in the end, he didn't call him.

He and Chloe took Katy to her hockey game on Saturday afternoon, and Mackinnon watched her run around like a lunatic, all the while thinking about Luke, thinking how hard it must have hit Bruce when his active, teenage son was suddenly unable to do even the most basic things himself.

Chloe could tell there was something bothering him. But Mackinnon told her it was nothing, that he was just thinking about how fragile life was.

On Monday morning, Mackinnon was very reluctant to get into work. He arrived later than usual, having driven from Oxford, and the incident room was already full of people when he turned up.

DCI Brookbank had had a huge result over the weekend, and his team had pulled in the suspects they thought were responsible for a string of armed burglaries in the area. Now everyone was working hard to file the reports and get the paperwork in order, so the prosecution could go through without a hitch.

Charlotte spotted Mackinnon from across the room and caught his eye. She nodded at him and gestured for him to follow her out of the room. Mackinnon took off his jacket and put it on the back of his chair, then started to cross the room.

DI Tyler intercepted him. "Mackinnon, have you heard?"

"What?"

"Heard about Bruce?"

"What about Bruce?"

"It is a bloody tragedy, that's what it is. He was a good man. But he was never the same after what happened to his son."

Mackinnon could hear the blood rushing in his ears. He knew what was coming, but it couldn't be true. He'd seen him on Friday night.

"Bloody tragic," DI Tyler said. "Hung himself in the early hours of Saturday."

Mackinnon pushed past Tyler heading for the door. He heard Charlotte's voice behind him.

"Nice one, Tyler. Tactful way to break the news."

"What? They didn't even get on. Bruce was a mate of mine. I'm the one who should be upset."

Mackinnon reached the gents' toilets, slammed open a cubicle door and retched. He couldn't stop.

Afterwards, he stared at himself in the mirror, at his pale face, his bloodshot eyes and muttered, "It's my fault."

CHAPTER NINETY-THREE

MACKINNON, CHARLOTTE AND DI Tyler all attended Bruce's funeral. About seventy people crowded into the hall at Mortlake Crematorium.

Mackinnon looked at the sorrow etched on the face of Bruce's wife and daughter, and thought it wasn't possible to feel worse than he did at this moment.

Bruce's brother made his way to the front, and read out a poem by John Donne. His voice wavered, but he read to the end. When he finished, he stood beside Fiona and hugged her.

DI Tyler stood up and walked a short way down the central aisle to the front of the room. His hands shook as he held his notes out in front of him. There was a long pause, then Tyler shoved the notes into the pocket of his trousers.

"I stand before you today with a heavy heart," Tyler said. "It is never easy to say goodbye to someone who meant so much to so many. Bruce Evans was a beloved husband, father, brother, friend and colleague. To his fellow police officers, he was a shining example of what an officer should be: brave and dedicated, yet understanding and compassionate to those who needed his help."

Tyler's voice cracked and he lifted his chin, paused for a moment then said, "In many ways, Bruce was a hero. But to me, quite simply, he was my friend.

"God bless you, Bruce. We will miss you, and we will never forget you."

Something had shifted in Mackinnon. He no longer saw things as either right or wrong, as black or white. He could see the grey, and Bruce Evans had definitely been grey.

He wasn't a bad man. He was a victim; and thanks to Mackinnon, Luke and his sister had lost their father.

CHAPTER NINETY-FOUR

RONNIE STOOD BY THE phone box not daring to get any closer. It was playtime at the school, and he could hear the squeals of laughter as the children ran around, trying to burn off all their pent-up energy.

He tried to pick out his daughter's voice, but of course, he couldn't, not this far away. He didn't want to get too close. He didn't want one of the teachers to spot him and think he was one of those weirdos. But maybe he could get a little closer, just so he could see her.

Ronnie walked along the street, past a row of parked cars, acting like he was just about to get in one and drive off.

He scanned the playground for his little girl, but he couldn't see her. What if she wasn't there today? What if she was off sick? Or at the dentist...

Then he saw her. Ronnie thought his heart stopped.

Standing off to one side, she was with two other girls. They were playing some sort of game, and Ronnie's daughter had taken on the role of leader, telling the other two girls where to stand. Ronnie smiled. That was his girl, bossy just like her mother.

He stood there watching them hold hands, perform a little dance, then drop to the floor laughing. She was so pretty, so perfect. Did she even remember him? The smile slid from Ronnie's face.

He wanted, more than anything, to go over there now, to tell her how much he'd missed her.

He looked down at his freshly laundered clothes, at his polished shoes. He'd made a start, but he wasn't ready yet. He wasn't good enough yet.

Ronnie turned and walked back to the phone box. He opened the door, stepped inside and picked up the handset. He caught a glimpse of his reflection in the glass door, and did a double take. He raised his hand to his newly cropped hair. He hardly recognised himself.

A woman's voice answered.

"Um, hello," Ronnie said. "Is that the St. Michael's rehab centre? I'm interested in attending your outpatient program."

CHAPTER NINETY-FIVE

IT HAD BEEN A long week, and Mackinnon had never looked forward to the weekend more. He spent a relaxing Saturday with Chloe and the girls. They had had a pub lunch at the Woodstock Arms, and none of them felt like eating a big dinner, so Chloe was in the kitchen making ham sandwiches for their supper.

Katy lay on her stomach, on the floor in front of him, watching a weird wildlife documentary on creepy-crawlies.

His laptop warming his knees, Mackinnon searched the internet. It didn't take him long to find the article he was looking for. Charlotte had sent an email earlier with the details. Mackinnon clicked on the link and began to read.

A bar manager who allegedly sold drugs alongside the drinks in a central London bar has been charged with supplying heroin.

More than thirty officers from the Metropolitan and City of London police raided the bar last week, after a covert operation. Drugs, with a street value of more than eighty thousand pounds, were seized from a nearby property in a related raid.

The accused is currently hospitalised with a severe form of pneumonia, and hospital sources confirm his condition is critical. A friend of the family confided they feared the accused would not live long enough to attend the trial.

DCI Rosser, who oversaw the operation, said, "This was a remarkable case. It seems the main reason for the existence of this bar was to supply drugs, rather than drinks. It was an unusual case, but in a joint effort, the Metropolitan police and the City of London police have shown that we will continue to stamp out the use of drugs in our city."

Mackinnon closed the article and shut down the laptop. There was no mention of the cause of Justin Theroux's pneumonia, no mention of how the drugs had been contaminated with warfarin and no mention of DI Bruce Evans. The whole story would come out eventually, but so far, the press office seemed to be controlling the release of information surprisingly well.

Sarah walked into the living room. Her hair was still damp from the shower. She settled on an armchair, tucking her legs under her.

"Thanks for lunch, Jack."

Mackinnon looked up, surprised. "You're welcome."

Mackinnon wished things could stay like this. He would prefer to be watching the cricket, rather than a weird documentary on bugs, but still, as Saturdays went, this was a pretty good one. His thoughts automatically turned to Bruce's family, how different their Saturdays would be from now on.

He picked up his empty beer glass and carried it out to the kitchen.

Chloe turned and smiled at him. "Do you want mustard on your sandwich?"

Mackinnon nodded. "Please."

"You know," Chloe said, spreading the yellow mustard on the ham. "I think we might be past the worst of it. I think Sarah is going to be okay."

Mackinnon leaned over, and kissed her on the cheek. He took the plates she passed him, then carried the sandwiches through to the girls.

He hoped Chloe was right.

He hoped they would all be all right.

THANK YOU!

Thanks for reading Deadly Revenge. I hope you enjoyed it!

The next book in the series is DEADLY JUSTICE.

Please sign up for my new release email at www.dsbutler-books.com/newsletter if you would like to know when the next Jack Mackinnon book is out.

You can follow me on Twitter at @dsbutler, or like my Facebook page at http://facebook.com/dsbutler.author.

Reviews are like gold to authors. They spread the word and help readers find books, and I appreciate all reviews whether positive or negative.

If you would like to read the first chapter of Deadly Justice, the next book in the series, please turn the page.

EXTRACT FROM DEADLY JUSTICE

1

1976

"You are a liar." The woman leaned forward and snarled at Mr. Johnson.

Her lips curved back over her small pointed teeth.

Mr. Johnson shifted back in his chair and placed his hands on the solid oak desk that separated them. He wished it was a little wider. In his thirty-year teaching career, the headmaster of White House primary school had never encountered a parent quite as aggressive as this young woman.

Strands of her light brown hair had fallen loose from the tight bun at the base of her neck. Her skin, usually so pale, was now red and blotchy.

Her hand shook as she jabbed a finger in his direction. "You are a disgrace. You're not fit to be in charge of innocent little children."

He had needed to discuss disciplinary issues with parents and guardians in the past, and no one liked to be told that their child was not perfect, but he had never come across a parent so determined to ignore the truth.

She shook her head vigorously, freeing more wispy strands of hair. "Junior would never do such a thing. I can't believe you could even suggest it."

Mr. Johnson took a breath and waited. He hoped she would run out of steam soon. Since she had stormed into his office five minutes ago, she hadn't paused for breath.

He glanced down at the small boy sitting by her side, the child they were discussing. His large grey eyes regarded the headmaster steadily. He didn't seem surprised or at all worried by his mother's outburst.

Finally, the woman seemed to gather herself, gripping the neck of her blouse with one hand and smoothing her skirt over her thin thighs with the other. She raised her chin. "I hope this is an end to the matter. I don't want to hear any more of this nonsense."

Mr. Johnson shook his head and said as gently as he could, "Another child saw him do it."

The woman gripped the side of her chair. "Then the other child is lying. Junior would never hurt an animal. He loves them."

"The hamster was..." Mr. Johnson hesitated over his word choice, but there really wasn't a pleasant way to put it. "The hamster had been cut... several times, and Junior was seen by the cage..."

"Oh, so Junior was seen by the cage, well that proves everything, doesn't it?" The woman snorted, then turned as if addressing an imagined audience. "Why don't you lock him up and throw away the key? He's a little boy, for goodness sake. He would never do anything like that."

The woman tugged the arm of the six-year-old boy sitting

next to her. His face was blank, seemingly the picture of innocence.

"You'd never do such a terrible thing would you, Junior?"

"No, Mother," the little boy said, his big grey eyes wide and serious.

This wasn't the first time the little boy had been in trouble. Since Junior had been admitted into the reception class, he had been known as a biter and pincher, and he was sly with it. The teacher would never actually catch him in the act. They only saw the results: a sobbing child with bruises or teeth marks buried in their flesh. But Mr. Johnson found it hard to believe anyone, even Junior, could do such a terrible thing to the school pet.

The children had spent the school year taking care of the animal, feeding it, watching it play and taking turns to stroke its soft fur. To think that someone could do that to the defence-less creature, something so inherently evil, let alone a child... Well, it was unthinkable.

The boy stared back at him, unblinking, with those huge, round grey eyes.

Could he be telling the truth?

"Junior doesn't lie. Do you, Junior?"

"No, Mother."

"You see. He's a good boy. It's the other children. They bully him. You need to talk to the other parents, not me." She smoothed the little boy's hair and reached over to straighten his school tie.

"Which child told you Junior had hurt the hamster?" she asked, in a deliberately light tone.

Not hurt, Mr. Johnson thought, but killed, sadistically.

He shook his head. "It won't do any good to bring them into this debate."

She pursed her lips together for a moment then said, "I see. So you're more than willing to spread these malicious lies about my son, but you won't give me a chance to defend him. How can I confront these lies if I don't know who is behind them?"

Mr. Johnson shook his head again. There was no way he would let this awful woman, or Junior, know which child had come forward so they could take their revenge.

"Why would you trust one child's word over another?" she demanded, leaning forward and clasping her handbag with white-knuckled fingers.

Mr. Johnson regarded her steadily. Because it isn't the first time, he thought. Because this little boy has serious problems.

"Have you ever considered taking Junior to a doctor to discuss his behavioural issues?"

She shot up from her chair and slapped her hands flat against the oak surface as she leaned over the headmaster's desk. "He doesn't have any issues. You're the one with the problem. He's a good boy." She looked over her shoulder back at Junior. "He's good with his reading. Good with his numbers and his adding up, aren't you, Junior?"

"Yes, Mother."

She turned back to face Mr. Johnson, triumphant. "See."

"It isn't a matter of intelligence. Junior is ahead of his peers in many subjects, but he doesn't make friends easily and has a tendency to be violent towards the other children."

She folded her arms and began to pace the office. "I knew it," she said, forced a high-pitched laugh and shook her head.

The little boy watched his mother. His eyes followed her across the room.

"I knew you'd bring that up again, even though I already explained this to you. Junior is the one who gets bullied. They call him names; nasty, cruel names, and when he stands up for himself, he gets into trouble."

She stopped pacing and turned to face Mr. Johnson with her hands on her hips.

"He hasn't done anything wrong. I told him to fight back. It's the only way to deal with bullies." She nodded, pleased with herself. "You lot don't do anything about it, so he has to deal with it himself."

"I can't condone that type of behaviour in my school. If Junior is bullied, then he must tell me or his teacher, Mrs. Adams."

"Mrs. Adams? Don't make me laugh." The woman folded her arms over her bony chest. "She's useless. She hates Junior. She won't do anything to help him. She has favourites."

"Mrs. Adams is an excellent teacher. I regard her very highly. I'm sure she'll do everything in her power to make sure Junior is well looked after and feels comfortable and secure during class."

The woman made a tutting sound then sat back down next to Junior. "She isn't a good teacher. Junior tells me everything, you know?" She leaned forward and lowered her voice to a whisper. "And Mrs. Adams doesn't like that."

Mr. Johnson wanted to bury his head in his hands. This wasn't working. There was no way he could get through to this woman.

He turned his attention to Junior.

"Would you like to say anything, Junior? If you know what happened to the hamster, you could tell me now. You won't be punished, but it is very important to tell the truth."

The small boy stared up at the headmaster with solemn eyes. He swung his little legs back and forth and tilted his head to the side. His big, grey eyes narrowed a little.

Mr. Johnson suppressed a shudder. Something in the way the child studied him sent a prickly chill over his skin.

He is only six-years-old, Mr. Johnson told himself, an innocent. A little boy who needs help. But he couldn't shake the overwhelming desire to shove both the little boy and his mother out of the office.

As if he read the headmaster's thoughts, the little boy smiled. Then he opened his mouth, "I..."

His mother yanked him by the arm. "You don't have to say anything, Junior. We've told the truth. We can't say more than that."

"Yes, Mother."

The little boy turned back to the headmaster with the trace of a smirk on his lips.

Mr. Johnson could almost believe the boy was laughing at him. He stared down at the papers on his desk, trying to collect his thoughts. He was clearly being ridiculous, and these fanciful notions weren't doing anyone any good. The boy needed help. Was it really a surprise the boy was struggling with a mother like that?

After a moment, he looked up to see Junior and his mother staring at him. The headmaster took a deep breath and tapped his pen against the pile of papers on his desk.

"I'll have to include it in my report."

"What? And have it on Junior's school record? How will that look?"

"It will look ... better than expulsion." He couldn't turn his back on the boy. He had to give him another chance. Perhaps if Mrs. Adams could give the boy a little more one-on-one time...

"Expulsion!" The woman reared back as if he had hit her. "You can keep your poxy reports. There's no way my Junior is coming back to this school." She sprang up like a jack-in-the-box and grabbed Junior's hand. "I'll put him in another school - something I should have done a long time ago."

"Of course, you must do what you think is best for Junior," Mr. Johnson said, feeling a surge of relief and hating himself for it.

"If there is any justice in this world, that little tattletale will get what's coming to him." The woman spun on her heel and stalked out of the office pulling Junior behind her.

For a few moments after Junior's mother had slammed the office door, Mr. Johnson didn't move. He set his pen down on his desk with a shaky hand and exhaled heavily.

The encounter had really shaken him. At fifty-two years old, he was no longer wet behind the ears. On a previous occasion, he'd had the misfortune to be grabbed around the throat by an irate father during a heated discussion at a parents' evening, and he'd even dealt with a ten-year-old boy trying to sell his mother's anti-depressant tablets in the school playground. After almost thirty years of teaching, he'd thought he had seen it all, but there was something about that little boy and his mother that chilled him to the core.

He took a deep breath and stood up, leaning heavily on his desk. Standing by the window, he looked out on a view of the playground and the school gates. The woman was striding across the playground to the exit, tugging at the boy's arm to make him walk faster.

Suddenly, Mr. Johnson felt incredibly sad.

"That poor boy," he muttered to himself. "That poor, poor boy..."

* * *

2

Present day

Vinnie Pearson stared across at the skinny Pakistani newsagent. He leaned in close then said, "I ain't paying a hundred quid. I'll give you twenty-five."

Syed Hammad puffed out his chest and straightened behind the counter. "On your bike, son."

Hearing that expression from Syed was so unexpected, Vinnie wanted to laugh. But he didn't. This was business, and Vinnie took business seriously. The newsagent had something Vinnie wanted.

Vinnie moved closer and peered over the counter at the cardboard box, resting by Syed's feet. "How many have you got down there?"

Syed kicked the box under the counter, out of sight, but not before Vinnie caught a glimpse of the shiny, black smartphones. "None of your business," Syed said. "Keep your sticky beak out." He tapped the side of his nose.

Vinnie gritted his teeth. He sensed a movement behind him, someone else had entered the shop.

"All right," Vinnie said. "I'll stretch to fifty, but it's daylight robbery."

Syed folded his arms across his chest. His sparse moustache stretched thin as he smiled. "You can take your money somewhere else. I don't want it."

Vinnie flushed. How dare the little bastard talk to him like that? If there hadn't been someone else in the shop, Vinnie would have taught him a lesson right then and there. Vinnie glanced back over his shoulder. The customer was a man of around forty, dressed in jeans and a dark jacket. No one Vinnie recognised. Still, Vinnie didn't want word to get out that he had been disrespected by Syed Hammad of all people.

"What's wrong with my money, Syed?" Vinnie's voice was low and dangerous.

"It's dirty," Syed said and screwed up his nose. "You and your lowlife friends robbing, stealing from hard working people like me. Don't think I don't know who trashed my shop and the others in this street last summer."

Vinnie kept his smile fixed in place. "You don't have any proof."

"I don't need proof. I know what you did, and I want you out of my shop now." Syed raised his voice, causing the customer to pause by the magazine rack and turn to look at them.

Vinnie could feel his cheeks glowing, and his mouth grew dry. No one spoke to him like that and got away with it.

"Watch your mouth, Syed."

"No. No, I won't. You can't push me around. I'll call the police. I pay my taxes, work hard and you..."

"You what?" Vinnie gulped down air as he tried to control his temper. "What do you reckon the police would have to say about them?" Vinnie jabbed a finger in the direction of the smartphones. "They're nicked, you bloody hypocrite. I'm sure the police would love to have a look at them."

Syed shrugged. "No. No. They aren't stolen. They are from my friend's sister's boyfriend's father. Perfectly legitimate."

"Bollocks. They are nicked. Stolen goods. You're no better than a thief!"

"How dare you. Get out!" Syed screamed. He was bouncing up and down on his toes. "Get out of my shop now. I'm calling the police. I have a witness," Syed pointed to the man still standing by the magazines.

"A witness to what?" Vinnie shook his head. "You're a bloody nutcase."

"Out! Get out!" Syed Hammad picked up one of the smartphones and made a big show of pretending to dial 999.

"I'm going," Vinnie said. As he turned to leave he kicked out at a pyramid made of carefully stacked packets of biscuits, sending them tumbling to the floor.

Afterwards, Vinnie stood outside the hairdressers and smoked a cigarette as he tried to calm down. That little bastard. Who the hell did he think he was?

The blonde woman who owned the salon kept shooting him nervous looks. Normally, Vinnie would feel gratified. He liked people being afraid of him. It showed respect.

He'd get back at Syed, but not now. Not when he was so worked up. He needed to make a plan. A plan that made sure the bastard would never disrespect Vinnie again.

As Vinnie walked back down the street, he kept his head low as he passed the newsagent's. The cafe next door was full to bursting, which was crazy considering the awful food it served. Even if he hadn't been banned from the premises after the riots last summer, Vinnie wouldn't have eaten there.

Mitch Horrocks, the cafe owner, stared out at Vinnie. He'd run the place for years. Mad Mitch, the local school kids called him. Vinnie and some mates had trashed the cafe last summer, and Vinnie had taken great pleasure in wrecking the joint. If anyone deserved it, it was Mitch. Vinnie smiled and waved and got a two-fingered salute from Mad Mitch in return.

Ahead of him, Vinnie saw a man dressed in jeans and a grey hoodie standing at the bus stop. He didn't recognise the man at first, but as he drew closer he realised it was the man who had walked into the newsagent's. The bloke who'd been hanging around the magazines. He'd pulled up the hood on his sweatshirt, but Vinnie was sure it was him.

The man slouched back against the glass panel of the bus

shelter, but as Vinnie approached him, the man straightened up and turned to face Vinnie.

Vinnie recognised a threat when he saw one. The bloke had obviously witnessed his argument with Syed and pegged Vinnie as an easy mark. There was no way Vinnie would back down. He couldn't, not if he wanted to keep his reputation.

Vinnie jutted out his chin and gave him the look. The look that said if this bloke was looking for trouble, Vinnie had plenty to supply.

The hoodie stepped forward blocking Vinnie's path.

This was a direct confrontation. Vinnie couldn't back down. If he wanted to get past, he would have to step into the road or shove his way past.

Vinnie shoved his hands in his pockets and felt the reassuring cool, smooth metal of the knife. If there was going to be trouble, Vinnie was ready for it.

The hoodie surprised Vinnie by smiling. The hood of his sweatshirt kept most of the bloke's face in shadow, but Vinnie could see the lower half of his face and he was definitely grinning.

Vinnie glanced across the road. Maybe he should cross the road and avoid the stand-off. That was the sensible thing to do. Vinnie wasn't a hot-headed kid any more. He didn't like to take on fights unless he was sure he could win, and this bloke looked a bit of a dodgy character. Besides, the police were just waiting for him to slip up again.

"What do you want?" Vinnie asked.

The hoodie looked up and down the street, his eyes shifty. "I've got a proposition for you."

"Oh, yeah?" Vinnie said. "Well, I'm not interested. I don't do business with people I don't know."

"You'll be interested in this," the hoodie said.

Vinnie scoffed. "I don't think so, mate."

Now he was closer, Vinnie could see the bloke was older than he first thought. He had at least ten years on Vinnie. That should have made Vinnie more confident. Vinnie was ten years younger and fitter, but for some reason it made him nervous.

Vinnie tried to sidestep the man but felt the hoodie's fingers dig into his shoulder.

Vinnie stared down at the man's hand. "What the hell do you think you're doing? Get your hands off me, unless you want me to break your fingers."

The man laughed but removed his hand. "No need to act like that, mate. If you're not interested..." He shrugged. "I'm sure someone else will be. Maybe the Brewerton brothers?"

Vinnie scowled. The Brewertons were his closest rivals. They wouldn't be happy until they had driven Vinnie out of the area.

"All right. What's this proposition? I'll give you two minutes."

"Money. An easy job. I saw you earlier, trying to get a phone off that newsagent." The bloke nodded down the street in the direction of Syed's shop.

Vinnie folded his arms across his chest. He hated the idea anyone else had witnessed his embarrassment. Who was this guy anyway? Some kind of spy for the Brewertons? Vinnie stared at him, determined not to show any reaction. He wouldn't give him the satisfaction.

The hoodie smiled slowly, as if he understood. "You were right. He was trying to cheat you. I wouldn't mind one of those fancy new phones myself, but there's no way I'm paying one hundred quid for it."

Vinnie shrugged. "They are nicked anyway. The dodgy bastard. It's a rip-off."

"So why don't we just take them?" The hoodie grinned. "It's hardly stealing if they were already stolen once."

Vinnie licked his lips. "Are you suggesting we rob poor old Syed?"

Vinnie tried to stifle his grin. He would enjoy teaching that stupid bastard, Syed, a lesson.

"Few of your mates, few of mine. We could do it like last summer. A smash and grab. In and out before he knows what's hit him."

Vinnie grinned. He liked that idea. But he wasn't about to let this bloke think he was a pushover. He shrugged. "I'm not sure it's worth my time for a couple of poxy phones."

The man looked around again nervously, as if he expected somebody to be watching them. "Your loss. But if you change your mind, we do it at six o'clock tomorrow night."

"Why are you telling me? Why not just do it yourself?"

"Strength in numbers," the hoodie said. "If there's a lot of us, the owner will back down. We can split the phones fifty-fifty. I bet some of your mates would do this sort of thing for a chocolate bar."

"Maybe," Vinnie said and side-stepped the man. He was probably right. Most of the kids he hung around with didn't take things seriously. They didn't see it as a career, more as a way to have fun. That was their problem. It didn't stop Vinnie using them for backup now and again. And the man was right. There was strength in numbers.

"Yeah, well, I might make it if I haven't got anything better to do."

"Your choice," the hoodie said. "But there's a whole box of phones, and he's selling them for a ton apiece."

"Like I said, I'll see."

Vinnie carried on walking and didn't look back. He didn't notice that the man was still watching him. He was too busy planning who to contact for tomorrow night.

There were lots of eager kids he could call on, but he didn't want to involve too many. The more people in on the action, the more they would have to divide the profits. And Vinnie didn't like to share. He pulled out his old Nokia and opened the Facebook app. It took ages to load, which was exactly why he wanted a new phone in the first place.

He decided to invite four others. Four others he could trust, and more importantly, four others who would be happy with just a few cigarettes for their trouble.

He typed their names into the search bar and sent each of them a message. Then he shoved the phone back in his pocket and smiled. Only one more day before he could dump that plastic piece of crap. Yeah, he would look a lot better with a brand-new, fancy smartphone clamped to his ear.

As Vinnie swaggered up the road, full of plans for tomorrow, he had no idea the man watching him had plans of his own.

Deadly Justice is out now.

ACKNOWLEDGMENTS

MANY PEOPLE HELPED TO provide ideas and background for this book. My thanks and gratitude to DI Dave Carter and Richard Searle for generously sharing their time and wealth of experience.

I would also like to thank my friends on Twitter, especially @886niko and @DS_Rosser, for their entertaining tweets and encouragement.

My thanks, too, to all the people who read the story and gave helpful suggestions and to Chris, who, as always, supported me despite the odds.